MW01443529

Braker Ford's Adventures in Space

Copyright © 2022 Braker Ford's Adventures in Space

All Rights Reserved.

No parts of this publication may be reproduced, stored in a retrieval system, or transmitted in any form or by any means, electronic, mechanical, photocopied, recording, or otherwise without the prior written permission of the copyright owner.

This book is sold subject to the condition that it shall not, by way of trade or otherwise, be lent, resold, hired out, or otherwise circulated without the publisher's prior consent in any form of binding or cover other than that in which it is published and without a similar condition including this condition being imposed on the subsequent purchaser.

This is a work of fiction. Any similarity between the characters and situations within its pages and places or persons, living or dead, is unintentional and coincidental.

Cover art by James A. Fyerman
Cover art Copyright © 2022 Braker Ford's cover art

Braker Ford's
ADVENTURES IN SPACE

James A. Fyerman

**8th Floor
PRESS**

Chapter One
Braker!

Out in the swirling depths of the shimmering cosmos, far away on the edge of creation, a speck of light cut across the yawning void. It was Braker Ford, space trucker, in his trusty galactic freighter *The Steak and Egger*. Beside him sat his best friend, the simple hillbilly space farmer, Wayne.

Inside the ship's cockpit, Braker Ford sat in an observation seat, his thin body shifting awkwardly under the weight of the white pressure suit that burdened his wiry frame. Braker was young and fresh-faced, with a permanent look of bewilderment stamped across his ruddy features. Fidgeting with nervous energy, he tugged at the battered utility cap that somehow always managed to remain perched at the most extreme angles on his head.

"Be sure you watch those propulsion dome-quats on that beam adjuster," Braker instructed his companion.

"Sure, Braker," Wayne answered, his big, calloused hand wiping a smudge from the monitor. Wayne wasn't much older than Braker although he possessed a body much larger than his friend's;

the sleepy-eyed man was built for farm work, heavy and thick, with powerful arms and shoulders. Yet he was gentle and slow-moving, as comfortable as a feather pillow in his worn overalls and padded work shirt.

"What's with all the extra precautions?" asked the farmer, surprised at the safety measures.

"Not sure, Wayne, I've just got a feeling something's gonna happen. It's a space trucker thing. When you've been out here long enough you start to get a feeling when something alien is about to happen."

"But, Braker, you've only been a space trucker for a week."

"It's a trucker thing," Braker insisted. "I'm turning on the 'Roving Eye.' We'll have a look around."

Braker sighed with satisfaction as he reached for the optic switch, slowly gliding his hand over the truck's gleaming dashboard. He loved this huge rig, from its triangulated oil tubes and dual-cylinder dry pans to its slab-covered rear scorchers. But, most of all, he loved its laser-propelled engines that could fly him from the nearest planet to the tips of the universe.

Not everyone had the courage to travel these vast realms. The black, misty highways of space had been known to swallow up even the hardiest of souls. The dangers were innumerable. There were ricocheting lava stars, interstellar tidal waves, and drifting clumps of radioactive space mites. A long-distance explorer might get caught up in an astral hydrogen river, stumble upon the majestic yet deadly twin cascading black holes of Klothorpe, or encounter the Plo, a wandering cloud of living space gas that loved to kill people with its toxic odor. But the list of galactic peril didn't stop there, not by a long shot—there were cunning gangs of starship hijackers, predatory bands of space cannibals, feral packs of interplanetary space chimps, and the occasional careless space jogger. But Braker didn't care; where others saw danger in crossing paths with alien civilizations and bizarre cosmic creatures, he saw opportunities and adventure—and maybe even a shot at greatness.

He yanked on the optic switch and suddenly a large white ball was launched from its steel housing on the *Egger's* flank. The ball floated into space, attached to the truck only by a thin wire. Braker had it orbit the ship once and was about to have it return when something caught the Eye's attention. Blinking its eyelid-like shutters, it sent a series of pictures back to Braker.

"What is it?" Braker exclaimed, studying the blurry images.

Wayne slipped on a pair of view-dar goggles. A glance out the window showed only the glow of afterburners fading into the distance. "Just some space traveler speedin', I guess," he said. "But they sure did have their haunches up. They were movin'."

The Roving Eye was blinking again. It detected a second ship approaching the *Egger* from far behind.

"Here comes another one," said Wayne. "And this one's trying to send a message."

An excited voice came piping in on the *Egger's* voice box. "Space truck, this is *Patrol Flight I-89* coming up on your tail; what are you doing way out here?"

Wayne spoke first into the voice box. "Hey, feller, this is Braker and Wayne in the good ol' *Steak and Egger*. We're just haulin' sunshine. That's what we're doin'. How 'bout yourselves?"

"Come again?"

"Well, Braker here, he works for a company that collects all the leftover energy from old stars and takes it back to be recycled. So, yup, we're just haulin' sunshine."

3

"Okay, that's weird," replied the voice, "but, whatever you're doing, we need your help. *Steak and Egger*, we're correctional officers with the Galactic Correctional Institute. And we're attempting to detain an escaped crew of convicts who have, well…escaped. We believe they have just crossed your path."

"Boy and how!" said Wayne. "They was splitting their pants from both ends at once."

"Okay, we're not sure what that means, *Steak and Egger*, but this is an emergency."

"You bet it is," said Wayne. "Imagine, a whole mess of dangerous outlaws bustin' free of a space jail right under your very own noses. That's what I'd call really spreadin' the stink."

"Hey, ask 'em how they escaped," said Braker.

"Say, how'd that gang escape, anyway?" Wayne said into the voice box.

"How'd they escape?" snapped the officer. "Who cares? They…they stole a guardhouse transport. That's all. Now listen, those convicts have outdistanced us, but from your position, you could possibly catch up to them and cut them off. That would give us time to arrive and apprehend them for the good of the galaxy."

Braker was fidgeting with his harness clip. "Can you believe it, Wayne? Those cops need our help. This is big."

"Yeah, well, should you tell them, or should I?"

"No, don't, I—"

"I'll tell 'em," said Wayne, leaning toward the voice box. "Hey, fellers, this is Wayne here. We sure are sorry, but we cain't help. Sure sorry, fellers."

"What do you mean you can't help?" replied the officer. "Sure you can. Just do a quick end-around that convict ship. You trucker types do that all the time."

"Yeah, well, the pilot of this truck cain't do it."

"Wayne, don't tell them that," Braker pleaded.

"What's wrong with your pilot?" said the officer.

"Ain't nothin' wrong with him," replied Wayne, "he just cain't fly the ship. Actually, he doesn't do much of anything. Machines do all the work. See, we're on one of those mechanically guided rigs that's on a set course. You know, the kind that don't really need a pilot."

"It's not exactly like that," said Braker, his voice cracking.

"Why, it sure is," Wayne shouted into the voice box. "In fact, the only reason Braker's even on board is to put out small cabin fires with this little fire extinguisher."

"I am a trucker, technically," said Braker.

"That's true," said Wayne, "but it weren't easy. You should of seen how many times he failed his trucker test before they give him this job. I'll bet he run near fifteen of 'em in the ditch. I think they just got sick of seeing him comin' back. But that's why we love him; good ol' Braker."

"*Steak and Egger*, please. We appreciate that your pilot is incompetent and all, but this is an emergency. These are dangerous escaped convicts. We're humble, law-abiding correctional officers. Don't say no. The bad guys are getting away. Just a little help from you could change everything. Listen, your pilot could end up being a galactic legend like Tuff Barlow the Asteroid Warrior, or even Skippy Dodge, the Galaxy Saver."

"Yeah, but didn't Skippy Dodge end up getting himself killed the last time he saved the galaxy?" Wayne asked.

"Nah, he just went missing, never to be heard from again by another living soul," replied the officer.

"I guess that's not so bad," Wayne muttered.

"And so what if he was killed, anyway?" the officer continued. "Skippy Dodge is a legend throughout the universe, isn't he? Doesn't your pilot want to be a legend? Or did he always dream of being just an average, ordinary space trucker?"

"Well, like I said, he's ain't even that really; most of the time he just stares out the window."

"Wayne!"

"Come on, you truckers, it's for the good of the entire galaxy. It will only take a minute. It'll make a great story to tell your friends. Everyone will love you. Our government will throw money at you. People will write songs about you. Please do it, this is getting rather humiliating."

"We'd love to help," said Wayne, "but Braker cain't fly. You have to understand. He cain't do it. He just cain't. Nope, he just cain't do it. He cain't—"

Braker switched off the voice box as Wayne went on repeating himself. The trucker was anxiously rocking back and forth in his seat, both hands pressed under his legs. "Wayne, we've got to help these people. It's my duty as a trucker."

"But you cain't fly."

"It's my responsibility. I'm a space trucker. We're kind of like guardians to the far-flung space regions."

"Not really."

"I want to do more than just put out small cabin fires."

"But that's the only thing you're good at."

"I can be a legend."

"Braker, you cain't fly the ship. The coordinates are locked into that there navigation drive. This may just be one chicken we cain't scratch."

Braker stretched his arms up over his head and then behind his neck. He stood up, then sat down, and then stood up again. Finally, he became completely motionless. Rolling his eyes toward Wayne, he said, "There's always The Box."

Both men slowly exhaled as they turned to stare at a small metal key hanging inside a glass box on the wall: The Emergency Manual Transmission Key.

"Braker, you cain't. Call your dispatcher first. Please."

"No time," said Braker, breaking the glass with a space helmet. "Those convicts are already getting away, probably endangering other travelers. Other guys have saved the galaxy. Like they said, Skippy Dodge even did it more than once. Why can't I? And I am a trucker. Technically." Braker grabbed the key and shoved it into a slot in the dashboard. One turn brought a blast of escaping drainage pressure as a large section of the control panel rotated completely around to reveal a gigantic steering wheel and gear shifter. Beneath the panel, a long row of clutches, brakes, and gas pedals dropped toward the floor. The section locked into place with a metallic click. *The Steak and Egger* was now completely in Braker's control. Unguided, it began a lopsided drift off its previous course.

A tiny bead of sweat rolled down Braker's forehead. "What do I do now?" he gasped.

Tim looked out the window. "Well, seeing as how we're 'bout to slam into that pack of floating moon rocks beside us, I'd say you'd better tilt this drum the other direction."

Braker lunged at the wheel, spinning it hard as he jammed the gearshift as far as it would go. The *Egger* howled with fuel-injected fury, quivering with new life as power-juice flooded its engines.

"Braker, a turn like that could rupture the harmozinite anti-bladders!" Wayne exclaimed, nearly tossed out of his seat.

Braker shot back a frustrated glance. "Wayne, I have nine gas pedals, fifteen clutches, and seven brakes to deal with, not to mention the pack of floating moon rocks; could you please not bring up the anti-bladders?"

"Don't forget you're also trying to save the galaxy," Wayne added.

Braker continued working the controls. The *Egger's* lurching and wobbling started to decrease. "Hey, I think I'm getting the hang of this," he said, smiling. "Hang on, I'm going to catch those jailbirds."

Braker opened the speed valve—they moved faster. He cranked back on the momentum rod—they moved even faster. He toggled into accelerated vitality mode—the other ship came into view. It was a large, luxury transport.

"Say, that sure is one fancy prison bus," said Wayne.

"That's no prison bus," said Braker. "That's one of those super expensive Milk and Honey space yachts everybody's been talking about. Just one of them is worth more than an entire supercluster of platinum stardust."

"Well, be careful then, you're gettin' awful close. You don't want to put a scratch on it."

"I'll take us down to sub-maniac speed," said Braker, pumping a row of brakes.

Wayne's eyes widened. "Better make it fast, Braker. We're fixin' to T-bone them boys!"

"Too late," Braker groaned as the engine's Fab-Drive kept them reeling forward.

They plowed into the space yacht at full speed. There were explosions, sparks, and a burst of inaudible space sound.

When it was all over, the runaway yacht lay motionless, its burned-out engines spilling fuel. Even worse, its fractured hull was leaking precious interior atmosphere. The *Steak and Egger* idled nearby, its transmission knocked into neutral by the blow; otherwise, the sturdy freighter appeared undamaged, its thick lunar grille guard having absorbed most of the impact.

Braker shifted the *Egger* into first, circling around until the two ships were viewport to viewport. Inside the pulverized space yacht, the pilot beat his head against the controls. Behind him, lights were blinking, dazed crewmen staggered, and, in the corner, two beautiful young women stood huddled together looking scared.

"Wow, check out those dolls," said Braker.

Wayne stared at the girls; they clung together tenderly, whispering encouragement to each other and the bustling crew. "Braker, I know we're supposed to be chasing criminals, and they're supposed to be tougher than backfirin' tornadoes full of dynamite, but them two gals don't look like they could turn a frown to a crawdad. Bad guys don't come that purdy. I'm figuring there's been some kind of mistake."

Braker remained plastered to the window. "You're right," he said. "And just look at their ship. Its life support systems won't last much longer. They need rescued."

"Ain't that the truth. You almost finished 'em off with one swat."

Braker glared at Wayne. "Well, it's not over yet. Maintain the *Egger*. I'm going to fix this."

"Hoo, boy, this should be interesting," Wayne said to himself.

Chapter Two
The Truth Revealed

Wayne took over the controls while Braker quickly donned his space suit and rocket pack. Then, cracking open the *Egger's* outer seal-lock the trucker stepped into space.

Maneuvering himself down to the ship below, he motioned for the crew inside to give him access to the disabled vessel. With nothing to lose at this point, they agreed, turning on the fan that would suck him through their matter conductor. Then, after a quick ride through an anti-pressure gasket, Braker found himself deposited in a sparkling hold that resembled a grand reception parlor.

Enormous chandeliers reflected shimmering light off glass walls. Long sofas and over-stuffed chairs were grouped into charming, cozy arrangements perfect for socializing. A trio of moon dwarfs played soft instrumental music from a platform in the back. Gleaming mechanical men wandered about the seating area, offering refreshments to crowds of impeccably attired crewmen.

Rendered speechless by the opulence, Braker grabbed a Cherry Fizz off a nearby tray. Downing it, he smacked his lips. "Somebody tell me what's going on here?" he shouted.

Two men in plush astro-suits came running forward. "What's going on here?" shouted the first man. "You just destroyed our ship. You ruined our lives, jerk!"

Before Braker could respond, the second man stepped up. "You'll have to excuse my co-pilot, he's a touch excitable. I'm Neal, the pilot."

"I'm Braker Ford, space trucker."

"Welcome aboard the *Shameless Indulgence*, or at least what's left of her," said Neal.

"Yeah, I guess I should apologize for smashing into you," offered Braker.

"Think nothing of it," said Neal. "Things happen."

"Neal's right," added the co-pilot, "sorry I popped off like that. It just seems like we can't catch a break today. I'm Herb."

Another crewman approached, saluting the *Indulgence's* pilot. "Sir, the engines are beyond repair, our last oxygen reserves are almost empty, and all the carbonated beverages have gone flat."

"Darn, it," said Neal. "If it isn't one thing it's another."

"You guys are actually taking all of this pretty well," said Braker.

Neal nodded. "Well, honestly, we're not quite sure how to act in a situation like this. We've spent most of our lives wallowing in sheltered prestige and comfort."

Braker studied the other crewmen—they were all soft-skinned yacht-boys with styled hair and monogramed uniforms. "Who are you people?" he asked.

"We're the only surviving inhabitants of the extremely wealthy and pampered planet, Diten," said Herb, "and this was our last chance at escape."

"Escape?" said Braker. "Escape, from what? What happened to Diten?"

"It was disintegrated by a vicious space fleet from the darkest corner of the universe," said Neal.

"Disintegrated?" gasped Braker. "Who would want to disintegrate your planet?"

Herb's face twisted in disgust. "Who else but Lord Preposterous, the evil dictator of Nebulous X."

"Never heard of him," said Braker.

"Never heard of Lord Preposterous?" Herb replied.

"Nope."

"Never heard of Nebulous X, either?"

"Never."

"And you call yourself a space trucker? It's a planet, you fool."

"Lay off, I'm only trying to help," said Braker.

"Quit acting working-class, Herb," said Neal.

"Sorry, sorry; it's just nerves," said Herb.

"So, anyway, why did Lord Preposterous blow up Diten?" Braker continued.

Herb sighed. "Okay, in answer to your question, it's because Lord Preposterous is a horrid, throbbing ball of royal space snot and he's lonely."

"Being a little over dramatic, aren't you?" said Braker.

"No, actually I'm being completely factual," Herb answered.

"Gross, but true," said Neal.

"Whatever," said Braker. "Still doesn't make sense."

"Just listen," said Herb. "Our planet is known for two things—how lame Ditenians are in a fight, and how beautiful our king's two daughters are."

"Don't forget we're also filthy rich," added Neal.

"Not anymore," said Herb. "The planet's gone, remember."

"Anyways…" said Braker.

"Anyways," Herb continued, "Preposterous decided he would steal the girls and choose the most beautiful one to marry him. When we tried to fight back, Preposterous got all peeved and ordered us zapped with a disintegration ray. There was just enough time to gather a crew and get the sisters to the ship. We're the only ones who got away; we were trying to make a break for it before you came along."

"So you're not really escaped convicts?"

"Not at all," said Neal.

"And you're not dangerous?"

Neal laughed. "Hardly. The last big dispute on our planet was resolved over a game of pass the hanky."

"And that means the guys chasing you aren't correctional officers?"

"Correctional officers!" exclaimed Herb. "They're not correctional officers. We're dealing with Nebulous X space soldiers—Goons of Doom. And you know who their leader is, don't you?"

"I'm sorry, I don't."

"Wow, you really are out of it," said Herb.

"Herb, you're sounding common again," said Neal.

Herb went on. "Does 'The Glamour Boy of Gunberry' sound familiar?"

Braker shook his head.

"Gunberry is a rather posh suburb just outside of the Nebulous X capital," explained Neal.

"Who cares?" said Braker.

13

"Maybe you should, trucker," said Herb, "because you just ran into a whole trailer-load of trouble. Gunberry produces more than its share of privileged bullies. And one of the worst is hot on our tails. We're being followed by a monster, a heartless, wild-eyed villain to make your blood run cold."

"Actually, he comes from a very good family," said Neal. "And aside from his sadistic tendencies he has a highly developed fashion sense."

"He's a beast," said Herb, "a horrible, salivating devil by the name of—"

"Prince Tony," said a smug voice.

Everyone spun around to see a tall, black-haired man in a spotless blue uniform and sapphire cape. A pompous sneer cut across his handsome face. It was Prince Tony himself—the Glamour Boy of Gunberry. Two soldiers stood behind him. Tall, metal helmets, like stovepipes, covered their faces, a small glass window in the front for vision. Their white uniforms were made of rubber along with their long, grey gloves and boots. Goons of Doom. An unwitting crewmember had let them in soon after Braker.

The debonair prince continued, "Gentlemen, please, let us not resort to calling names or making harsh judgments on others before we have all the facts."

"Facts, you murderer!" screamed Herb. "You destroyed our entire world."

"Don't be bitter, Herb," said Neal.

"Thank you," said Prince Tony. "Gentlemen, again, I plead for fairness. I have no quarrel with you personally; I've simply been assigned to escort these ladies back to Nebulous X. A special marriage selection is to be held in their honor at the palace of Lord

Preposterous. I'm told it's to be quite the party, with an open juice bar and everything."

"That sounds great," said Neal, "but at this point it's really hard to trust you. You did blow up our planet, you're forcing one of our princesses into marrying your slimy dictator, and who knows what will happen to her sister."

"Well, the last part's easy," said Tony. "The sister not selected will be quickly executed due to her loathsome hideousness."

"That does it!" growled Herb. "Now we know your hospitality is insincere."

Prince Tony caressed his narrow mustache. "Come now, my good man. Your boorish incivility is hardly appealing. Tell me, why such a buggery attitude toward Lord Preposterous's love overtures?"

"He is an oxygen-sucking mucus sac!" shouted Herb.

Tony nodded. "True, figuratively and literally. In fact, he makes us all rather queasy. Clearly then you can see why he is in need of companionship. You should be honored that your princesses were even chosen for the task."

"Wait a minute," said Braker. "How come Preposterous doesn't just marry a girl from his own planet?"

Prince Tony sniffed, giving Braker a cold once-over. "Because all the eligible females exiled themselves to the forgotten nether-dimensions when they realized a royal marriage to Lord Preposterous might be imminent."

"Oh, come on," said Braker. "The guy can't be that bad."

"Want to bet?" said Neal. "He's an alien space tumor on legs."

"That's disgusting," said Braker.

"Yeah," said Neal, "but that's not all. Imagine being soul mates with a pale, baggy-faced blister that smells like bad fish."

"Kind of makes my throat tight," said Braker.

"Sure, but I'm not even done yet," Neal continued. "He's also crude, obnoxious, cross-eyed, bald with a lumpy scalp, dirty, slovenly, constantly sweaty, bigoted, and insane."

"Truly sad," said Prince Tony.

Herb nodded. "And don't forget he chews with his mouth open, wears his pants embarrassingly tight, and always sneezes into his hands before reaching into the candy dish."

Braker shook his head. "Wow, you've convinced me, that's a list of shortcomings it'd be hard for anyone to overlook."

"Quite right, gentlemen," said Prince Tony. "And that's not even taking into consideration his reputation for mistreating the girls he does manage to take out. Does anyone remember that one girl he took to the annual Dictatorship Ball several years ago?"

"Ahh, yes," said Neal. "The Duchess of Trenchmoor, I believe. Whatever happened to her? She was lovely."

Prince Tony rocked lightly on his heels. "If I remember correctly, Preposterous sentenced her to life in gravity prison for slurping her drink too loudly."

"That's horrible," protested Neal.

"Yes," giggled Tony, "and the best part is she wasn't even the one doing the slurping—Preposterous was. Such a gagster, Lord P. Your princesses will just love him—they'll have to."

"Never," said Herb. "We'd sooner die than let you take those girls."

Prince Tony stroked his fur-trimmed collar. "I must say I anticipated such a fanatical response from you, although I had hoped you would be more reasonable. But, out of fairness, I will comply with your wishes for violence."

"Bad form, Herb," said Neal. "I told you that temper would get us into trouble one day."

"Sorry," said Herb, hanging his head.

"Now here's what we'll do," Prince Tony continued, "in two minutes I'll have my Goons spray you and your crew with a special blend of my very own Sauna Gel. I have it imported from a lava planet on the galactic rim; very expensive. I use it myself when I want to relax and don't have access to a spa. The only difference is that this mixture is extremely spicy. In fact, once contact is made, it will trap all the heat inside your bodies until you explode. Afterwards, while your gooey remains slide down the walls, I'll return to my ship with the ladies as planned. How does that sound?"

"Your lousy hot sauce doesn't scare me," said Herb.

Prince Tony smoothly drew his pistol, vaporizing Herb's head. "Gentlemen, I will not stand here and endure such profane abuse. My Sauna Gel is not lousy hot sauce. I assure you it is the finest toxic body oil in the universe. I don't use it on just anyone."

Neal looked at Braker. "Herb never did appreciate the finer things."

Prince Tony's Goons were already assembling the Sauna Blaster they had brought with them in big packs on their backs.

"Umm, perhaps we can negotiate after all," Neal suggested.

"Too late," said Tony. "I'm feeling very miffed."

"Well, we tried," said Neal, dashing from the hold.

"That appears to take care of your captain and first mate," said Prince Tony, addressing Braker and the remaining crewmen. "Does anyone else have something they wish to add?"

An awkward silence echoed through the room. Only the mechanical servants' constant offer of refreshments continued.

Braker knew it was a moment that begged for a final word of heroic, doomed defiance. "I...don't really work here," he stammered.

Prince Tony ignored the trucker. He had already turned his attention to the two princess sisters cowering behind a loveseat. One was red-haired, the other blond; both were gorgeous, with long legs and flowing gowns.

Tony was stunned by their beauty. "My dear maidens, you are without a doubt the most charming creatures in the universe." Purring, he extended his elbows. "Please join me, my ferry awaits."

There was nothing else for the sisters to do. They stood, each reluctantly taking an arm as the prince performed his high-heeled strut to the transportation hatch. The trio was almost to the threshold when one of the sisters shouted, "Please, someone, do something! Do anything!"

Braker looked at the Ditenian crewmen—they were all holding hands and crying; he knew she must have been talking to him. Emboldened by her confidence, he lunged for one of the Goons' pistols. Grabbing it, he shoved it into the soldier's belly and pulled the trigger. Nothing happened. He whirled, trying his luck on the other Goon—again nothing. Braker was holding the gun backwards. Behind him terrified Ditenians leapt for cover.

Prince Tony, cursing his Goons for their incompetence, now used his own custom-made sidearm to send a cluster of precisely aimed death beams at the trucker. Braker managed to avoid the barrage by throwing himself to the floor—only to watch helplessly as his own gun skidded back into the hands of its delighted Goon owner.

Both Goons' now joined their leader in firing, shattering the *Indulgence's* glass wall partitions and exquisite Ditenian furnishings. Sizzling destruction was everywhere. Showers of glowing sparks rained down on the mechanical men still trying to distribute drinks to the terrified crew who were snatching them up and downing them as quickly as they could while simultaneously running for the exits.

In the commotion, the princess sisters tried to make a run for it, but Prince Tony stuck out his leg, tripping them into each other; such was the prince's skill that he was able to divert the sisters' escape, take a few sips from a quickly snagged Black Hole Slammer, and continue firing all at the same time. He smiled to himself.

Meanwhile, Braker was busy squirming across the floor in an attempt to get control of the half-assembled Sauna Blaster. Upon reaching it, he flung the strap over his shoulder and lifted the heavy steel tube.

"Now you'll see what a space trucker can really do!" he shouted, pulling the trigger. The incomplete weapon exploded, spewing its noxious mixture in every direction, and coating Braker's spacesuit in a thick layer of the scalding red gel.

The last of the terror-stricken Ditenian crewmen had already abandoned the room when the Blaster went off. Only the moon dwarf musicians remained, but the eruption of Sauna Gel quickly cleared out the trio of dawdlers; they exited at a dead run with high-pitched squeals and waving hands.

The only other participant actually affected by the gel was one of Prince Tony's Goons. A glob of the deadly lotion had landed on his back and was already giving off the scent of burnt rubber. His partner had fared much better, somehow avoiding the blast while beating a retreat to the transportation hatch. Prince Tony was right beside him, dragging the sisters back to the shuttle by their hair.

For his part, Braker was on the floor again, this time trying desperately to get out of his smoking, gel-covered space suit. Being so distracted by this frantic work, he didn't notice Wayne's unexpected appearance at the transportation hatch, halting Tony's escape with the girls.

"Who are you?" snorted Prince Tony, disdainfully appraising the big man.

"I'm Wayne," said Wayne. "I'm with that feller over there on the floor, the one all covered in red paint."

"Destroy the peasant," Tony ordered his remaining trooper.

The Goon growled, drawing closer. Wayne just smiled—then smashed in the Goon's helmet with a monkey wrench.

Prince Tony watched the Goon collapse in a heap. "You have no style," said the prince, gracefully aiming his pistol at Wayne. "You're obviously a hillbilly space farmer."

"Well, this space farmer is about to milk your face," said Wayne, giving Tony a wrench wallop so colossal that it sent the prince cartwheeling through the air.

"You pitiful man," Prince Tony moaned, sinking against a wall, "your metaphor makes no sense, and your tool-wielding sadism cannot save you from your doom. The rest of my fleet is following and will soon be here to destroy you. It will be a fitting end to men of your brutality."

Braker had just shed his burning space suit when he heard Wayne's happy voice call out to him. "Braker, I've wrastled with the best they've got, and it ain't much! Let's go! I brought the *Egger's* rescue shuttle!"

"Perfect timing, buddy!" Braker shouted, running to the escape hatch. Passing the *Indulgence's* viewport, he could see Prince Tony's war fleet coming in from the distance.

"Listen," Braker exclaimed to the sisters, "this crate won't stand a chance against that fleet; you ladies should come with us. The *Steak and Egger* is waiting!"

The sisters watched the few remaining Ditenian crewmen frantically trying to get the ship's defense weaponry ready for one last fight; the trembling group stood in a circle, arguing over who would actually have to load the portable space mortars they had positioned in the *Indulgence's* portals.

Knowing their ship's destruction was inevitable at this point, the sisters quickly agreed to accept Braker's offer. The foursome piled into the waiting shuttle and prepared for launching. At the last minute, Braker ran to the rising gangplank.

"Let this be a lesson to you!" the trucker shouted to the groggy Prince Tony. "When you mess with Braker Ford, you're messing with class!" Then he turned and tripped back into the shuttle.

Chapter Three
A Little Romance

It took only seconds to reach the *Egger* by shuttle flight. As the escaping foursome of Braker, Wayne, and the two princesses squeezed into the hold, they witnessed the last moments of the *Shameless Indulgence* fighting it out against the Nebulous X war fleet. Leading the attack was Prince Tony's enormous personal command ship, the *Maiming Lily*—equipped with multiple flight decks, hundreds of fighter craft, portable siege equipment, medical facilities, a gift shop, and a night club, its size alone was intended to shame and humiliate any who were audacious enough to oppose it.

Every weapon from the *Indulgence* was firing now, but since the kind-hearted Ditenians guns only fired soap bubbles, the *Lily* completely disintegrated them with one simple Zero-Ray.

"We've got to move!" exclaimed Braker after witnessing the *Lily*'s incredible fire power. "They'll be coming after us next."

"We can't outrun them!" cried one of the princess sisters.

Braker gave her a sly look. "Not by conventional speed, baby, but once we blast into Psycho-Space, there's no way they can track us."

"Braker, you don't know how to navigate into Psycho-Space," said Wayne.

Braker rolled his eyes toward the princess sisters behind him. "Wayne, I am a professional," he said through clenched teeth. "Of course I can navigate through Psycho-Space."

"But you don't even have a license for Psycho-travel."

"Wayne…the girls," Braker pleaded.

"You can get six months in Solar Prison for Psycho-traveling without a license."

"Solar Prison doesn't sound so bad right now," said Braker as he flipped switches, turned knobs and scanned navigation charts. Wayne didn't answer; he was busy reading the owner's manual he found in the glovebox. Minutes ticked away; the *Lily* was right on top of them at point-blank range.

Braker slammed his fist on the control panel. "Alright, alright, I admit it. These rotten navigations are so complicated it would take a genius to figure it out."

Wayne was silently reading his booklet, moving his lips to what he was reading when he suddenly looked up, removed a small panel on the wall, and pulled back on the handle inside marked "Psycho-speed."

Instantly the ship was propelled forward with a burst of mind-crushing power.

"Thanks, Wayne," said Braker, trying to keep from losing his lunch in the surging Psycho-energy.

"No problem," said Wayne, retching into a nearby trash can.

Eventually, their bodies adjusted to the acceleration, and they were able to function normally again. Far out of reach of their enemies, Braker turned his attention to the princess sisters.

"So," he began, lifting his hat to wipe the sweat from his forehead, "let me introduce myself—I'm Braker Ford, space trucker. And you are?"

The blond princess spoke first, her blue eyes twinkling. "I'm Princess Babe, daughter of the good king Albert Fairlite." She hesitated as she stared with affection at the trucker. "Braker, I just want to thank you from the bottom of my heart for saving my sister and myself. We're the only Ditenians left in the galaxy now, and I want you to know I consider myself indebted to you forever." Her eyes closed slightly as she reached out to touch Braker's hand.

"Thanks, Babe," Braker coughed, surprised by such unabashed devotion.

Babe's sister spoke up now, not nearly as silky in her vocal tones as Babe, but still carrying a regal quality to her voice. "You'll have to forgive my sister," she began. "Babe's been given to excessive sweetness her entire life. In fact, it's so bad that if she actually hates something, the worst she can say is that she loves it only a little bit."

"That's weird," said Braker.

"Believe me, it hasn't been easy," replied the princess, "but somehow I've managed to endure it."

"Well, let's not get carried away," said Braker. "I mean, there's got to be a lot worse personality traits."

"Sure, that's what everybody says," said the princess, "but I can't stand the taste of all that sugar. Kind of like being forced to drink maple syrup every day of your life. Ticks me off. It just isn't fair really, of all the sisters in the universe, I get stuck with a perpetual ray of sunshine. Day after day, no matter how crummy the date or stale the party; no matter how lousy the food, or doltish the conversation, I have to tolerate her sickening gloss about thinking positive and loving everybody. It's like a cruel joke."

"I guess I don't get it," said Braker.

"You wouldn't," the princess continued. "But don't be concerned about me, I can handle it. Anyway, I'm Princess Contentious. And just so you don't think I'm overly critical based on my appraisal of my sister's annoying habits, I want to say it was very brave of you to come rescue us like you did, Braker—even if you did look like a spastic baboon fighting off our captors, and your lumbering friend was a little slow in coming to help out."

"Golly, thanks fer noticing," said Wayne, his mind clouded with visions of love for the crimson-haired beauty.

"Say," Braker giggled, "your name isn't really Contentious, is it? I mean that's just got to be a nickname or something, right?"

"I'll have you know it's an old family name held with great esteem, passed down from countless generations."

"A name like 'Contentious'?" Braker snorted. "Come on. Doesn't that mean 'argumentative'?"

Contentious put her hands on her hips. "I beg your pardon."

"He means 'crabby'," said Wayne.

"I know what he means," replied the princess, jutting her chin forward, "and for your information, on our planet it means 'one who is contented'."

"Well, everywhere else it just means 'crabby'," said Wayne.

Braker kicked Wayne in the shin.

"Sorry 'bout that," Wayne told Contentious, "what I meant to say is that's a right highfalutin' label you got, all right. It don't sound stuck-up, cranky, or ornery at'al."

Contentious sniffed and looked out the window. "Dishwater."

"What 'bout yer name?" Wayne continued, turning to Babe. "What's yer call-tag mean?"

"Oh, Babe's not actually my name," said the blushing princess. "When I was born my father christened me Effervescence. But of course that's not nearly as splendid a designation as my sister's, and as time went on everyone just ended up calling me Babe."

"Oh, I get it," said Wayne, "'cause you turned out to be such a fine-spun beauty, right?"

"Because she's the baby of the family, duh," said Contentious.

Braker gave Wayne a look of disgust. "Come on, Wayne, you should have known that."

"Yeah, I guess I should have," said Wayne scratching his head.

"So have we finished with the interrogation?" asked Contentious.

"Conty, please," said Babe, "they're only being polite." She gazed adoringly at Braker. "I think it's very thoughtful of you to inquire as to some of our family heritage."

Braker cleared his throat, glancing toward the blinking lights on the dashboard. "Oh, sure; we'd actually love to talk more but right now I'm afraid I probably really need to get back to the controls. It's highly unlikely, but I'd hate to see something go wrong while you're with us. Space trucker precautions, you know. In the meantime though, if you ladies are tired, please feel free to use the sleeping quarters in the back."

"Oh, how generous," cooed Babe.

Contentious stood up. "Yes, Braker, I believe after tonight's events we would appreciate that. Perhaps you could have what's-his-name show us the way."

"Oh, my handle's Wayne, Wayne Musher," said the farmer.

"Are you a space trucker too?" Babe asked.

"Nope, I'm a hillbilly space farmer. Braker and I are second cousins. His Uncle Earl married my Aunt Slucey; real nice folks. Aunt Slucey's been known to get mean grumpy, though. She got a growth on her hip that bothers her; moves on its own sometimes. Anyways, Braker just brought me along to see his nifty new space truck. And what a nifty truck it is. He run his last one in the ditch."

"These girls aren't interested in all that," said Braker, a smile covering his suddenly red face. "They need rest."

"Why, shore," said Wayne, jumping up. "That's enough yakkin' for tonight. Follow me, ladies. You'll be asleep faster than two hogs in a haystack."

The princesses bowed politely before following the farmer down the darkened hall.

A short time later, Wayne returned to the cockpit feeling rather dreamy after walking down the corridor with the one and only Contentious Fairlite. The big farmer plopped into the seat beside Braker.

"Braker, you might not understand this being a city boy like you are and all, but I feel like I just crammed my bare feet into a pile of creamy moon mud. I feel like I just hitched myself to the back of a coarse-haired sowbelly. I feel like I just bit into a warm stack of homemade lard-cakes. I guess you can tell those are all just different ways of saying—I'm in love. The only question I have is if the young lassie feels froggy herself."

"Contentious?"

"That's the one."

Braker shrugged, "Sure, you're a big sturdy guy; that's what princesses like— big sturdy guys to protect 'em from stuff."

"Well, if that's true then I ain't the only one on board who's found himself a little prairie apple."

"What are you talking about?"

"Braker, if that Babe Fairlite ain't pining for you then I got a buck-toothed grin."

"Think so?"

"Come on, Braker. She thinks you're a hero."

"I must admit I did feel some chemistry between us."

"Shore you did, you silly hay rake."

Braker tapped his fingers on the fractured dashboard. "I want to believe it, Wayne. But look at me. You saw the mess I made of things today. I'm no Asteroid Warrior, and I'm sure no Skippy Dodge. I'm just what they said earlier—an ordinary, insignificant space trucker; barely even that really. And don't forget Babe's a princess."

"You saved her life. That's bound to tickle her feet. Just don't give up, no matter what. She'll see the hero behind that bad haircut and clumsy stride."

"I might have agreed with you before I destroyed her ship."

"Braker, you can only chew yer cud fer so long before it loses its flavor. And you got to salt a fish before you fry it. And you shore cain't stack oats in a windstorm."

Braker nodded. "Wayne, I have no clue what you just said."

"All I'm saying is don't lose yer confidence. You're right, you are a space trucker—technically. That counts fer something. And you did save her life."

Braker scratched his chin. "Yeah, I guess I did."

"Shore you did. It ain't your fault you almost killed her first."

"Thanks, Wayne. That helps."

"Aw, don't worry about it. She ain't got nothin' else going fer her right now. Yer probably lookin' purdy good."

Braker thought of Lord Preposterous and his brazen kidnapping attempt. "Say, that's right. It's either me or marrying a walking space wart."

"Right, and I'm bettin' she'd probably choose you."

"She does need a protector," Braker agreed. "That Nebulous X war fleet is still out there. And those aren't the kind of guys who give up easy. They blew up an entire planet just so their leader could get a date."

"She's hopeless without you."

"I might actually be the one thing that poor girl has going for her."

"It ain't much, but she won't sneeze at it."

Braker smiled to himself. "You're right, as usual, Wayne. This is my chance; this is my shot. I could be space hero to a princess and become a galactic legend in the process. This is what I've been waiting for." He paused. "You really think I can do it?"

"Braker, she's gonna cling to you like a stink-lovin' tick on a skunk's hip."

"Then it's settled, I'm gonna wrap her up with all the true love and devotion a courageous space hero can give."

"'Course you are," said Wayne, "there shore ain't no real heroes around to do it."

Braker thrust his fist in the air. "Look out, Babe, 'cause you just hit the mother lode of love!"

Back in the *Egger*'s sleeping quarters a similar conversation was taking place.

"Oh, Conty, isn't he just wonderful?" Babe asked her sister as they sat on the edge of the bed.

Contentious began pacing the room. "I can't believe you, Babe, I really can't. You break up with a guy like Hunk Wilson and now you're falling for a greasy trucker like Braker Ford? Don't forget you're still royalty."

"Well, Braker should be royalty too," Babe responded. "He risked his life to save us. When have you ever seen a man do that?"

"But what about Hunk? Daddy scoured the planet to find the perfect specimen for you."

Babe nodded sadly. "I know. Hunk was a fine man; he just seemed a little self-centered at times. He would make me change my dress if he thought it clashed with his tan."

"But Hunk was perfect. Braker's skinny and his clothes don't fit well."

"Conty, maybe I can just see qualities in Braker that aren't as apparent as Hunk's muscles and naturally curly blond hair."

"Babe, this guy's a goof. Don't tell me he's fooled you with his pathetic posturing."

"Of course not, but underneath, there's something genuine. Something I've never seen before. It's ragged and real, and completely beautiful."

Contentious shook her head. "A trucker; Daddy would never approve."

Babe leaned forward, sobbing quietly. "Conty…Daddy's gone, and so is Hunk, and everyone else. We're all alone. Braker's the only one I can trust now."

Contentious sat down beside her sister, holding her close. "We've still got each other."

Babe looked up, smiling through the tears. "Sisters to the end."

Contentious held Babe's face. "Babe, you're right. Trust Braker. I think he is a good man—maybe a bumbling clod—but a good man. And he cares for you."

"Thanks, Conty, but you know Wayne seems to care for you too."

"That overall wearing farmer?"

"Of course; he's very sweet."

"He's a walking corn cob."

"Conty, he's simple and decent; obviously of a more rural tradition than ourselves but you can't hold that against him."

"Babe, he has the intelligence of a dog biscuit."

"So he's plainspoken, big deal; at least he's authentic. Do you really think any of your fancy party boys would have come to your rescue?"

"Maybe not, but you realize you're asking me to give my heart to a billy goat."

"No, I'm asking you to give your heart to a dependable, back-porch philosopher; a man raised in the arms of nature."

Contentious wrinkled her brow. "He is primitive, but when you put it that way, he does seem to have a certain noble savagery about him."

"Then it's settled? You'll love him?"

"If I have to."

"Conty, that's wonderful. Now try and say at least one good thing about him. He is your boyfriend, after all."

"Well, he is big and sturdy; I suppose that could come in handy for protecting me from stuff."

Chapter Four
Raising the Stakes

The small metal door slid open with a hiss, revealing the inner sanctum to the evil leader of the mysterious planet known only as Nebulous X. Into this dark chamber came the frail, elderly manservant to the planet's great dictator.

A booming voice called out from the towering throne, "Benchworth, what have you to report?"

The drooping steward gulped before giving his response. "I'm sorry, my Lord, but the news has not been good."

"Curses on you," came the reply as the shadowed figure rose from his throne, revealing the most feared tyrant in the universe—His Majesty, Lord Preposterous!

"Forgive me, my Lord," begged the assistant.

"This time, my faithful doormat, this time, and only because I need to solely concentrate on my great quest to find a suitable queen to join me in my power-mad lifestyle of conquest, destruction, and self-serving luxuries."

"Yes, I know how important this is to you and how frustrated a man of your quality must feel in these circumstances."

"Quit stalling, gas pouch," said Lord Preposterous. "Get on with it; what's the latest report?"

Benchworth gulped. "It appears Prince Tony was ambushed by a pair of random, wandering space trash. During the encounter, your prospective brides were abducted by the thieving duo. Thankfully, Prince Tony managed to survive and is organizing a pursuit as we speak."

Lord Preposterous rapped his jewel-encrusted fingers on the sides of his throne. "And just who were these hijackers who dared to steal the very princesses I was daring to steal?"

"We don't know that yet," said Benchworth, "although one was reported to be extremely inept and the other was an overgrown yokel."

Preposterous rose from his throne. He stepped close to his wobbling aide, his heavy black boots ringing on the ground with each step. "Benchworth, I am feeling cruel. My evil intentions are in danger of being compromised."

"It was indeed a brazen pilfering."

"So it was," said Preposterous. "And we must take desperate measures to prevent the successful escape of those two bandits."

"What do you propose we do, O Perfect Mind?"

"You know what we must do. I want those girls. And I want the schemers who stole them. We must call on The Doctor."

Benchworth managed a gasp of apprehension. "Oh no, please not The Doctor. He's too dangerous."

"Certainly he is," answered Preposterous, "but we have no other choice. With him on the case, I'm sure to win."

"Perhaps you could reconsider, just this once. The Doctor is scary, and he treats me like something he just stepped in."

Preposterous squeezed tight on Benchworth's scrawny throat. "You heard my desires. Are you with me, my friend?"

"Sire, I cannot, Benchworth squeaked.

"Then you die."

"I'm with you forever, my Lord."

"Good," smiled the pimple-covered ruler. "Now go, and inform The Doctor I request his presence at once."

Benchworth exited Lord Preposterous's throne room with a nervous knot growing in his stomach. A ring of sweat spread around his collar. He tapped The Doctor's code number into his handheld voice box while scurrying down the corridor. A stale voice received the call.

"You have reached the labs of Doctor Joseph P. Wilde, scientist, surgeon, master criminal, and micro-specialist in maiming technology."

"Good afternoon, this is High Secretary B.F. Benchworth, personal aide to his majesty, Lord Preposterous. I seek an audience with Dr. Wilde, please."

"'Kay," replied the disinterested voice.

A few moments later Dr. Wilde spoke into the line. "Benchworth, you bag of sludge, how dare you interrupt me! For what possible reason would an amoeba like you even try to distract my precious attention?"

Benchworth's left eye twitched. "The great and unholy Lord Preposterous sends a most cordial invitation for your immediate presence in his throne room."

Dr. Wilde snorted. "Again? How many times must I waste my invaluable talents in boring discussions with that dim-witted, child-brained emperor of yours? I am a busy man; it's not easy for me to just leave my experiments at a moment's notice!"

"But you are on Lord Preposterous's personal staff; you must comply with—"

"Don't try to manipulate me!" Dr. Wilde fumed. "Don't you realize I could have you killed in a million different ways? I'm not kidding. I have them categorized. I am a man of considerable brilliance and I refuse to be treated like a common servant!"

Benchworth felt his bowels about to give way. "Oh, my good doctor, I can assure you that you are highly respected."

"No, I'm not."

"Alright, if you say so. But may we expect you in an hour?"

"Make it two, but don't hold your breath."

The line went dead and Benchworth walked away with a newly developed limp, but quite thankful that the conversation went so well.

Three hours later Dr. Wilde made his entrance into the throne room, screaming as he came. "Thanks so much for ruining my entire day, you fat-mouthed little dictator! If you wish to stay in good standing with me, you had better pray this visit was quite necessary!"

"I assure you it is of the highest priority," said Lord Preposterous.

Dr. Wilde stopped short of the throne and folded his arms. "Spit it out, Preposterous."

Lord Preposterous began, his voice trembling with emotion. "Our revered kingdom of Nebulous X has been insulted, Dr. Wilde; my great name slobbered upon. Someone in the galaxy didn't let me get my way."

Dr. Wilde faked a yawn.

"This is serious," Preposterous continued. "Your esteemed emperor has decided it is time to seek a royal marriage."

"That's not news; you've been trying to get hitched for years, only you can't find anyone lame enough to go through with it."

"That's not true."

"Oh yes, it is. Everybody knows it."

"Will you listen? For your information, just today your colleague, Prince Tony, was escorting two young princess sisters here for the prospect of matrimony to me. Unfortunately, due to the unexpected interference of two rather low-living space travelers, the sisters have fled. Prince Tony is now hunting for the sisters. But I wish to take no chances in their return. Therefore, I am sending you to assist Prince Tony in their capture."

Dr. Wilde cut loose with an ear-piercing scream. "Prince Tony? You gave the job to Prince Tony? I could have told you this would happen. Prince Tony is so hilariously overrated. Give me just one example of a time he succeeded on a mission. You can't because he's not really interested in the advancement of your villainous causes. Not the way I am. All he cares about is decorating that tasteless bachelor castle of his and increasing his exotic shoe collection. Yet somehow, he always gets the good jobs while I'm the one who is always left to do his dirty work! Do you really think all I'm good for is running around behind that pretty-boy prince and cleaning up all his mistakes? I'm a fabulous scientist who has a special gift for creating weapons of gut-wrenchingly destructive capability!"

"Dr. Wilde, I'm tired of arguing. I want to get married. Now take a bunch of angry lab assistants, and that giant robot of yours, Buckmaggot, or whatever you call him—and go. Time is wasting."

"His name is Bullmack, and he's more than a giant robot. He's my greatest creation. In fact, if you must know, I almost view him as the moronic son I never had."

"I don't care," Preposterous boomed. "Go and assist Prince Tony in whatever way he desires. I want those sisters."

"Yeah, but afterward Tony will get all the glory for capturing them. Prince Tony always gets the glory, and all I get to do is scuff around that dingy lab of mine. I should be the one soaking up the well-deserved praise of an adoring population."

"Dr. Wilde, do you wish to continue receiving funds for your experiments?"

"Of course!"

"Then you will do as I say and join Prince Tony."

"Help Prince Tony, help Prince Tony, that's all I hear! Alright, I'll go, but mark my word, that prissy foot's not nearly as perfect as you seem to think he is. That's right, someday you'll see what your golden boy is really made of and how much I'm really worth."

Dr. Wilde turned abruptly, stomping out. When he was gone, Preposterous eased his gelatinous body back onto the throne. "So, how do you think it went?" he asked Benchworth, who was hiding behind the great chair.

"Just splendid," replied the cowering assistant. "I think things can only get better from here on."

"Me too," said Preposterous, his thick green lips quivering with joy. "Soon the universe will never be the same. Soon the interlopers will be punished, and I will begin selection of my bride. Soon I will no longer be the only galactic tyrant without a miserable wife to serve his every reasonless need."

The emperor began to laugh, an enormous gap-toothed grin crossing his pitted, blobish face. "Soon I will no longer be seen only as a seething pile of rancid, bologna-like flesh, but will instead be known for who I truly am—Lord Preposterous, Master of Evil Love!"

Chapter Five
Shipwrecked

An entire cosmic night had passed as the *Steak and Egger* coursed through Psycho-Space. Braker and Wayne were dozing in their observation seats when the anchor alarms began flashing. Braker shoved his hat to the back of his head and sat up straight. "Wayne, wake up, the engines have maxed out. We've got to go sub-Psycho—like right now!"

Wayne smacked his lips. "Sub-Psycho, shore enough," he said with a yawn. He ran his fingers through his hair. "So how we doin' that again?"

"How do we do it?" said Braker. "You're the one that read the instruction book. You tell me."

"Oh, right," said Wayne, rubbing his eyes. "Umm, well, them pages said you just activate the curb harness and then—hey, you're the space trucker."

"But you read the book!" shouted Braker. "Listen, we don't have time to argue about it now. If we overheat, we'll burn to a cinder."

"Right, right," said Wayne. "Well, it said we just activate the curb harness and then do something with a cinch binder."

"Okay," said Braker.

"Okay," said Wayne.

"So, what does any of that mean?" Braker shouted.

"How should I know, you're the—"

"Don't say it."

Wayne noticed a restrainer clamp on the dashboard. He quickly snapped it shut. The engine temperature decreased. "Well, that's a start," he said with a smile.

"Yeah," said Braker, "let's keep doing stuff like that."

They began searching the dashboard, adjusting anything that looked like it might slow the *Steak and Egger* down.

Braker opened a repressor panel. Wayne lit a suppression bulb. The *Egger* slowed, but not enough; they were still moving at Psycho-speed—only now the ship was rattling from hyper-turbulence.

"We're right on the edge of Psycho-Space," said Braker. "Our balancers are coming unhinged. We've got to commit to one stream of travel. It's sub-Psycho or nothing."

"Hey, here's a thing called a velocity strangler," said Wayne.

"That sounds useful," said Braker. "Try it."

"It's got a tag on it saying only for authorized use."

"What do we care?" Braker exclaimed. "We've got to stop! Try it."

Wayne turned the control dial. Nothing happened. Then the motor turbines began whining. Soon they were clanking. After that they were banging. A few unnerving minutes later it sounded as if something large and heavy broke loose. The *Egger* dumped a hot cloud of engine fumes and came to a dead halt.

"Well, we're stopped," said Wayne.

A quick assessment showed they were now in a new sector of the galaxy, hundreds of light years from where they started—and so far removed from Braker's hauling route that his limited computer mapping didn't even recognize the surrounding star system. As for the Psycho-braking, a few solar panels had come off during re-entry, along with the portside engine, but for the most part Braker felt things had gone well. The local cosmos itself was tranquil in its silent beauty. As far as the eye could see, only velvety blackness shrouded the sparkling stars. The calm weightlessness of space seemed to blanket all life within its floating, gentle caress.

Contentious and Babe entered from the sleeping quarters. They glistened with fresh beauty after a long, restful sleep.

"Good morning, gentlemen," said Contentious, with a curtsy.

"Well, good morning," said Braker.

Wayne slammed out of his chair, scrambling across the floor to present himself directly in front of the princess. "Howdy-do, frilly-girl. You shore do glow ripe purdy enough to make sore eyes water."

Contentious looked pleadingly toward her sister—Babe squeezed her hand and Contentious continued. "Alright, whatever you meant by that we can see you boys are quite enamored with us, so let's just get right to the point. Babe and I discussed our present situation last night. Your efforts to save us yesterday, though extremely muddled, were highly commendable. You're both young, and in the right light, could be considered somewhat cute. Therefore, we have decided to have affection for the both of you."

"Decided to have affection?" said Braker.

Babe took the trucker's arm, snuggling close. "My sister's training in courtly manners can make her appear cold, but believe me, she means each of you have won our hearts completely. Especially mine. We're your girlfriends now."

Wayne looked to Braker, then back to Contentious. "Did you mean what yer sister just spoke, girl?"

"Of course we mean it," said Contentious. "You have our full devotion. What's your problem?"

Wayne shuffled his feet. "Well, them's kindly things to say and all, but it's just that when yer sister's talkin' it sounds all huggy, but when it's your turn it sounds like you don't really mean it."

"What more do you want me to say?"

Babe frowned at her sister. "Conty, Wayne, comes from an entirely different culture. You have to learn to communicate on a level he's comfortable with."

"I don't think I can go that low."

"Love tries, Conty."

Contentious sighed. "Wayne, you're a low-functioning piece of cornbread, but I've come here to offer you a genuine portion of my fondness."

Wayne stuck his hands in his pockets. "I sure enough appreciate the sentiment, Princess. But I still ain't feelin' what yer drivin' at."

"Conty, a rung lower," said Babe.

"This is ridiculous," said Contentious. "He knows what I mean."

"It's not just about the knowledge, Conty. It's about connecting emotionally. Adjust your vocabulary for your beloved."

"Oh, I hate this," said Contentious, clawing at her face.

"Focus on the love, and just let it out," said Babe.

41

Contentious rolled her eyes. "Plowboy, I done come up in here to be your one-and-only honeycake 'cause your beefy man-scent straight-up horse-stomped my heart. Take me like I'm the last dinner dumplin' on the gravy plate."

Wayne let out a long whoop, slapping his knee. "Now them's lovin' words, gal! Sure bet, I'm yer man." He turned to Braker. "Hot potatoes! Ain't this better than a pan full of squat?"

"It sure is," said Braker, looking at the sisters. "And believe me, girls, we're going to treat you like precious cargo. You won't have to worry about a thing from here on out."

"Yer my rosy-haired tootsie," said Wayne, puckering up.

"Don't push it," said Contentious, elbowing the farmer. "Now listen. Since we've finally got all those love negotiations sorted out, let's move on to more important matters. We're still in deep trouble. Lord Preposterous's Goons could show up any time. What are you guys going to do to protect your girlfriends?"

Braker pulled away from Babe's embrace. "Hey, wait a minute. Are you two just warming up to us so we'll protect you?"

"No, Braker, not at all!" exclaimed Babe. "This is genuine love. Dangerous circumstances brought us together, yes, but we're with our perfect counterparts. I'm sure of it. We just have to survive the journey, that's all."

Braker turned from Babe to study Contentious. "Is that the truth?"

Contentious nodded. "Unfortunately, yes. Babe clearly needs the honest companionship of a common slob, and Wayne needs housebroken. Obviously, we've found our perfect counterparts. I apologize if I sounded insensitive."

"That's as dead-on a reckoning as I've ever heard," said Wayne. "Love's got us pegged alright."

"I can't argue with it," said Braker.

Babe squealed with delight. "Okay, so where do we go from here?"

Braker grinned. "Well, I figure this shouldn't be too hard of a jam to get out of. We've got a decent head start, so I've come up with a couple options I think are pretty good. Now the first one is the simplest—we'll just get you girls to the nearest law-enforcement satellite as quick as we can and let the police handle it; they're trained at this kind of stuff and it gets you girls into some immediate protection. What do you think?"

"The cops?" said Contentious. "That's your plan? Please. What good will some space cops do? Lord Preposterous blew up an entire planet to snag us. You think a thousand ship space fleet will hit the brakes just because we're clamped up in some copper's outpost?"

"Okay, well—"

"I mean, what are the cops going to do against a space warlord and an army of smokestack-headed gunmen? This isn't just your average crime gang. These are planet-scrapping wife-snatchers. No, sir, this is way out of their league."

"I said, okay."

"I just can't believe you would even suggest a course of action so incredibly feeble. This is our future we're talking about. Me and Babe, the last of our kind. If that's the best you've got, we're in real trouble."

"Alright, I get it!" Braker exclaimed. "Forget I even suggested it. I said it's not our only option. I've got others."

"Hey, buddy, don't bite my head off," said Contentious. "You blue-collars are so hot-tempered."

43

"Conty, you're being snippy," said Babe. "Remember your poise." She turned to Braker. "Pay no attention, it's a fine suggestion, that's just my sister's anxiety talking."

"It really wasn't a very heroic plan, anyway," Wayne whispered into Braker's ear.

Braker took a deep breath, grinned, and began again. "Okay, so here's my other plan. Wayne and I are not from around here; Lord Preposterous doesn't even know who we are. And you two don't even have a planet to go back to, so—we just fly back to our corner of the universe and take you with us. You'll never be found again."

"That's your other plan?" said Contentious. "Just run away? That's not even a plan, that's just…running! We're doomed."

"Yeah, that's not really a very heroic plan, either," Wayne whispered into Braker's ear.

"Can you believe it?" Contentious continued to wail. "Babe, this guy's plan is to just keep doing exactly what we're already doing! Tell him that's not a plan!" She grabbed Babe by the shoulders. "Tell him!" Spinning, she pointed at Braker. "You're a goof."

Babe looked at Braker, her eyes shining. "Braker, you're right, Lord Preposterous doesn't know who you or Wayne are; a space trucker and a farmer can just fly away and never be found again. And Contentious and I have nothing—no planet, no family, not even a kingdom; in a way we're not even really princesses anymore. What I'm trying to say is—your plan is marvelous! So yes, please, take us with you. Conty and I will start our new lives as hard-working common space women. I'm ready to learn about space trucking."

Braker stifled a gasp. "You mean it? You really like the plan?"

"It's perfect."

"Babe!" cried Contentious.

Babe took her sister's hand. "You know it's true. Everything is gone. It's time to start over."

"But as common space women?"

"A life filled with love is never truly commonplace, Conty. Together to the end?"

Contentious groaned. "I suppose."

Wayne let out a joyous howl, sweeping Contentious up in his arms. "We's gonna raise us some chickens, gal!"

Contentious hung limp in the embrace. "Maybe we should've checked in with the cops after all."

Braker smiled at Babe. "From here on in it's you and me, Princess. And don't you worry, I won't let you down."

Just then every light, alarm, and siren went off in the freighter at once.

Braker dashed to the controls. "What the heck? Everything's jammed!"

"What's wrong?" Babe asked, leaning in beside the trucker.

"I don't know," said Braker. "All the instruments just locked up."

"Braker, I'm scared," said Babe.

"Don't worry," Braker replied, flashing a weak smile, "it's probably just something simple like an over-cranked gravity spring or a sticky blitzar valve."

"Or it could be the way you almost ripped the ship in half coming out of Psycho-Space," said Wayne.

Braker sighed. "Yeah, it could be that too, Wayne."

"Hey, just what kind of a pilot are you?" asked Contentious.

"Not a very good one," shrugged Wayne.

Braker shot Wayne an angry glance. "Don't everyone get hysterical. Just give me a minute. In fact, why don't you girls just go on back to the sleeping quarters and relax while I figure this out."

"Sure, why not," said Contentious. "What's more relaxing than drifting in the black hollow of space while our pilot tries to figure out why all our controls are frozen?"

"Conty, this is no time to be sour," said Babe.

As she was speaking, all the lights in the Egger went out. A moment later the artificial gravity broke, leaving everyone to spin helplessly in the darkness.

"How about now?" asked Contentious.

Babe slowly drifted across the hold. "Conty, must you always be so negative?" she said just before her beautiful face thumped off the windshield.

"Girls, relax. Really, it's not that bad," said Braker.

"That's right," said Wayne. "I honestly expected Braker to have made it a whole lot worse by now."

"Thanks, Wayne," said Braker.

The back-up generator systems suddenly came on, illuminating the control panel with a dim green light. Even a thin layer of gravity reinstated itself across the floor.

"Hey, we've got some power back," said Wayne. "Maybe Braker was right; things aren't that bad."

"Uh, no, they're actually pretty bad," Braker moaned. "That's the emergency reserves."

"Shore it is," said Wayne. "But how's that a bad thing?"

"It means we've reached terminal operation mode. We have ten minutes before everything shuts down again permanently—including our air."

"Well, there's just no way I'm relaxing now," said Contentious.

"Braker, I'm sure you can fix it," said Babe, drawing close.

"I wish I could, Babe, but when a big rig like this is forced to use its emergency reserves, it's just not a simple matter anymore. This is complicated high-tech stuff. It could take a certified technician weeks to find the cause of the problem."

"Uh, Braker, can I talk to you for a minute?" said Wayne in a hushed tone.

They moved to a corner where Wayne whispered into Braker's ear. "I was just thinking, remember how you woke up late this morning?"

"Yeah."

"And how you said there wasn't time to go through the standard truck checks before taking off."

"Yeah."

"Well, I don't remember you winding the Trip Timer after you turned on the power."

Braker slugged Wayne in the arm. "Wayne, look at me—Space Trucker. Think about it. Even the least experienced space traveler knows you have to wind the Trip Timer every day."

"Oh yeah, that's the one other thing you get to do besides waiting to use the little fire extinguisher."

Babe and Contentious were still standing at the controls, studying the console. "Braker," Babe shouted, "are you sure it's not your Trip Timer? It looks like it could use winding."

Wayne stared at Braker.

"Shut up, Wayne," said the trucker.

47

Braker hurried over to the control console and winced. "Alright, if it makes everybody feel better, it's possible I *may* have forgotten to wind it this morning."

"What kind of a pilot forgets to wind their Trip Timer?" said Contentious.

"Not a very good one," said Wayne.

"Wayne!" shouted Braker.

"Please, quit complaining, everyone," said Babe. "Don't you see? Our trouble's over. We can just wind it now and be on our way."

Braker winced again.

"Braker, what's wrong?" asked Babe.

Contentious stepped forward threateningly. "Say it, buster."

"Well, that's just it," said Braker, "even if we do wind it now, the sub-grafters won't have time to recharge before we lose all power."

"Yup, you really blew it this time," said Wayne.

Babe was staring out the windshield when she suddenly whirled around. "Hey, wait a minute, everybody—is that a planet below us?"

Braker leaned forward. Dangling beneath them was a tiny, bleached dot surrounded by a ring of glowing suns. "It sure is!" the trucker smiled. "And if I can steer us down to it, we may just have a chance after all."

"Well, don't just stand there lookin'," Wayne shouted, "drive this plow!"

Braker maneuvered the *Egger* into a steep descent. Without propulsion they crept forward at a sleepy pace until entering the alien atmosphere. Suddenly their lethargic slide turned into a furious, fiery plunge. The small white planet drew closer until details of its desolate chalky surface rushed into focus.

"Slow down, Braker!" shouted Wayne.

"I can't," Braker replied. "There's no power to the brakes."

"You're trying to land a spaceship and we don't have any brakes?" said Contentious.

Wayne shrugged. "Well, he also forgot to wind the Trip Timer, so…"

"Is there anything else we should know about that might kill us?" Contentious asked.

Braker sighed. "Alright, we're hauling leftover sunshine, and when we crash all that energy is probably going to make for one big explosion."

"Sunshine!" shouted Contentious. "You guys are hauling sunshine? You gotta be kidding me!"

"Nope, it's gonna get real shiny," said Wayne.

"There's got to be something we can do!" Babe cried.

"Run to the back!" Braker shouted, leading the stampede to get as far as possible from the nose of the ship.

Babe and Contentious ducked off into the sleeping quarters, slipping under the mattress while Wayne dove headlong into the rear storage compartment. Braker, way ahead of them all, never slowed down until he reached the exit ladder at the farthest end of the corridor.

"Braker, what are you doing?" Wayne shouted.

"Looking for the fire extinguisher!" Braker replied.

The ship pierced the ground with all the power of a charging missile. Two-thirds of the *Egger* were pulverized instantly, erupting into a deadly fireball as the solar shielding gave way.

"Help us, Wayne!" cried Babe, flinging open the burning door to the sleeping quarters.

Wayne butted his head over the side of the doorway amid a shower of sparks from above. The long, heavy freighter was rammed into the ground like a stake, sticking straight up into the sky. Babe and Contentious were now below the farmer, with a rising tide of exploding gas making its way towards them.

"Hold on, you gals!" Wayne exclaimed. "I'll get ya out of there; these star freighters are just loaded with all kinds of helpful outer space gadgets." He whirled around searching for something to lower to the women. He was in luck—on the wall was an Emergency Rescue Cabinet. Reaching inside, he was elated to discover an old-fashioned Distance Extender; his joy was short lived— it was a non-retractable model. Tossing the Extender aside he reached back into the cabinet and pulled out a Personal Transporter Canister, but the can opener was missing. Flinging it into the fire, he dug into the cabinet once more, this time finding something labeled as an Anti-Gravity Device. Hastily aiming it at the dangling sisters, he squeezed the trigger. "Here comes help!" he shouted to the sisters just before the container shot out of his hand and went floating into the upper portions of the ship. "Doggone it, space can be frustrating," said the farmer.

With alternatives running out, Wayne whipped off his shirt from under his overalls. Holding the tip of one sleeve, he lowered it to the sisters. "Cain't you reach it?" he blared.

Babe stretched her arms up as far as possible; there was a good five feet in between.

"No, it's not long enough," said Babe. "Try something else."

"And hurry," added Contentious. "It's getting hot down here!"

Suddenly, there was a crashing from above, followed by the sight of a screaming Braker tumbling from his ladder. He dropped past Wayne and was about to pass the princess sisters when he caught hold of Wayne's dangling shirt. By the time the trucker regained his senses, the girls were using him to fill in the gap. Babe started first, crawling up one leg while Contentious took hold of the other.

"You saved us, my hero!" squealed Babe, as she and Contentious each kissed Braker on the cheek during their climb over his back.

The girls gave Wayne a slightly different reception upon reaching his level. "Thanks for trying," Babe said softly, too compassionate to look the farmer in the face.

"Massive fail, Clyde," said Contentious, smacking him on the ear. "Try not to be a total disappointment next time, please."

"Conty, that wasn't polite," Babe scolded. "Wayne did his best; he can't help it if he's not as resourceful as Braker."

Contentious rubbed her forehead. "Babe, let's be honest, I'm not convinced *either* of them are that resourceful—let alone competent—but at least give me room to communicate my frustration with Wayne's failure; like you said, we've got to understand each other if this relationship is going to work. I've got a feeling it's not going to be easy getting through to this hayseed."

"She touched me," said Wayne, smiling to himself. "She actually touched me."

Babe stared at the delighted farmer. "I see your point."

As the sisters conferred, Wayne hoisted Braker back to the ledge. It was a short distance to the escape ladder; soon all four were crowding the hatch.

Braker took a quick look through the opening. Nothing but sand dunes swept out toward the blazing, sun-drenched horizon.

"It's a long drop, but there's no other choice," he said. "Maybe the sand will cushion our fall."

With that, Braker bounded out of the hatch, through the flames encircling the ship, and finally sunk neck deep into the soft, white sand below. The remaining threesome did likewise.

"Nice beach," said Contentious, popping her head above the sand.

The *Steak and Egger* exploded, sending hot shards of steel far across the desert along with seemingly endless beams of sunlight that rose toward the clouds. The charred superstructure would continue to burn like a flaming geyser for days to come.

Braker plucked his arms from the shifting sand and began swimming away from the wreckage.

"Looks like we're gonna be here awhile," he coughed, spitting out small bits of metal, "we might as well get acquainted with this place."

As the group pulled themselves through the sand, Wayne looked over at Braker. "Braker, I'm just realizin' something."

"What's that, Wayne?"

"Well, remember how you run your last truck into the ditch?"

"Yes, Wayne."

"Well…you shore got that story beat."

"Be quiet, Wayne."

Chapter Six
A Day in the Sun

J. J. Whammo leaned across his weather-beaten desk. "There you go," he said in his high-pitched, squeaky voice, "that beauty is all yours, and I'll tell you what, I can't remember when someone made a better deal on one of my ships."

The blue-skinned alien sitting across from J.J. was feeling quite pleased with his purchase. Even as he walked out of the office and squeezed into his newly acquired sky-speeder he couldn't help but congratulate himself on his shrewd handling of the transaction. He might have felt slightly different if he had seen the fast-talking salesman behind him trying frantically to replace the dented rear bumper that kept falling off the old vessel's exhaust port. But for now, the alien was pleasantly ignorant of any such shortcomings as he blasted off in a cloud of smoke and sparks while J.J. strolled back to the office counting his money.

J.J. was a short little man with short little arms and a round little face, but perhaps that's why he worked so hard to develop his oversized attitude, along with that handy ability of convincing others that he always had something they couldn't live without.

It was J.J.'s space-lot that Braker Ford and his company found themselves on after several hours of swimming through the deep desert sand. Overjoyed at reaching solid ground a mile back, the group was even more ecstatic at the first sight of J.J.'s flashing neon sign, indicating some kind of life.

"'J.J. Whammo's Used Spaceship Palace ahead one dune'," read Braker. "Well, if we're going to run into any people on this planet, I can't think of any better than a spaceship salesman." He pulled his wet shirt away from his chest.

"Not unless it was a spaceship salesman with a pool," said Wayne.

Over the next hill, they arrived at J.J.'s Spaceship Palace, which wasn't much of a palace at all, but merely a half-dozen space wrecks scattered around an old wooden shack. A big yellow flag was planted at each corner of the lot with little glowing lights stretched from pole to pole. The decorations didn't help much, despite their gaudy ornamentation the place still looked like a long-forgotten desert outpost.

The group was barely within visual range when the door of the shack flew open and J.J. came scampering into the daylight. "Hello, friends!" he called out when they got closer. "What can I do for you fine desert travelers today?"

"We need us a ship," said Wayne.

J.J.'s keen eyes paused on the farmer. "Well, you certainly know how to pick the right place. I'm prepared to satisfy any of your space-traveling needs, from simple hydraulic thruster converters to the most lavish star mufflers. I like to think I dangle the universe at your fingertips; what's your price range?"

The sweaty group stared at each other.

"My wallet was in the glovebox on the *Egger*," said Braker.

"I've only got some change left over from lunch," said Wayne.

"Don't look at us," said Contentious, "royals don't carry their own money."

"I could donate my earrings," said Babe. "They cost daddy several moons."

J.J. chuckled. "All right, kids, all right, I get it. You want to finagle the best deal you can, but let me give you a word of advice—don't try to bluff a bluffer. The old, 'we don't have any money, but I'll trade you my priceless jewelry' bit is the creakiest sucker play in the book. You're dealing with J.J. Whammo now. It'll take real cash to gain yourselves one of my star rockets. So, let's dispense with all the flimflam and get down to talking actual dollars and cents."

"But, honestly, Mr. Whammo," said Babe, "the jewels in my earrings were mined from the stellar mass of black holes. They could easily pay for your entire inventory."

"Of course they could, child—if you really had them. Such jewels, as I'm sure you know, are very rare. Despite what your daddy told you, I doubt either of us is lucky enough to be in the presence of the genuine articles."

"Listen, mister," Braker interrupted, "we don't have time to haggle about money and jewels. If we don't get back into space, we're all going to die!"

J.J. threw his arms toward the trucker. "Whoa there, youngster, you're sounding just a wee bit emotionally disturbed—and you're wrong on two counts. First, there's always time to haggle about money and jewels. Second, nobody's going to die. Now tell ol' J.J. what's got you so strung out."

Braker sighed. "We're on the run from a crazed dictator who wants to kidnap our girlfriends so he can force one to marry him.

Our ship was destroyed when we crashed here and I'm sure there are patrols looking for us right now. We need a ship to get us back into space, but we really don't have any money; how's that?"

J.J. nodded. "Okay, listen, you're obviously easily excitable and prone to acting like a baby—although my heart is breaking for you. I've dealt with softies like you many times before so just listen to everything I say and I'm sure I can work a deal out of you. I have an excellent time payment plan for people in your position."

"Please, sir," said Babe. "What Braker said is true, we're not here to make deals; we simply need your kindness. We barely survived a terrible crash and then had to swim half a day through this thick desert sand."

"Boy, you kids really are mixed up," said J.J. "Everyone knows this planet's not made out of sand."

"It's not?" said Braker.

"Far from it," said J.J. "Why do you think I have a space lot out here? It's because most sensible people know it's not made of anything remotely like sand and want to get as far away from this planet as possible. They'll pay anything to go. It's life or death."

"But what's the planet made out of that's so horrible?" Braker asked.

"Well, it's certainly not sand," said J.J., laughing to himself. "Actually, it's a sugar-like substance created by the planet's unique super-abundance of core vitamins and minerals."

"You mean this planet is made entirely of sugar?" said Braker.

"Basically, yes."

"Oh, how sweet," said Babe.

"Say, that's my kind of planet," said Wayne, scooping up a handful of the white grains and licking it from his palm.

"Well, it's not exactly sugar," J.J. went on. "I said it's a sugar-*like* substance. Its main difference is its highly addictive nature that leads to near instant stupidity followed by incurable insanity. Worse yet, if you don't kick the habit, you'll eventually die."

Wayne stopped in mid-lick, spitting the sticky droplets all over J.J.'s shoes.

"Thank you, my boy," said J.J. "You're another fine example of why dog collars shouldn't be just for dogs."

"I can't believe it!" exclaimed Braker. "Now we're marooned on a Poison Sugar Planet; what could be next?"

With a burst of ear-splitting noise, a squadron of Nebulous X warships suddenly came swooping down from the clouds. In the lead was the unmistakable *Maiming Lily*, Prince Tony's personal, city-sized warship. The *Lily* landed directly on top of J.J.'s compound, smashing it and his collection of used spaceships beneath its massive bulk.

As the *Lily's* gangplank slammed down at Braker's feet, a mechanical voice boomed through a series of loudspeakers. "Worthless space trash, prepare to surrender yourselves to the mercies of the most awesome ruling force in the galaxy!"

J.J. leaned over to Braker. "Do you know these people?"

"Who do you think they are, considering we just told you we're on the run from an evil war fleet?"

"Okay," said J.J., putting a hand on Braker's shoulder. "You are a person completely incapable of dealing with stress. Take a two-minute vacation and let me handle this. Situations of this magnitude are merely a matter of communication; my specialty."

"Hello, friends," said the salesman, waving as dozens of Goons filed onto the white plain. "You seem to have had a problem with your landing navigations, you accidentally crushed my business.

I'm sure you're planning on fully compensating me for my loss, but in the meantime, could I help in giving some directions?"

A tall, silhouetted man stood at the top of the gangplank. Stepping into the afternoon suns, he was revealed to be none other than Prince Tony, Glamour Boy of Gunberry! The prince was attired in the finest of royal desert wear: an ivory silk shirt, thin linen cape, soft felt boots with turned down cuffs, and a bright red sash hanging at a fashionable slant from his waist. J.J. began to introduce himself but was cut short when Prince Tony stiff-armed him out of the way.

"It's him!" Babe gasped.

"But we saw you blow up on the Ditenian ship!" Braker exclaimed.

Prince Tony put his hands on his hips. "My dear intellectual sapling, you will soon learn that Prince Tony is not so easily defeated." He offered his hand to the princess sisters. "Ladies, once again I offer you transport to the home of Lord Preposterous. You shall be quite comfortable on the journey, I assure you. And one of you will even become his future soulmate if he orders you to be."

Babe pressed closer to Braker while Contentious lashed out, striking Prince Tony across the cheek.

Prince Tony snatched her by the wrist, squeezing hard. "You little vixen, I'll soon break you of that high-spirited pride."

"Braker, we cain't let that snooty bacon-sniffer take our gals," Wayne gulped.

"I know, just gimme a second," said Braker.

Before Braker could make a move, another gigantic spaceship appeared in the sky. This one rivaled the *Lily* in sheer size but was bristling with telescopes, radar dishes, and little wiggling antennas that shot bolts of high-voltage lightening. It was the *Flying Electric Laboratory,* Dr. Wilde's personal spacecraft, layered with deck after deck of gadgets and unlicensed weaponry.

When the landing maneuvers were complete, the doctor himself strode out from within the ship's sterilized confines. A monkeyish aide stumbled along behind him. "Say it!" growled Dr. Wilde, slapping his helper in the chest.

The aide sneezed, wiping his nose with the palm of his hand. "By order of the Great Lord Preposterous, the inadequate Prince Tony is to be relieved of this holy mission of wife-hunting and for none other than our beloved Dr. Wilde to be passed the staff of leadership. How was that?"

"Good, boy, good," Dr. Wilde complimented, rumpling the orderly's hair. "Well, Prince Tony, I don't think any more needs to be said. As you just heard, Lord Preposterous has fired you from the case and left me in charge. You can take your disgrace of a unit back to Nebulous X, I'll finish this job."

Prince Tony laughed. "You liar, Lord Preposterous didn't give you that order; I just spoke with him, and he told me he dispatched you as mere reinforcement on this case. I'm still in charge here."

"He changed his mind!" Dr. Wilde roared. "Now I don't have time for any more of this foolishness! Give me those girls!"

"I won't do that," said Tony, "but I will make a call to Lord Preposterous. I have the strongest notion that this is just another one of your pathetic schemes to see your name in the papers instead of mine, and I want to be the first to inform our commander of your self-serving, traitorous ways."

Dr. Wilde exploded. "Filthy simpleton! Do you really think I can be dusted off so easily? I am a scientific genius; brilliant! You will respect what I say!" He lunged for Prince Tony's throat. "Respect what I say!"

Prince Tony slapped the raving doctor down, smacking him back and forth soundly across the face. "I'm sorry, but as I said before, there are just some things I won't do, although I will bid you farewell as I return with my trophies."

Dr. Wilde rolled over in the sugar dust, a trail of blood running from his lips. "I'll kill you; I swear I'll kill you."

Prince Tony flicked a booger at the ancient man.

"Bullmack will be your executioner," Dr. Wilde whispered, turning on a small beeper strapped to his belt.

And then it came, a monster, an unstoppable, towering behemoth—Bullmack, a flesh-covered robotic creation from the early days of Dr. Wilde's dark-shrouded career. The android looked deceptively like a man—enormous arms and legs protruded from a block-like torso while an overgrown beard sprouted from his otherwise bald head. His wardrobe consisted of a leather vest, pants, and a pair of heavy moon-scraper boots. He was completely indistinguishable from a human except for the loud, annoying squeaking of his mechanical joints.

Prince Tony had no idea how much fear should have been streaming through his body at that moment—Bullmack was the most ferocious killing machine he, or anyone else, had ever seen in the universe. The beast enjoyed inflicting pain; his only flaw, and one Dr. Wilde had never been able to correct, was how to increase his intelligence without stealing away some of his wild brutality. Eventually though, to the regret of any who crossed paths with the robot, Dr. Wilde chose to leave Bullmack a mindless, blood-loving punisher, while doing most of the creation's deep thinking for him.

"I get killing done," said Bullmack in a husky, yet jovial tone.

Dr. Wilde jumped to his feet. "Exactly right! Kill Prince Tony and any fool who gets in your way!"

Bullmack laughed a jolly belly laugh as he threw his arm around one of the nearby Goons. The soldier crumpled to the ground—broken neck.

Prince Tony snapped his fingers. Three Goons stepped up from behind him, each carrying a heavy weapon. "Not another move," Tony told the doctor. "I trust you recognize these devises."

"Of course I do; I'm the one who invented them," said Dr. Wilde. "That's a Shrivel Gun, a Trample Beam, and a Mood Cannon. How dare you use my own weapons on me!"

"It's your own fault for creating them," said Tony. "Besides, you made them for our service, so keep your monster away."

"Heel, boy," Dr. Wilde ordered.

"But I was fighting the men," said Bullmack.

"Heel!" the doctor snapped.

Bullmack sighed and plopped down in the dust.

Dr. Wilde glared at the prince. "So, what's your next move, Fancy-Pants?"

"Just this," said Tony. He nodded toward the *Lily*. In response, a long, metal arm unfolded from the side of the ship, grabbing Contentious and drawing her, kicking and screaming into its steel belly. Babe was snagged next. The beautiful blond was stunned with fear, unable to even utter a peep.

Braker, without stopping to think, turned and leapt, grasping tightly onto the mechanical arm that was carrying the princess away.

Braker's daring heroics quickly melted Babe's paralyzing terror. "Braker," she gasped, gulping in air, "Braker, ooh, I love you!"

Those three simple words slammed into Braker's skull like a renegade meteor; he saw stars, flowers, rainbows, and fuzzy little puppies. The beauty of life flooded his very soul. He opened wide his arms to embrace the universe…and fell twenty feet to the sugar below. The metal arm finished pulling Babe inside and shut the door behind itself.

"Is that really the best you could do?" said J.J. as Braker lay groaning in the dust.

Prince Tony pumped his fist in the air. "My dear Dr. Wilde, as you can see, I have accomplished my task after all. And so, I shall go. But do not fear, I know how eager you are to contribute to our Majesty's great mission. I will leave these three meddling interlopers to your handling. I'm sure Lord Preposterous will be glad to hear they have been adequately punished for their interference."

With that, Prince Tony and the rest of his Goons disappeared into the *Lily*, the squadron soon heading into the stratosphere unhindered.

Down below, Wayne stood straight up on the white sugar plain, arms hanging down and jaw open while Braker ran in circles, punching himself in the head.

Dr. Wilde watched the sky until his rival was too far away to be seen. Grinding his teeth, he motioned for Bullmack to round up the prisoners.

J.J. Whammo saw the robot coming. "Say, friend, perhaps we could negotiate a solution to this slight misunderstanding."

"I don't think so," said Bullmack. "I'm just a dumb robot. Everything to me is a misunderstanding."

"Well, perhaps then I could convince you that I'm actually on your side."

"Nope, I'm usually too confused to be convinced of anything."

"I see, well—"

"Prisoners aren't allowed to talk to me," said Bullmack. "If you talk to me again, I'm allowed to pull your lips off."

J.J. slapped his hands over his mouth.

The robot quickly collected J.J. and his two companions, dragging them into Dr. Wilde's presence. Although not yet acquainted, one look into the doctor's bulging, bloodshot eyes and the three prisoners knew nothing could prepare them for the horrors about to be unleashed upon them now.

Chapter Seven

Here Comes Knothead!

Braker, Wayne, and J.J. Whammo dropped painfully back into consciousness after each had been knocked out by a single finger flick from Bullmack.

"What's going on?" Wayne asked groggily.

Dr. Wilde's hot face appeared before him. "You have just awakened from the sleep of the ignorant, weak, and pathetic."

Wayne thought for a moment. "Well, good morning then," he said, smiling.

Dr. Wilde stared at the farmer. "You are incredibly stupid. You are obviously a hillbilly space farmer."

Wayne frowned. "Mister, you're about as friendly as a flat-footed man walkin' on sharp rocks."

"Get away from me!" yelled Dr. Wilde.

"I cain't," said Wayne after trying to do just that, "I figure to be strapped to this giant bomb-shaped object."

"It is a giant bomb," groaned Braker, strapped in line next to Wayne and J.J. The trucker looked at Dr. Wilde. "And I suppose now you're going to detonate us at any minute, right?"

Dr. Wilde laughed. "Not that simple, meatball. That would be much too easy on you; the fact is I'm not going to detonate it at all—you are! You see, you and your friends are strapped to my brand-new invention, the Plasma Heat Atomizer; I created it while you were still knocked unconscious."

"What exactly does it do?" J.J. asked.

"Very simple," said Dr. Wilde. He pointed to a long tube that extended from the middle of the gigantic bomb, running along the ground until terminating several feet in front of the three prisoners. "That tube, as you can see, connects to a scale at its end; on one side is a cup with a tiny portion of plasma-globylene, a substance that expands in heat. Due to the heat on this planet, it will soon weigh down the cup it is contained in, hitting the trigger mechanism that will activate the bomb. On the other side of the scale is an empty cup, which, if filled, will outweigh the plasma-globylene and tip that side away from the trigger, therefore saving your worthless skins."

"Great," said Wayne. "How do we fill the cup?"

Dr. Wilde grinned. "That's up to you, but if you've got any spit in that empty head of yours, I suggest you use it. If you try really hard you might just hit the rim a couple of times."

"Thanks for the advice, jerk," said Braker.

Dr. Wilde sneered at the trucker. "I will excuse you that remark this time, dead man, only because I have more important business to attend to."

"Your business is over," said Braker, "Prince Tony just spoiled your entire plan."

"You would like to think that, scum, but I have some news for you—I left several busloads of angry lab assistants in space to ambush Prince Tony. Perhaps I'll get the girls yet. How do you like that?"

"That's a joke; he's probably called Lord Preposterous already and told him what a traitor you are. And once Preposterous finds out about that, you're through."

"Wrong again," said Dr. Wilde. "I've had Prince Tony's voice boxes jammed ever since we've had sight of the planet. Obviously, my whole story about Tony being fired was a lie, but I was hoping the prince would fall for it just long enough that I could get the girls and then massacre him in space; do you think I would be so dense as to let him get back to Lord Preposterous, even if I did get the girls?"

"Alright, so what does that mean to us?"

"Not much, except maybe a little something to think about before you detonate. Ha, ha, ha!" Dr. Wilde was climbing the stairs into the *Flying Electric Laboratory*. "Oh, and by the way, buried under the bomb you're strapped to is a bomb even ten times bigger! Bye, bye, losers."

Dr. Wilde's ship lifted off, leaving Braker, Wayne, and J.J. alone with the Plasma Heat Atomizer.

"Hawk-pit-owee!"

"What was that?" asked Braker, trying to stretch as far away from the bomb as possible.

"Hawk-pit-owee!" The grotesque sound came again.

"Wayne, you're not trying to spit into that stupid little cup, are you?"

"Sure am," said Wayne, his chin covered in slobber. "There ain't nothing else to do out here."

"Oh, come on," said Braker. "J.J., tell him it's not going to work."

"Hawk-pit-owee!"

"Oh no, not you too, J.J.!"

"Well, it's our only chance," said the salesman. "It's simply a matter of production meeting demand."

"What's that supposed to mean?" said Braker. "That doesn't even mean anything!"

J.J. hung his head. "I know, but that kind of business talk usually makes people think I know something they don't."

Braker scowled. "Forget it; it's pointless."

Wayne shook his head. "Naw, try it Braker; actually, it's kind of fun!"

J. J. agreed. "Yes, it is, and it does take a measure of skill…See, I made one. I just think Braker's afraid to try."

"Maybe I'm just trying to think of a better way."

"Trust me, kid, there is no better way," said J.J. "Start hacking."

"It's like pitchin' horseshoes," said Wayne, "'cept these come outta yo mouth."

"Hawk-pit-owee!" Braker finally gave in, adding his drool to the effort.

"Nice try," encouraged J.J., "but a little too much arc."

"Lower huh?" said Braker. "Alright, wait a second, I can do better…"

This bizarre contest went on for some time before a sudden flash of light and an explosion of noise broke the trio's concentration. Flying out from behind the white, congealed sugar cliffs to the north, came a single-seater, motorized skycycle piloted by an uncommonly filthy man. His long red hair and mustache whipped about his face while he struggled to maintain his hold on the handlebars. At first it appeared that the triple-piped, anti-matter engine was too powerful for the cycle's pilot to retain control. But it soon became evident the guidance difficulties were not a result of the overpowered motor, or even the pilot's ability, but it was instead because the rider was being chased. Behind him, a hoodless, low-topped sky skimmer was surging forward in repeated attempts to ram into the cycle. Worse yet, the skimmer was directing withering laser blasts toward its fleeing target by way of the gun emplacements it had welded beneath its front-end grille.

Despite the mounting damage to his vehicle, the cycle pilot almost made it across the sugar field before a wild shot sent him and the cycle careening nose first into the ground. Howling as he went, the pilot flipped over the fuel tank, landing on his back. Braker, strapped next to Wayne and J.J., stood exactly six feet from the cycle wreckage. Each one strained for a better look at the unfolding scene.

A short distance away, the pursuing sky skimmer made its landing. The exit portal opened, and two strange creatures appeared in its hatchway. The occupants of the sky skimmer came into full view as they crossed the field. The approaching creatures were nearly twice the size of the cycle rider; both were identical, possessing muscular, feather-covered upper bodies balanced upon scrawny stick-like legs and clawed feet. Teeth sharp as razors rotated continually in their mouths. And, despite the searing effects of the burning desert sun, the skin on their faces remained soft and pink, highlighted by rosy red noses and cheeks.

The red-haired cycle pilot rose from the ground, ready for a fight. At his hip dangled a beautifully fashioned Molarkian hatchet, its shiny blade offsetting the dingy grey of his cut-off mechanics pants. "Who are you?" he growled.

"I'm Buck."

"And I'm Helbus," each alien said in turn.

"And we're the Precious Brothers," they finished simultaneously.

The cycle rider scratched a patch of dirt from his chin. "The Precious Brothers, huh? I've never heard of that clan. How'd you come by that name?"

"We don't know," shrugged Helbus, "that's just what our momma always called us."

"So, what do you uglies want?" the rider snapped.

"We're here to rob and kill you," Buck replied.

The human drew his hatchet. "And what if I resist?"

"Then I'll grab you and shake you until all your life is gone," said Buck.

"That's right," agreed Helbus, "and Momma says the only one stronger than Buck is me, and the only one stronger than me is Momma."

Buck nodded. "It would be much safer to not interfere." The creature reached out toward his victim—and was greeted by the flat side of the rider's hatchet smashing across his face.

Buck staggered back as the human struck again, this time laying the big alien out cold. Unfortunately, the blow also sent the hatchet spinning out of the cycle rider's hand.

"Dropped something," said Helbus, returning the weapon to its owner.

It was the last thing the alien did before being pounded into unconsciousness.

With the Precious Brothers out of the way, the human adjusted his armor-plated shoulder pads and turned his attention to his smoldering skycycle. A brief inspection confirmed that it was beyond repair. Disgusted, the human silently loaded his saddle bags into the Brother's skimmer, never bothering to acknowledge the presence of Braker and his friends.

"Do something," Braker whispered.

"You do something," Wayne said.

"Be quiet both of you," J.J. demanded. "If you're not careful you'll get us killed."

"But he's got a hatchet, he might cut us loose," said Braker.

"Listen, kid," said J.J., "this guy's a killer, one of the worst I've ever seen, you saw what happened to the Precious Brothers. He'll cut our heads off if you don't watch it."

"He's our only chance," Braker insisted. "It's him or the bomb."

"Alright," said J.J., "just let me do the talking. I don't want him to get a bad first impression. I'll make it smooth."

"Just hurry, please," said Braker.

J.J. looked up to find the cycle rider distracted by their conversation, silently staring at them.

"Hello, friend," said J.J. "Fine weather we're having, aren't we?"

"Just fine," said the man.

J.J. gulped. "I couldn't help but notice how good you are at killing people," he continued.

"Smooth," whispered Braker.

The cycle rider laughed. "You mean the Precious Brothers? Why, I didn't kill them. I just knocked those boys out."

"But they wanted to rob and murder you."

"Well, I can't blame them for that."

"You don't?"

"Not at all. Their only problem is they're beginners. They're only learning; just babies really. We barbarians have to stick together. I'm gonna give them another chance."

"You're a barbarian?"

"Knothead Madhouse, space barbarian, at your service."

"A space barbarian!" said J.J. "Now that's a rarity. What are you doing on this planet? There's nothing to pilfer out here."

"Aww, I've just been slumming it for a while."

"Well, we don't mean to spoil your shiftless vagrancy," said J.J. "so, please, feel free to just ignore us and go on your barbarian way, looting and wrestling and all that."

"J.J.!" said Braker.

"He's a barbarian," responded the salesman, "a savage, bloodthirsty—"

"And we're strapped to a bomb," countered Braker. He looked to Knothead. "We're pleased to meet you, Mr. Madhouse, we really are, and we don't mean to be an inconvenience, but we've had a few problems recently, and we were just wondering if you could do us a little favor as long as you're here?"

"Sure, what is it?"

"Well, you see, this bomb is gonna blow up if we don't fill that cup with spit, and we haven't been very successful at filling it so far, so if you could just...."

"Say no more," said Knothead, "I gotcha covered."

As Braker and the others watched, Knothead snorted and growled, working up an unbelievably thick wad of saliva into his throat. With one shot, and a stomach-disturbing splat, he filled the cup and tipped the scale into a safe position. "How was that?" he asked, satisfied with his performance.

"That was great," gagged Braker, "but actually we were hoping you could just cut us loose."

"Should have said so in the first place; that's even easier," Knothead replied, cutting them free. "Now tell me, you guys sure you're okay?"

"Absolutely," said J.J. "Thanks so much for everything. We'll be seeing you; bye now."

"Give it a break, J.J.," said Braker. "To tell you the truth, Mr. Madhouse, things are looking pretty bad for us at the moment."

"Braker, why don't you just keep quiet there, boy," said J.J., smiling apologetically at Knothead. "Mr. Madhouse is a busy barbarian, I'm sure he has more important things to do than listen to your whining."

"Nope, not really," said Knothead. "I'm just like every other space barbarian; I got nothing important to do. Tell me your sad story. And call me, Knothead; I ain't nobody's boss."

"You heard him, Braker," J.J. ordered. "Tell the man all your afflictions."

Braker scowled at J.J. and began explaining, Knothead listening transfixed until the account was finished. Then, without a word, the barbarian stomped over to the sky skimmer and climbed into the pilot's seat.

"Get in," he shouted, "we don't have to stand for this. We're gonna get those princess sisters back."

"We are?" said Braker, J.J., and Wayne, simultaneously.

"Sure, why wouldn't we?"

"Well, you're a barbarian," said J.J. "Braker didn't think you'd care."

"Of course I care," said Knothead. "I know what it means to love someone. I've got a mother, don't I?"

"Not if you're from the planet Sorok," said Wayne. "They ain't got mothers there. Strange planet Sorok; babies grow on trees. Look just like little apples. Almost ate one once; I didn't know."

Braker ignored Wayne. "We appreciate the concern, Knothead," said the trucker, "but we just need to put some distance between us and that bomb. Honestly, if you can just drop us off on the edge of a town somewhere that's more than enough to ask of anyone."

"Thoughtful," said Knothead, giving Braker a slap on the back, "but hop in, I'm driving."

"Really, Knothead, you don't have to—"

Knothead pulled out his Molarkian hatchet, waving it dangerously close to the end of Braker's nose. "You act like you don't want me around, like you were scared of me or something."

"I'm sure he is," said J.J. "The kid's afraid of everything. The sissy."

"That settles it," said Knothead, laying a finger to one side of his nose and blowing hard through the other nostril. "I'm going all the way; you flimsy boys need me. And besides, I've been meaning to get back into long-distance space traveling. I've got to get out of here; I'm starting to become known as the sugar-planet barbarian. And that's not a very commanding title, if you know what I mean." Then, forcing his newfound friends into the skimmer, Knothead super-charged the engines. Soon the strange company were on their way, leaving the Plasma-Heat Atomizer and the Precious Brothers far behind.

First on the agenda would be to find some type of spacecraft to get them into the chase, not an easy feat considering they had hundreds of miles of empty desert to cover before touching even the most remote edge of civilization. But there was one outpost, one solitary oasis which shimmered temptingly in the suns, one terrifying place where only the most desperate or most insane would go. Here, and only here, was their last chance at finding a suitable ship. And they would have to steal it. Knothead loved the idea, Braker and Wayne were ready to do whatever it took, and J.J. was just stuck with these crazy people.

Chapter Eight
Ambush & Intrigue

Deep in space, Prince Tony's fleet was already under attack from Dr. Wilde's ambush team. The lab buses, armed with Dr. Wilde's specially designed Mayhem Spreaders and Chaos-Chuckers, were wreaking havoc on the unsuspecting armada. Even the mighty *Maiming Lily* was feeling the effects; the giant warship rocked back and forth under the continuous bombardment. And yet, as the great ship battled the threat from outside, there was another fight, one possibly even more dangerous, brewing within. A little man wearing thick space goggles and a business suit burst into a darkened storage closet. Standing in the corner was Roger Godsend, Nebulous X space soldier, lowest class. Godsend was tall and thin, with neatly trimmed grey hair and mustache. Unlike the elite armor-wearing Goons of Doom, he wore the standard space trooper's blue coveralls and black boots. Despite this, he somehow appeared remarkably dignified. He stood arms crossed, looking down on his companion with a noble air.

"Call off the revolt, sir! We're under attack," the diminutive man shouted.

Godsend rolled his eyes. "Nub Niblet, you are a gentleman. I'm surprised at you. You know such a display of emotion should be contained until all the details are given. Now let's hear your report."

Nub continued to bounce around the room. "All we know is several busloads of Dr. Wilde's lab assistants have ambushed us from all sides. And I can't believe it. And what next? And how much longer must we wait?"

Roger Godsend leaned his long, lean body against the wall. "Young Nub, you must learn that a true revolutionary's food is patience, and restraint is his drink. In due time we shall properly begin our secret rebellion against Prince Tony."

"But it's taking so long. Why does it seem so far away?" groaned Nub.

"Justice is never far away," said Godsend. "Don't forget that we are to be the heralds of a new and brighter future for all of Prince Tony's accountants, bookkeepers, and otherwise abused office staff like yourself. And with that honor comes responsibility. For only a short time longer will you be forced to manage Tony's vast, galaxy-wide investments and financial statements. So, straighten your back and look on toward victory. Prince Tony's evil rule over you and your pathetic coworkers will not last. I shall see to that. In the meantime, we must guard our secret, now is obviously too risky a time to commence the revolution. Send out the delay signal and return to your post. I'll contact you later. Don't worry, once we get started, I promise we'll really mess everything up for everyone."

Nub nodded and scurried down the hall to an elevator that unloaded him on the Trammel deck, just outside the secretaries' lounge. Nub retrieved a tiny message machine from behind a hidden panel and sent out the postponement notice to all the accountant insurgents scattered throughout Prince Tony's fleet.

Meanwhile, the flamboyant Tony was hopelessly unaware of any internal rumblings—he was standing at the helm of the *Lily's* navigation center, a ferocious space battle raging around him and two angry young princesses at his throat. The prince had chosen to wear a simple yet elegant white turtleneck coat, grey pin-tucked slacks, and sensible low-heeled shoes during the crisis.

"A thousand curses on that crazy fool," said Tony, pacing behind the *Lily's* row of pilots. "It must be that maniac Dr. Wilde again!"

Contentious leaned back on a guidance console, her clenched fists chained together. "Good, I hope he blows you and your lousy ship to atoms!"

"An hour in my torture chamber will tame you," said Tony before turning to Princess Babe, who was seated politely in the corner. "I see that you, at least, have sense enough to remain respectful in the presence of your superiors."

Babe smiled. "I like to think all people are equals. But I don't see how someone can call himself a prince and behave so horribly."

"It's an honorary title actually," explained Tony. "My father ran a highly successful deodorant factory on Nebulous X—"

"Your father ran a deodorant factory?" laughed Contentious.

"It was no joke," Tony snapped. "Especially considering all the space trolls and squid men on Nebulous. Anyway, he was known as the Deodorant King, and I, as his son, came to be known as the

Prince. When I began competing in beauty contests, I used it as a stage name, and it's just stuck ever since."

"Beauty contests?" snickered Contentious. "You get more lame all the time."

"It's just a hobby," said Tony.

A monstrous explosion hit the navigation center, instantly wiping out all of Tony's pilots. Babe leapt to the sparking controls.

"Quickly, Contentious, we've got to help fly the *Lily*!"

Contentious snorted. "Not on your life, sis. I'd rather die with this crumb than help him."

"I don't care for him either," Babe shouted over flaming control circuits, "but Braker's going to save us, and I'm going to do whatever I can to keep us alive until his arrival!"

"Well, I'm going to do whatever I can to make Tony sweat," said Contentious, reclining on the floor.

Prince Tony ignored Contentious's taunting; he was too busy watching in awe as Babe struggled alone to work what was left of the ship's controls. The beautiful blond princess's irrepressible courage and poise overwhelmed him. In one dream-like moment he realized he was in love.

"Oh, my darling, how blind I have been!" he cried. "Perfection has been standing right before me, and only now do I see. Yes, I see. Your charm has convinced me. We are meant to be together; your excellence reminds me of myself, and I must have you. The undeniable voice of infatuation demands it."

"What are you talking about?" said Babe, fighting to maintain the ship. "I love Braker. Now help me with the controls."

"Darling, in time you will see we were destined to be love mates. But, for now, yes, I will help you, though it won't be at the controls. I have something much flashier in mind. I'm going to lead the counterattack in my own single-man fighter ship. Don't be surprised if you are inflamed with passion after witnessing my death-defying stunts."

"Please, just do *something*," said Babe as the controls continued to smoke.

Prince Tony swept his arm across his forehead. "Do not plead for me to stay, my darling. I must go, sacrificing myself for your dazzlement; yet I shall return. Fight on, fight on!"

Contentious scowled as she looked up at the prince. "So just go already; like anybody cares."

Tony left in a huff, quickly slipping into his satin flight suit before hurrying down to the launch deck and into his private fighter ship. He was lucky to make the lift off—several of Dr. Wilde's Vertigo Torpedoes zoomed into the hanger as he was launched.

Instantly, Prince Tony was thrown into a terrifying new reality, the horrors of Dr. Wilde's space weaponry almost beyond comprehension. Spoil Rays, Nausea Bombs, and Fumble Bolts brought disaster to all who came within their terrible reach. None of this really bothered the prince though—he was an excellent pilot, and more importantly, convinced the danger would help in impressing Babe. He swept through flaming ships and debris, picking apart the lab buses one by one.

Racing into the battle zone now was Dr. Wilde himself in the *Flying Electric Laboratory*. "Keep fighting!" Dr. Wilde instructed his troops over the voice box. "We must wipe them out completely. And make sure all their voice boxes stay jammed in the meantime, I don't want them contacting Lord Preposterous!"

Bullmack stood behind his hunchbacked creator. "But, Master, the girls are on that ship. We going to kill them too?"

Dr. Wilde didn't even turn around. "Of course, idiot. We can't worry about them now. Prince Tony and everyone with him must be destroyed or Lord Preposterous might discover we disobeyed orders by lying about our orders."

"Ah ha!" said Bullmack as if he understood, although he really didn't.

"Message for you, sir," announced an aide, handing Dr. Wilde a battle report.

"What does the little paper say, Master?" inquired Bullmack.

Dr. Wilde crumpled the report, stuffing it into the attendant's ear. "It says that the *Maiming Lily* has been expertly piloted out of the conflict and most of our buses have been destroyed in a counterassault personally led by Prince Tony!"

"I don't know what that means," said the robot.

"It means we've lost!" screamed Dr. Wilde. "It means Lord Preposterous will know we betrayed his orders. It means that from this moment on our future is of less value than a rotting foot fungus salad!"

"Umm, now you're making me hungry, Master," giggled Bullmack.

Victory was within Prince Tony's grasp, and even as his enemies watched their hopes fading, the Glamour Boy of Gunberry was returning to the *Lily* with love on his mind.

Chapter Nine
Duel in the Dust

Back on the Poison Sugar Planet, Braker and his crew were skimming across the dunes at breakneck speed as Knothead filled them in on where they were going.

"Listen, fellas, we're heading for Holly Blackguard's WaterWorks, an illegal sugar-water factory Holly runs from a secluded mountaintop fortress. From there her water freighters distribute the nasty mixture to all the sugar addicts throughout the universe."

"Pardon me, but how exactly does one go about marketing a deadly poison?" J.J. asked, wondering if being a sugar baron wouldn't be such a bad move now that his business had bit the dust.

"Pretty easily, actually," said Knothead. "She just packages it in brightly colored 24-ounce cans with different, snazzy sounding names, like Brain Glaze, Mind Flush, or I.Q. Hammer. You've probably seen at least one version in a vending machine here or there. She's cornered the market because there's no other planet in the universe with this kind of sugary soil."

"Well, why don't those addicts just move here themselves?" J.J. continued. "Then they could have all the sugar they wanted for free by eating it off the ground."

"It's not that simple," Knothead shouted over the engine's roar. "First of all, they'd have to know what planet it came from, and that ring of scorching suns surrounding us wards off most explorers. Second, even if they did figure it out, this planet's pretty much devoid of life, and Holly runs a vast army of enforcers that scan the planet looking for any half-insane sugar addicts. Then, once she finds them, she has them shipped out to faraway moons. Those sugar-heads are too out of it to find their way back; they simply spend the rest of their sorry lives scrounging for money to pay for the next can of juice."

J.J. shook his head. "I've been on this planet for quite a while now and I've never heard about any of this."

"Of course not," said Knothead, "Holly likes to keep a low profile. She's the only one who's ever been smart enough to figure out a way to make a profit from this stinkin' place; she sure doesn't want the news to get out."

"The way we heard it," said Wayne, "this here sugar is guaranteed to leave a man silly-faced and dead."

"You betcha," said Knothead. "But that's Holly's game."

"Well, that shore ain't nice," replied Wayne.

"Ain't nothing nice about the Sugar Planet," said Knothead in a dark voice.

Soon, they crossed the tip of one last frosty white dune and arrived at Holly Blackguard's WaterWorks. The factory was indeed built like a defensive stronghold. Behind its weaponized barricades, silhouettes of huge water silos dotting the skyline; freighters and security barges crisscrossed above the compound.

"So how do we get in, Knothead?" asked Braker.

Knothead squinted. "There's a tiny entranceway down there among the rocks. We'll have to sneak our way in."

Braker raised an eyebrow while staring at Knothead. "Say, how do you know so much about this place anyway?"

Knothead tossed Braker a sly glance. "Holly and I used to date."

The tiny group left their sky skimmer in the dunes above and crept through the sugar until coming to rocky, congealed ground. A perimeter guard bearing a long-barreled vaporizer leapt up from behind a huge pile of crumbling sugar cubes.

"Halt, I want to ask everyone who is going here."

"It's just us," Wayne blurted out.

J.J. glanced at his companions. "This tuber's easy pickings. Watch this." The salesman quickly jumped to the front. "Hello, friend," he said with a big smile, "we'll be more than happy to tell you who we are, but it would only be polite for you to introduce yourself first. Don't you agree?"

"I'm Fug," said the man in a superior tone. "Fug is guard. More better than you. Fug very important. More than you."

"Say, are you sure you're really a guard?" J.J. asked.

"Yeah, you seem kind of stupid," said Knothead.

"Fug is guard," replied the man. "Fug important guard. Fug in charge of protecting top-secret door in the rocks."

J.J.'s grin grew larger. "Fug, I get the impression you may have started snacking on sugar dust recently. Am I right?"

"Just little bit," said Fug.

"You know that's not such a good idea," said J.J.

"But it get so boring out here for Fug."

"And that dust probably starts looking just so yummy-yummy," said J.J. in a babyish voice.

"Yump," said Fug, licking his lips.

Knothead rolled his eyes. "This joker flaked his brain out on sugar dust. Forget him. Let's go."

Fug leveled his vaporizer at Knothead. "Fug guards door. Don't make Fug be shooting."

"Take it easy, boy," said J.J. "The truth is we can see how important your job is, and we were going to let ourselves in the secret entrance because we didn't want you to get in any trouble."

"Why Fug be in trouble?"

"Well, Fug, because everyone knows Holly Blackguard doesn't want her guards eating sugar dust. It makes them stupid."

"And you're a moron," said Knothead. "Lousy sugar hound."

"Quiet! I'm working here," said J.J. "Fug, do you remember being informed that we were coming today?"

"Fug not remember that."

"Exactly," said J.J. "That's the sugar dust getting to ya. In fact, you were told to expect three very important new pilots—that would be us, Fug, stay with me—and that you should let us through. But you don't remember that because you're way too scorched on sugar dust. Now, Fug, that's why you'll be in trouble—you weren't paying attention. If the water queen finds out you wouldn't let us in, she'll figure you can't be trusted anymore. You'd probably be sacked."

"Fug not want water queen mad at him."

"Oh, she will be, son, she will be. You'll be the boob of the whole operation."

Fug was grief stricken. "What Fug do?"

"I'm glad you asked," said J.J. "It's simple really, although it might be kind of difficult for you. Anyway, to keep your job all you have to do is let us through. And then if anyone asks you about us, you just tell them we're the important new pilots Holly hired. More important than you."

"And that will solve Fug problem?"

"Well, partially," said J.J. "Then you just have to stop eating sugar dust and spend the rest of your life trying to increase your intelligence. Go to night school. Get a tutor. Read something."

"That good idea. You go through. Fug have to think about being smart."

"Wise decision, Fug," said J.J. as he and the others filed by.

"You should have just let me smash him," said Knothead, tromping through the rock-covered entrance.

"And pass up a chance to practice my manipulation skills on an unwitting dunce?" said J.J. "Hardly."

Soon the group was in the busy compound, trying to look casual and not attract any attention—Braker looked thoughtfully at the farmer, salesman, and barbarian next to him. "Better find us a ship, fast," he whispered to Knothead.

The barbarian scanned the enclosure. Several ships were nearby; most were the large water freighters. No good—too large and bulky—they needed something lightweight and quick. He pointed toward an interstellar cargo van; it was double-wide and high-topped, but still much smaller than the other options.

"Over there," said Knothead. "Our best bet."

The foursome scampered up the ship's ramp and through the outer passageway. For what appeared on the outside to be just another delivery vehicle, the craft's interior was curiously extravagant. Warm, decorative wall paneling, a set of lounge chairs, and a padded sofa gave a sophisticated, laid-back charm to the internal hold.

"Weird set up for a delivery wagon," said Braker.

"Who cares?" said J.J. "We don't have time to admire the aesthetics. Just get this thing fired up."

Braker took his place at the driver's seat, his heart beating faster as he examined a whole new set of controls. "I'm not quite sure what to do," he whispered to Wayne.

"Don't let that panic ya," said Wayne. "Why, just look at ol' Fug, he's doin' a job he ain't qualified for, neither."

"Thanks, a lot," said Braker, turning on the power. The ship immediately rose off the ground. They were ten feet in the air when the real pilot burst in from a back extension nobody had bothered to inspect. "What's going on here?" he shouted, calling for the co-pilot who immediately came charging forward.

"Get him off me!" Braker exclaimed as the pilot tried to throw him from the seat.

"Just keep flying, kid!" J.J. instructed, darting behind Knothead. "We'll cover you."

While J.J. cringed, Knothead and Wayne battled the other crewman. Unfortunately, Wayne had a habit of closing his eyes when he fought; he ended up spending most of his time pounding on Knothead.

Braker was left to resist the pilot on his own; he wasn't even trying to steer the ship at this point—he was using both hands just to hold on to the seatbelt hanging next to him.

The ship roared forward, blasting through a row of Water Silos and sending huge bursts of sugar-water raining down onto the workers below.

At that moment a new enemy entered the cockpit. Dressed in black and wickedly beautiful it could have been only one person—Holly Blackguard, the Water Queen! Braker had not just stolen any spacecraft—he had stolen Holly Blackguard's personal starship!

"You will all stop fighting now," she commanded in an icy tone.

As if controlled by her voice, everyone stopped what they were doing. Holly stepped further into the hold as Braker kept the craft hovering just above the ground. "So, it appears we have a pack of spaceship thieves in our midst" she said, inspecting the faces surrounding her. She froze when she saw Knothead.

"Hi, cutie," winked the desert bandit.

Holly punched the barbarian straight in the mouth. "Knothead Madhouse? What are you doing here?"

Knothead laughed. "Well, I was just in the neighborhood and really needed an ugly fix so I decided to drop by and see ya."

"Kill them," Holly ordered. "Kill them now."

"Not yet!" exclaimed Braker, slamming on the thrusters.

Everyone tumbled backward; Holly, closest to the hatchway, hit her head on the exit switch and flew outside. She would have fallen to her death if Wayne hadn't been rolling along behind her. With expert reflexes, she reached out at the last second and latched onto Wayne's overall strap. "Pull me up!" she shouted.

"Don't do it!" said Braker. "Don't you even do it!"

"Pull me up!" Holly cried.

Wayne gulped. "Braker, I've got to save the lady; how could I live with myself if I don't save a lady?"

"How can any of us live if you do?" Braker shot back.

Wayne ignored him and pulled Holly back up. Safely inside, the ungrateful water queen laid Wayne out with a couple of quick jabs to the stomach. Then, spinning on one foot, she reached for a secret panel in the wall. An instant later she was leveling a mini-water slinger at the hijackers. "Knock it off," she said, emphasizing her seriousness by blowing a few holes through the roof.

"Knock this off, honey!" Braker exclaimed, banking the ship on its side. Everyone tumbled to the floor. Then, before anyone could regain their footing, Braker drove the ship straight upward.

Holly dug her long fingernails into the ship's thick carpeting. "Oh, how I will stop you," she said, crawling toward the controls.

"Braker, look out!" shouted Wayne as Holly moved closer.

Braker whirled to find Holly looming behind him, clinging to the back of his seat.

"Bite it, twerp!" said the water queen, aiming her deadly handgun at his head.

Without thinking, Braker slammed the ship into a steep descent, only leveling out when they were inches from the ground. Holly was pitched into the dashboard and then back to the floor.

"I think I'm going to be sick," said J.J., as he and Knothead, Wayne, and the terrified piloting crew all clung to the bolted down furnishings.

Holly blew a strand of tangled hair from her eyes. "You're all going to pay for this," she said raking the inside of the ship with a long burst from her water slinger.

"Only if you can hold on to your cookies, lady!" said Braker, angling the ship into a sharp turn. They scraped the ground as Holly once again tumbled toward the open hatch. She popped off a few more shots before spilling out of the ship and onto the compound.

"Braker, I can't believe it," J.J. cried. "You actually did something right! You dumped that evil empress out of here and saved us!"

"Don't celebrate too soon," said Holly, her voice broadcast into the ship by way of a handheld voice box. "Your joyride is over. Stop now, or I will use my remote-control self-destruct button to detonate the ship." The resilient water queen was standing defiantly in the center courtyard, her dark beauty nearly hidden beneath a sheet of white mud.

"Braker, you better put it in park," said Wayne. "She's gonna blow us up."

"Fat chance," said Braker. "She wouldn't blow up her own ship."

"Sure I would, idiot," Holly replied through the voice box. "I'm an evil space queen. I've got plenty of ships."

"Just ignore her," said Knothead. "What's the big deal?"

"What's the big deal?" said J.J. "What are you talking about? We'll all be killed—*I'll* be killed!"

"What do I care?" said Knothead. "I'm a space barbarian. I like dangerous stuff."

"Don't worry about it," said Braker. "I'm betting her remote control won't work if we're too far away." He mashed the accelerator. "We're outta here."

"That's it," said Holly announcing her final threat, "I'm blowing you up."

The water queen pressed the button that would start the self-destruction of the cargo van. Inside the craft, the control panel began to spark, its internal temperature gauges shooting into the critical zone.

"Braker, I think we's about to get put in the smokehouse," said Wayne.

"Okay, I am actually starting to get worried," said Knothead.

"Oh, someone please stop this fool!" cried J.J.

Braker gingerly reached out toward the crackling control panel, only to yank back his hand after receiving an electric shock. Braker was now no more than a mere passenger as the ship continued across the compound until crashing head-on into an enormous Water Barn. The storehouse exploded from the impact, drowning the van under countless tons of water. The runaway ship came to an abrupt stop, its engines—and more importantly—its lethal self-destruct circuits, flooded beyond repair. The ruined engines choked a final motorized gasp and flamed out. Braker's desperate flight was suddenly over.

As Holly's guards surrounded the ship, Wayne put a reassuring hand on Braker's shoulder. "You know what I'm thinkin'?"

"What's that, Wayne?" said Braker.

"Well, I'm just thinkin' this is one time I'm actually glad you crashed the ship."

"Be quiet, Wayne."

Chapter Ten
Lies, Lies, Lies

On the other side of the universe, Prince Tony, soaring triumphantly in his personal fighter craft, howled with glee as he saw the last of Dr. Wilde's disabled lab buses spinning off into space. "I've beaten him again," he laughed. "Oh, the joy of inflicting such disgrace on one as deserving as Dr. Wilde. Oh, the joy!"

"The *Lily* is ready for the jump to Psycho-Space at your command," came a voice over the prince's voice box. "We've supplied a fresh crew of navigators at the controls, sir."

"But what of Princess Babe?" asked Tony. "What about the savior of our beloved *Maiming Lily*?"

"She's here. We were about to take her to the confinement center."

"Never!" shouted the prince. "Would you stuff a rose under your armpit? Leave her, I'll be but a moment." Tony quickly touched down in the *Lily*'s landing bay. Once there, he ordered the jump to Psycho-Space. The prince chuckled knowing there was no way for the mad doctor to catch him now.

Inside the *Flying Electric Laboratory* there was one last flurry of activity. Dr. Wilde himself ran to the launch bay. "Scramble every remaining lab bus we have! We must stop their jump to Psycho-Space."

An aide bowed low. "I'm sorry, doctor, but it will take fifteen minutes to ready another attack wave."

"Fool!" Dr. Wilde growled, shoving the man into the path of a speeding transport shuttle.

The furious doctor gazed out the launch bay's space window, watching as Prince Tony and his fleet disappeared into Psycho-Space.

Bullmack trudged over to his creator. "What now, Master?"

Dr. Wilde clenched his fists. "I don't know. Just let me think. Go kill someone and come back later."

"Okay," obeyed Bullmack, wandering off.

Far away now in Psycho-Space, Prince Tony rushed into the *Maiming Lily*'s navigation center with love in his veins. Clothed in a soft, intricately woven crimson pullover and a billowing wine-colored cape, his choice of attire aptly expressed his amorous intentions.

"Darling," he cried out to Babe, "I have returned safe and secure; oh, how I missed you so. If only you had known the unfolding blossoms of love I felt while watching you steer the command to safety. Your piloting was almost as good as my own." He took the struggling princess in his arms. "O my shining trophy of desire, you are like a vision of my own reflected glory. Imagine it—the chances of someone as extraordinary as myself finding the perfect complement to such flawless beauty. And best of all, after witnessing your bold resistance to our destruction, I sense that beneath your silky exterior there may perhaps lurk that same unyielding yet tender spirit which I myself embody. Be honest now, darling, and tell me of your same feelings for me."

Babe groaned. "If you have a tender spirit, I have yet to see it. Since I first met you, I have seen only coldness, conflict, and bloodshed. I find such behavior sickening."

Tony chuckled. "Don't play bashful, darling. I know women adore garish displays of masculine military potency."

Babe shook her head. "Tony, listen to me. I'm sorry, I don't wish to be impolite. You do have many worthy attributes—outstanding leadership skills, piloting expertise, and groundbreaking fashion dominance, but you only use those things in order to bully your enemies and rule over a brainwashed fleet of toy soldiers."

"Groundbreaking fashion dominance?!" cried Tony. "You really do love me!"

"What?" gasped Babe.

"Admit it, you said it yourself, I have a groundbreaking fashion dominance. What else could that mean but that you love me?"

"No, that's not at all what I mean."

"Of course, it is. Admit it, you've exposed your true feelings. You love me."

"No, it's just not true."

"Then tell me, what are your truest deepest feelings for me?"

Babe lowered her head. "I do not wish to say."

"But you must; I insist. Your truest feeling from the bottom of your heart."

Babe looked away. "I love you only a little bit," she whispered.

"Ah ha!" laughed the prince. "You've confessed it with your own lips. Joy over joy! I am rolling in clouds of golden love. It is settled—we were forged for each other in an eternal shower of frothy molten ardor."

"No, you misunderstand me," said Babe. "Besides, how could I ever love you when my true hero man is on his way to rescue me even as we speak?"

Tony stepped back. "To whom do you refer; certainly not that uncoordinated oaf that tried to free you from the clutches of the *Lily's* electro-arm?"

Babe nodded. "One and the same."

Tony squealed with laughter. "Darling, that is the man worthy of the name coward, not I. Did you not see him leap to safety as you rose into my ship? If ever there was a more flagrant example of selfish cowardice it is certainly dispelled under that man's shadow."

"He wasn't afraid…he just lost his grip."

"Oh, come now, darling, any Goon in my fleet could tell you they saw the same thing as you and I—the man left you to the cold hands of fate as he scampered away for his own safety."

"Well, he's coming back for me."

Prince Tony spun around, pretending to search the room for Braker. "Darling, let's be logical here, don't you think he would have come already? Do you really think he intends to find us after a trip through Psycho-Space?"

"Braker can do it. He's saved me before."

"Of course he did, my darling. But did you ever stop to consider that he did those things because he was in danger himself—you just happened to be there. He was only looking after his own skin. Tell me, what did he do in the end when he had the actual choice between saving you or looking to his own safety? Darling, the coward abandoned you."

"I...I just can't believe it," Babe sobbed.

"It's better to learn the truth now," said Tony.

Babe ran to the navigation screen. "Braker Ford, where are you?" she cried.

Prince Tony put a white-gloved hand on her shoulder. "Braker's not coming, darling, he's just not the kind of man he led you to believe. Let's face it, you really haven't even known him for that long, have you? No, I believe what you're looking for is a man of great quality and achievement. Darling...I'm that man. I'm the one who saved you from Dr. Wilde, and I'm the one who brought you along with your sister when Lord Preposterous ordered your planet destroyed." Tony paused for dramatic effect. "You see, the truth is Lord Preposterous only intends to marry Contentious—he knew you were unworthy. He only had you brought along to use as a kitchen slave. But I am willing to have you, to give you more than you deserve. I'll take on the burden of stealing you to safety. Yes, I will disobey Lord Preposterous for you. So, if it is a hero you truly desire, I'm your man."

"Can I say something now?" Contentious asked in disgust, rising from where she had been resting on the floor.

"No!" shouted Prince Tony, summoning a nearby Goon. "Guard, remove this woman, she is obviously suffering from Space-Sickness."

"The only one who's sick is you, Prince Flub—sick in the head. Let me give you a little clue about my sis, when she tells you she only loves you a little bit, it means you make her want to puke out of her ears."

"You're very ill," said Tony. "My honey-cup would never mean to say that love is like puking out your ears."

"Pay attention, sis," said Contentious, pushing the Goon away. "Princey here is lying to you. Never trust a man with a more expensive wardrobe than your own."

"Why, you hateful little she-devil," said Tony. "Guard, get her out of here."

"Let my sister stay!" Babe pleaded as Contentious was dragged away.

Tony cradled the blond princess in his arms. "Darling, it's all too plain to see, your sister's mind has become distorted by all the sudden space travel. It happens from time to time; there's nothing she could say to help."

"But I want to be with her—and Braker; you're just a callous soldier."

Tony stroked the princess's forehead. "Darling, you mistake efficiency for brutality. I'm not truly quarrelsome. I use strong, refined power to bring order where there is none. And that, darling, is a good thing. Give up Braker Ford and your girlish infatuations; you have a real man with you now."

There was a long silence. "So what happens next?" said Babe.

Prince Tony's face was stretched tight with satisfaction. "Not to worry, my dear, when we arrive on Nebulous, I will present your sister to Lord Preposterous as planned. Afterwards, I'll sneak you away to my private castle where you shall be perfectly safe with me."

Slowly, Babe quit fighting against the prince's embrace as he wiped away the last of her tears.

Chapter Eleven
Frozen Death

Braker watched warily as the ice-cold water rose inch by dangerous inch around his ankles. He looked around one more time, hoping to find some way of escape. He was strapped to a wall at the bottom of a fifteen-foot-high water basin in a freezing cold room. Moments ago, gallons of frigid water began pumping into the bottom of the pool. Like himself, Knothead, J.J. Whammo, and Wayne each hung from thick, chain-bolted shackles attached to the side of the tank.

"Comfortable, boys?" Holly Blackguard's voice echoed through the huge speakers in the ceiling. "This is where we mix our sugar water before shipping. We decided to let you get a firsthand look at the process since you're obviously so interested in our operation. Only difference today is we've turned the temperature down to sub-zero. But don't worry, if you're unhappy with the accommodations you won't be for long. Soon we'll be shipping you out of here—on the rocks!" The Queen of the WaterWorks walked away laughing.

In the silent freezing chamber, the water was rising higher.

"Great," Braker groaned, "first I almost get baked alive on this crazy planet, now they're trying to turn me into a giant ice cube!"

"Yeah, but you have to admit this cold water is great for yer sunburn," said Wayne.

J.J. looked over to Knothead as the water reached chest level. "Knothead, you know everything about this place, tell us what to do."

"Hold your breath," said Knothead.

"We could all try drinking the water," Wayne suggested.

Everyone just stared at the farmer for a moment.

"Come on, guys, we can figure a way out of this," exclaimed Braker, squirming under the grip of his bonds.

Crystal clear water was pouring in on the prisoners, the chill of the water so extreme that it was nearly impossible to think. Their tortured bodies were numb, their teeth chattering uncontrollably.

J.J. continued to focus on the barbarian next to him. "Knothead, you can do this," he said. "There's no one else I'd rather be trapped with. You can use your brute force to break us loose. This is what you were born for—this is your moment. Break free and claim your destiny." He was going to say more but gave up because of all the water running into his open mouth.

"I appreciate the pep talk and all," said Knothead, "but it's useless. Holly only uses the best shackles in the galaxy. These things are made from a patented blend of anarchy molecules and galvanized distemper electrons. Even I can't bust through a combination like that. Face it—we came up short on this one. It was bound to happen sometime. Take it like a man. That's what I'm gonna do."

"Take it like a man?" shouted J.J. "We're talking about dying here! I'll never take it like a man. Now bust those cuffs."

"No, it's useless."

"Would it really hurt to try?" said J.J. "I mean you already said we're all going to die anyway."

"Yeah, but I don't want to die a failure," said Knothead.

"Just try it, you bum!" shouted J.J.

"Well, alright, if you're going to get all grouchy," said Knothead.

Using all his strength, the barbarian pushed against the bonds. His arms swelled under the strain, his powerful muscles flexing and bulging until it looked as if his skin would burst. And yet the shackles remained.

"Can't make it," he conceded. "These cuffs are just too strong."

"Too strong?" exclaimed J.J. "Those spindly bracelets aren't too strong! It's just that you're too weak! You're a wimp! A lousy, pus-armed wimp!"

"Pfftt. You call that an insult?" said Knothead. "I've been welcomed home to worse than that."

"Oh, there's worse coming, fella. I'm just getting started. These are our lives you're dealing with! We're all going to drown because underneath all that leather and dirt you're really nothing more than a butter-spined muscle cramp!"

"J.J., are you crazy?" asked Braker. "Isn't drowning enough? Do you really want Knothead to beat you up first?"

"Yes. Yes, I do," said J.J. "I want that barbarian so furious that he's willing to bust those clamps just so he can beat my sassy mouth shut."

"Hey, I get it," said Braker. "Good thinking. Hey, Knothead, you're a soggy piece of gristle. Come on, Wayne, help us get Knothead mad."

"Hey, Knothead," said Wayne, "your mustache looks like it hasn't been trimmed in months."

"That's it?" said Braker. "His mustache is too shaggy? That's the best you've got?"

"Well, I'm not used to this insult business," said Wayne. "Okay, how about this? Hey, Knothead, you've got a shaggy mustache, but I bet your momma's is even shaggier."

"Better," said Braker.

"Aw, I appreciate it, guys," said Knothead. "But I don't think it's gonna work. I'm a barbarian. Really, we insult each other all the time."

"Don't give up," said J.J. "It's our only chance. Knothead, your face is greasy, your hair is slimy, your teeth are yellow—and those are the only good things that can be said about your mother. Come on, guys, keep it going."

"Knothead, if ugly was a color, your momma would be every shade of the spectrum," said Braker.

"I don't mean to be negative, fellas, but the mom jokes won't work," said Knothead.

"What? Those were pretty good," Braker protested.

"Yeah, but they're all true," replied Knothead. "Try again."

"Okay, no more mom jokes," said J.J. "Go for something more personal."

"Knothead, you're completely brainless—and still manage to be weak-minded."

"Knothead, you're so dumb you could fall inside your own empty head."

"Knothead, you're so stupid that every time you get an idea it's considered a special occasion."

"Knothead, you're so dumb you could lose an argument with yourself."

Knothead grinned. "Ha-ha. You guys are great. Gimme some more. You're a riot."

"It's not supposed to be funny," said J.J. "This is about igniting your barely suppressed barbarian rage. We've just slandered your one precious slice of intelligence. Where's your hostile caveman pride? Braker, you and Wayne have got to do better. Get mean, guys. Get nasty."

"Knothead, your head is so lumpy it looks like a moldy sack of potatoes got sick after getting a glimpse of itself."

"Knothead, you're a spongy, germ-filled ball of fish gas with legs."

"Knothead, I heard your handwriting is bad."

"Wayne!"

"Well, I'm tryin'."

"Knothead, your muscles look like soft, meat-paste leftovers shoved in saggy plastic bags."

"Knothead, you're face looks like a half-eaten breakfast burrito—with mumps."

"Knothead, your breath's so bad it smells like you swallowed a pile of regurgitated frog guts—even *after* you've brushed your teeth."

"Knothead, you're the only guy I know who braids the hair on his head—*and* on his back."

"Knothead, you're a liar, you're a fool, and you're sub-human."

"Knothead, your dad just called. He wanted to remind you that he still hates you."

"Knothead, you're so weak you can't even feed yourself."

"Wayne, just stop."

"Knothead, you're a roach-faced, prehistoric, cave dwelling she-ape."

"Knothead, you are the biggest pile of congealed belly fat and dog slobber that ever dragged its sorry carcass out of a can of worms."

"Knothead, you're not as tall as some people."

"Wayne!"

"Wait, I wasn't finished. Knothead, you're not as tall as some people…and, uh…sometimes your feet stink."

"That one would have been better left unfinished," said J.J.

Knothead's face suddenly turned red, his breathing heavy, nostrils flaring. "Nobody calls my feet stinky!"

"Wait a minute," said Braker. "After all that, you're upset because Wayne made a crack about your feet?"

"You bet," said Knothead. "We space barbarians are very sensitive about our feet."

"Really?" said Braker.

"Yes, really! Do you have any idea how hard it is for a barbarian to find clean socks?"

"That's it, boy!" said J.J. "Let that anger fester right down in your heart."

Knothead strained against the cuffs. Slowly, they began to tear.

"Yay!" said Wayne "We did it. Let's hear it for Knothead's rotten feet."

"Laugh now, plowboy," growled Knothead. "'cause in a minute I'm gonna belt you right in your cud masher!"

"Hey, don't get mad at me!" said Wayne. "I was only tryin' to help. Tell him, fellers."

"No, get mad!" said J.J. "Get smokin' mad. That hillbilly weed puller has no right to pass judgement on anyone's feet. Imagine what he's got stuffed in those oversized mud grinders he's wearing."

"Hey, Braker!" said Wayne. "Tell Knothead I didn't mean it. I don't want to get belted in my cud masher. I mean, I don't think I do; he's talkin' about my mouth, right? I mean that's where the cud goes. Hey, Knothead, what's a cud masher?"

"It's that stupid hay hole your words come out of!" said Knothead.

"That's your mouth," said J.J.

Braker was encouraged by the way Knothead was fighting against the cuffs. "Sorry, Wayne, I gotta go with J.J. on this one. Knothead, I wouldn't stand for that kind of talk, either. It isn't fair; I've seen Wayne's feet. That's a hideous mass of tangled tree root down there, boy."

"He's got no right," said J.J.

Knothead gave one last push against the chains, tearing them from the wall. The triumphant barbarian then snapped his cuffs and headed for Wayne.

"Hold it, big guy," said J.J. "Take a minute to liberate Braker and myself while you're still jacked up on that anger juice you've got flowing. Then you can make hamburger out of the ol' seed dropper over there."

"Yeah, makes sense," said Knothead, quickly ripping his companions loose. He was on his way toward the cringing farmer when Braker swam between them, waving his arms.

"Don't hit him," said Braker, "pop him loose!"

"Oh, I'm gonna pop him, alright!" replied Knothead.

"Listen to Braker," said J.J., already lying beside the pool. "You can give him a better thumping on dry ground."

"Good thinking," said Knothead, shoving Braker out of the way and braking Wayne free. He tossed the farmer over the side, following right behind before he was stunned motionless by the frigid temperature of the freezing chamber.

"Brrr, that's a cold slap in the face," said Knothead.

"I think it was warmer in the water," said Braker, climbing up and huddling on the floor.

"Scoot over," said Knothead, crouching down next to Braker. "Gotta get out of that nasty breeze."

"Make room for me," said J.J. wedging himself in beside the others. "You guys make good insulation."

Wayne plopped in beside them. "Good idea, fellers. Let's cuddle."

Everyone just stared at the farmer for a moment.

Soon all four soaking derelicts sat shivering beside the deadly ice pool, the freezing chamber humming ceaselessly from the sound of refrigeration units set to full strength.

"This is ridiculous," said Braker, frost beginning to form across his nose. "It's like a blizzard without snow."

"I think it's all that cold air blowing out of those vents," said Wayne.

Everyone just stared at the farmer for a moment.

"Weren't you going to belt him?" said J.J., turning toward Knothead. "Please, belt him."

"Nah, I'm just not feelin' it anymore," said Knothead, hugging his knees. "The chill in here kind of takes the fight out of a body."

"Well, that's right good news to my ears," said Wayne. "You had me feelin' like a bull in a butcher shop there for a moment."

"Ah, don't worry about it," said Knothead. "It all worked out in the end. You helped get us out of that ice pond. And I can still smash you some other time if I want."

"Right neighborly of you," said Wayne.

"We were promised a thrashing," said J.J. "And I expect to see you churn that bumpkin like butter. What kind of a barbarian are you?"

"How bout I give you a churning instead, big mouth?" said Knothead.

"After my strategy led you to feats of superhuman strength? I think not."

"Let's just forget about it and get out of here," said Braker, jumping to his feet. "We can't just sit here and turn into icicles."

"Easy for you to say," replied J.J. "But we're locked in. How do you plan on getting us out?"

"A little smarts and a little force," said Braker. "Watch this."

"Now, wait just a minute, Braker," said J.J. "Up to now everything you've done has resulted in disaster. I don't know if you should be the one leading the way. This is my safety we're talking about."

"So I suppose you'll be leading us, then?" said Braker.

"Not in a literal sense," said J.J. "I mean, I am the most qualified, but that makes me too important to risk being up front. I'll make the decisions from a safe position in the rear."

"Well, if you're not willing to lead from the front, I don't think you should lead at all," said Braker. "Besides, I don't think I've done so bad."

"Me neither," said Wayne. "Believe me, he's capable of much worse."

"You may have a point," said J.J. "I'll concede leadership for now if that means Braker accepts the responsibility of detonating whatever booby traps lie ahead so the rest of us can pass safely on."

"Then it's settled," said Braker, shaking the water from his hair. "We haven't got a moment to waste. Don't worry about a thing, just follow my lead. I've got a plan." He jumped up, pounding on the heavy steel door that led out of the death chamber.

The door flew open, and a guard rushed in.

"Now, Knothead!" Braker shouted. "Clobber him!"

"Hey, tell a guy when he's part of the plan next time!" said Knothead, still sitting on the floor. "I wasn't even ready."

"I knew it! I knew it!" said J.J. "He blew it again!"

"Yeah, that wasn't really a very good plan," said Wayne. "Or at least not a very good execution of a plan."

"Nobody move!" ordered the guard, drawing his weapon.

Braker looked around quickly, and then leapt onto the man's back, attempting to throw him off balance. The guard simply backpedaled, slamming Braker against the wall repeatedly until the trucker let go, slouching to the floor. In the meantime, Braker's three friends went racing through the open doorway and down the hall.

"Brilliant!" said J.J. as he and his fellow fugitives scrambled madly ahead. "Braker knew his bumbling had us defeated, so he sacrificed his body as a distraction for the rest of us. Told you the kid was special. Don't foul it up now, guys, split up and try to find a ship to get us out of here!"

As soon as the guard realized he was losing most of his prisoners he abandoned Braker and gave chase.

Alone now in the freezing chamber, Braker lay on the floor rubbing his chest. Slowly rising to his feet, he achingly joined in the breakout, hoping to eventually catch up to the others. Rounding a corner, he could hear muffled voices further down the corridor. Unsure if they were friendly, he moved cautiously as he grew closer to what he could tell now was a conversation. A dim light was coming from a nearby room. He listened to the discussion from just outside the door.

"Yes, I will keep it," stated a sultry-voiced woman. "This is one of the most attractive pieces I have ever seen."

"I quite agree," said a male companion. "It would never do in a long-range engagement, but at close quarters it would prove most effective."

It was Holly Blackguard and Stud Bracer, her handsome head of security. They were talking about Knothead's distinct Molarkian hatchet.

Braker heard the weapon being laid down as Holly and Stud walked to the back of the room. Deciding a weapon was just what he needed to ensure an escape, he dropped silently to the ground, his face pressed to the floor as he peeked through the doorway. Directly in front of him lay the hatchet on the corner of a desk. Holly and Stud were facing the opposite wall as they discussed some imminent business.

Braker slid through the doorway on his belly. Without a sound, he reached up and snared the weapon. He was almost out of the room when several guards went running down the hall. The noise alerted Holly and Stud who turned just in time to see Braker's heels as he dove under the desk.

Holly crouched low to the floor, fingering a tiny coat-sleeve laser nipper, the kind the tricky gamblers around the Asad Star

Casinos used in tight situations; her eyes were mere slits as she examined the silent room. "Stud, you're my chief of guards, what was all that commotion about?"

"Not sure," said Stud, "but I'll bet it has something to do with our little friend under the desk. And that probably means the freeze chamber is empty."

"You hear that?" Holly called out. "We know you're in here. Give yourself up before we're forced to do something you may find vile and treacherous."

There was no movement, no answer.

Stud unholstered his big irrigation gun, locking a cartridge into the chamber.

"Your time is up," Holly announced. "My bodyguard is going to irrigate the desk. Pity we'll never know who you were since most of you will be washed away with the rest of the debris."

There was no time for caution—using the desk as a battering ram, Braker pushed himself and the desk further into the room with massive backward lunges of his legs. Moving fast, he kept pushing until the desk slammed into the stunned Holly Blackguard, knocking the laser nipper from her hands.

Braker scrambled over the desk, gripping Holly in a tight headlock. Stud had his sights on Braker but couldn't shoot—Holly was positioned directly in front of him.

"Put the gun down!" Braker shouted.

"And what if I don't, hero?"

"Then you'll have to shoot through your boss to get to me."

Stud grinned as he set his sights directly between Holly's eyes.

"You idiot!" Holly complained to Braker. "Now you just gave Stud the perfect chance to take over the WaterWorks. Don't you know anything about crime?"

Braker knew his only chance was to abandon Holly and make a dash for the door. Tossing the water queen aside, he sprang forward, attempting to leap over the desk before tripping over his own feet, bouncing off the desktop, and onto the floor. He rolled over to find the long barrel of Stud's irrigation gun pointed in his face.

Suddenly an electronic whistle pierced the air. Holly threw herself on top of Braker as a flash of red light whirled once around the room. When it was over, Braker stood up to find Stud lying on the floor—split in two.

"You are amazing," said Holly, breathless with awe. "Somehow you noticed the secret laser-splitter button on my desk and used your body to set it off. Stud never had a chance. How heartless."

"That's right," said Braker, looking for the secret button, "and that means you're coming with me. I'm making you my hostage."

"Take me," said Holly.

Braker grabbed Holly's arm and led her into the hall. He never even noticed the delight in the water queen's eyes.

Chapter Twelve
Space Hostage

Holly Blackguard watched silently from the cockpit of the water freighter as the last of Braker's friends hustled in. Holly's entire operation was at a standstill. Holly Blackguard, herself the very heart of the organization, was now a hostage, about to be whisked away into the unknown by the man who had broken her. The only people moving in the compound were the workers Braker had ordered to prepare the starship for flight.

"Where we going now, Braker?" asked Wayne.

"We're going straight to Nebulous X," Braker answered. "Hopefully there's still time to stop Lord Preposterous's wedding."

"Now just a minute," said J.J. "We should be trying to get away from these Nebulous X characters, not stopping by for an afternoon visit."

"But they've got the princess sisters," said Braker.

"Well, drop me off somewhere along the way," J.J. replied. "You guys have become too reckless with my safety in your mad thirst for glory; I shouldn't have to keep pointing this out."

"What are you, some kind of a creep?" asked Knothead. "Don't you want to find those girls?"

"Certainly I do," said J.J. "I'm just suggesting that I be the rescuer who goes for help. I'll call the police, organize a bail-out party, assemble a therapy team."

"We cain't drop you off. We ain't got time," said Wayne. "While we're doing that, one of them gals may end up married to Lord Preposterous."

"But if we go to Nebulous, I may end up hurt by Lord Preposterous," said J.J.

Knothead stuck a fistful of knuckles in J.J.'s face. "You're real close to getting hurt by *me*," said the barbarian. "Those girls need our help."

J.J. clapped his hands. "I've always wanted to see Nebulous in the springtime. What are we waiting for? Let's go rescue those girls."

After the last worker had exited the ship, Braker steered into the sky.

Knothead sat close to Holly, holding his big hatchet in plain and threatening sight. She ignored him completely, instead staring with steely eyes at the pilot.

"Anybody hungry?" Wayne called out, digging into the food crates placed on board.

"Say, a bite to eat doesn't sound too bad, right now," said J.J., pushing Wayne aside. "Let's see what goodies these folks packed for us." J.J.'s face turned sour as he dug into the crate. He spun around, flipping open a couple more box tops. "Those no-good finks," he cried.

"What's wrong," asked Wayne.

J.J. threw a chunk of brown cheese across the hold. "This food is spoiled. All of it. It's garbage. They gave us garbage! That's false advertising."

Knothead looked at Holly. "Rotten food and not even an attempt to bust you loose? Boy, those folks just love you don't they, honey?"

"Don't worry," said Braker. "Before long we can stop at some Greasy Space Spoon and grab a bite—it's open galaxy from here on in."

They hadn't gone very far before feeling the shudder of choking engines.

"Now what?" J.J. asked, looking to Braker.

The trucker opened the reservoir slats. "Looks like our friends back at the WaterWorks conveniently forgot to load us up on fuel. We're stranded."

J.J. sat with his head in his hands. "Braker, weren't you supposed to oversee the flight preparations? First the food and now the fuel; those are necessities for long distance space flight. I thought a pilot would know to double check those things."

"Didn't nobody tell you?" said Wayne. "Braker ain't no…"

"I am a pilot—technically," said Braker.

"Technically!" shouted J.J. "Technically! This is a fine time to define yourself as 'a pilot — technically.' That word does not instill confidence. That word does not project experience. That word does not promote a professional-type status. That is a word that is only used when someone isn't really something they want to be. 'Technically' is not a good word, especially not now. No, it is not."

"That's what I keep trying to tell him," said Wayne, shaking his head. "It just don't sound right."

"Quit whinin', all of you," said Knothead. "Braker, don't these long-range ships have back-up fuel flooders?"

"I think so, but they're only supposed to last for so long. You know, maybe long enough for a nearby rescue crew to…" Braker stopped in mid-sentence. Every eye looked to Holly Blackguard who sat stoically in her seat.

"To come take her back!" everyone shouted at the same time.

Braker pulled out a stack of old star maps. "Okay, listen," he said, "not too far from here is a filling station; maybe I can use the last of our back-up power to get us down there."

Braker guided the sputtering ship until the floating filling station came into view. The station was of average size, able to service about three space freighters at once on its black, disc shaped platform. To the far side of the fuel pumps was a small restaurant protected by a space-bubble canopy. Ships on the platform remained outside of the bubble and could only be fueled by a trained technician in a space suit; self-service had been outlawed in the galaxy after several distracted customers had mistakenly attached the fuel hose for their ship to the air-intake valve in their pressure suits.

Braker made it to the landing platform and soon the group was hustling out of the ship's exit hatch and into the restaurant through a small portal extension in the space-bubble canopy. The friendly pump technician on the platform smiled from behind his space helmet and began fueling right away.

Inside the restaurant, the thick aroma of fried food and bad plumbing assaulted the travelers.

"Give us meat!!" Knothead shouted at the greasy short order cook behind the counter. "Don't care what it is, just give us lots of it."

113

While the hungry crew awaited their house specialty order of Gut-burgers and Moon Chips, J.J. Whammo posted himself at the window, looking for signs of Holly Blackguard's rescue party. Everything was going smoothly until the cook noticed Wayne dragging the shackled Holly Blackguard to a booth. Expecting trouble, he told the waitress to wait outside.

"I know it's none of my business," the saggy-jowled cook said, tapping Wayne on the shoulder, "and I'm sure you're going to hate me and think I'm stupid for being such a bother, but why are you shoving that handcuffed woman around?"

Wayne smiled. "Oh, I'm just trying to get the little thunderbolt to sit down and eat something. She's kind of stubborn you know."

"Well, you can't just be hauling a woman around in shackles," the cook whined, his sad eyes glistening under the diner's humming florescent lights. "She looks like she could be in trouble. Reminds me of when my life-long dreams were shattered, and I was forced to become a space cook. I was on my honeymoon..."

"Look, guy," interrupted Braker, "we're sorry about your honeymoon, but we're kind of in a hurry so could you just mind your grill and give us a break, okay?"

"Hostility!" complained the cook. "Great, now I'll probably have to stand up for myself for the first time in my life."

"Just get the food!" shouted Knothead.

"We really are in a hurry," continued Braker.

"Better listen to him," Holly told the cook, a deviant smile on her face, "I'm his prisoner, and he's a very bad man."

"Here they come—Water Troopers!" shouted J.J., stationed at the window. "And there's a potful of 'em!"

Holly Blackguard's rescuers were making their attack, a large water freighter and space barge bearing down on the fuel station.

As Braker turned toward the window, the confused cook decided to take a chance on defending the seemingly oppressed water queen. With a murmur of self-encouragement, he reached for a chair to heave at Braker's head. As the steel bludgeon was almost released, Holly Blackguard threw herself between Braker and the cook, knocking the chef onto the counter with a flying elbow.

"Ouch, ouch!" whimpered the cook. "I was only trying to help. I should have known I'd get beat up by a woman."

The attacking ships fired a couple of warning shots at the restaurant. The bolts sprang off the protective outer bubble, but it was obvious it wouldn't withstand many more hits. Everyone in the restaurant was on the floor scrambling for cover. Braker pulled the bruised Holly Blackguard under a table with him.

"Why did you protect me like that?" asked Braker. "Are you crazy, lady? We're enemies, remember."

Holly looked deep into Braker's eyes. "No, I'm not crazy," she said boldly. "I'm in love—with you, Braker."

The trucker's mouth fell open, as did everyone else's in the room.

"You *are* crazy," Braker stammered.

Holly shook her head. "No, not at all. You've got guts, Braker. And you're ruthless. I've waited a long time for a man like you. Don't you see, I wanted to come with you, that's why I didn't resist."

"You've got me all wrong," said Braker. "I'm not ruthless. I'm barely even a trucker if you must know."

"You can say that again," shouted J.J., tucked under a nearby table with Wayne.

115

"You're not fooling me," said Holly, stretching out toward Braker on her hands and knees, "you're heartless; just the man I need."

"The only one who's heartless is you, lady!" Braker exclaimed. "You deal that deadly sugar-water to down-and-out addicts."

"Don't believe everything you're told, dear," said Holly, "I do have a reputation to keep. Oh sure, I sell them the water, but the sugar's not addictive and it's certainly not poisonous."

"It's not?" gasped Braker.

"Nah, I just made that up so nobody else on the planet would get any bright ideas about selling it themselves. You'd be surprised how many people are scared away by rumors of poison death."

"But if it's not addictive, what about all the sugar-heads who would do anything to get ahold of your products?"

"Well, it tastes great. The rest is all labeling though. Power of suggestion is a wonderful thing."

"Are you saying it doesn't actually turn anybody into mind-addled zombies?" said Braker.

"Maybe a little indigestion and brief paranoia," said Holly, "but other than that, no."

"So that means Fug isn't stupid?" shouted Wayne.

"That guy?" said Holly. "No, he just thinks he is."

"Wow, that's stupid," said Wayne.

"Look, it's deceiving, I know, but it's not like I'm hurting anyone," said the water queen. "It's what I'm good at."

"I'm not the man for you," said Braker. "I'm in love with Princess Babe."

"Any man who could split Stud like you did is just right for me. Stop playing hard to get, it just makes you more attractive."

Braker peeked over the table; Holly's rescue ships were landing around the fuel pumps. "Well, if that's really how you feel, lady, call off your dogs."

"I can't," said Holly, for once not looking strong, "they're very loyal and they'd never believe me. They'd only think you were forcing me to turn them away."

"They're coming in!" shouted Wayne, rushing over to block the door with a pile of empty pie boxes.

"Braker, over here, quick!" called Knothead from the other side of the room.

Braker dashed across the restaurant. He found the barbarian crouched in a corner booth, a young space traveler he'd never seen before huddled beside him. "Who's this?" the trucker exclaimed, sliding in beside the pair.

"This is Johnny Comet," said Knothead, introducing the smiling ten-year-old boy. "He's a space orphan."

"Wait a minute, shouldn't he be in school?" said Braker.

"No way!" Johnny shot back.

"Just listen," snapped Knothead. "Of course he doesn't go to school, school's a drag. He hangs out in dives like this all day and begs for change when he's not playing video games."

"Okay, whatever," Braker sighed, taking another look at the doorway. "What does that have to do with us?"

Knothead smiled. "Well, this kid says there's a back way out of here and he has a ship parked—"

Knothead wasn't even finished by the time Braker was on his feet. "Everybody follow the kid!" he shouted, motioning for the others to head for the back. "There's a spaceship out there!" Reacting to Braker's hopeful cry, the others hurried toward the exit.

Behind the restaurant, their hopes were shattered by the sight of an old interplanetary star shuttle lying collapsed on a huge grease stain. The dilapidated heap occupied a spot just outside the bubble canopy, a sagging inflatable corridor connecting it to the ship's rusty side portal.

"Hey, that's an old *TS-Asylum*," said Braker. "That's a school bus!"

"Yeah, ain't it the coolest?" said Johnny.

"What's a kid doing with his own school bus?" asked Braker.

"Think about it," replied Johnny, "the authorities would never look in a school bus for a kid playing hooky."

"Yeah, but don't you think they might get suspicious when they see a little kid *driving* the school bus?" said Braker.

"Whatever; a guy has to get around somehow," said Johnny.

"Who cares?" said J.J. "You can discuss the boy's extracurricular activities later. Just get in the bus!"

"But we can't ride in this," said Braker.

"What's wrong with it?" asked Wayne. "Looks pretty good to me."

Braker looked with horror at the bus. "Those *TS-Asylum's* got recalled years ago because their engines had a tendency to spontaneously explode."

Just then fifty Water Troopers came charging around the far side of the restaurant.

"Get in!" J.J. exclaimed. "I've sold a million of these. We'll get around alright."

"You've got to be joking," said Braker. "This ship, it's, it's…"

"A wreck?" suggested Knothead, running through the bus's corroded doorway.

"'A bomb' might be more appropriate," answered Braker.

"Let me out of these shackles, you maniacs!" screamed Holly. "If Braker's afraid of this ship it must be bad!" She was still shouting protests even as Johnny Comet and the cook shoved her through the hatch.

Braker remained outside the bus, watching the last of his fellow refugees run aboard. "You know they say all but one of these has blown up."

"Hey, that means my ship is one of a kind, then," said Johnny, leaning out the passenger side window. "I'll bet it's worth a bundle."

"I'll make you a deal for it later, kid," said J.J. "Right now, how about you just cut the chatter and make sure it runs, okay?"

Johnny Comet hopped into the driver's seat and fired up the *Asylum*'s engines; they whined and screeched, throwing fiery sparks until, with a loud boom, they finally belched a cloud of black soot and turned over. The Water Troopers were left blinded and choking; Braker, still standing at the hatchway, was finally startled enough to jump in.

With everyone now onboard, Johnny Comet put the ship in drive and tore away from the canopy extension.

"Hey, you didn't seal the canopy corridor before you pulled out!" Braker exclaimed. "That space bubble will collapse in the vacuum."

"Them ol' water boys is 'bout to get straight up dry gulched," said Wayne. "What a way to go."

"Whoops," said Johnny Comet.

"So what?" said Holly. "All my soldiers are more than willing to die for me."

"Really?' said Braker. "I get those guys chasing after you and all, but are they really *that* loyal?"

"I guess I don't really know," Holly admitted, "but that's what they always say at the monthly meetings."

"Yeah, a paycheck can get you that kind of response," said J.J.

"It's too late to save those bums," said Knothead. "The bubble's already collapsing."

"Maybe it's too late for them," said Wayne, "but the waitress and pump technician are still down in front of the restaurant and the bubble ain't deflated there yet." The two station workers stood pressed to the front edge of the rapidly drooping canopy, frantically waving their arms. "We cain't leave 'em, fellers; this here bubble's 'bout to turn into a giant flapjack."

"But what can we do?" said Braker. "There's only seconds left!"

"Hang on, gang!" shouted Johnny Comet, making a sharp U-turn. "I'm gonna try something!"

Johnny banked hard, mashing the gas with one foot an instant before activating the emergency brake with the other. Near-perfect timing brought the *Asylum* back to the platform in one swift maneuver that placed them directly in line with the canopy's front portal entrance. The pump technician immediately locked the seal in place and ran through with the waitress beside him. Once they were safely in the *Asylum's* confines, Johnny sped away, shredding the canopy's airlock. The space bubble's last bit of interior pressure rushed out, bringing certain doom to the Water Troopers who remained there, and ensuring the *Asylum* an unhurried getaway.

"Can anyone please tell me why Braker can never seem to do something like that?" said J.J.

"Probably for the same reason he cain't ever make a clean landing," said Wayne.

"Hey, are you a pilot?" asked Johnny.

"Sure, am," answered Braker. "I'm a space trucker."

"Technically," mocked J.J.

"Great," said Johnny. "You can help me drive the *Asylum*. It gets a little tough to handle sometimes when the transmission starts choking, but it's sure to be a cinch with an experienced set of hands guiding it."

"Uh, sure," said Braker, gingerly taking a pilot's seat. "No sweat."

"Don't worry," Wayne told Braker. "I'm sure Johnny can teach you anything you need to know."

Able to relax now for the first time, most of the passengers collapsed into the *Asylum's* double-rowed bench seating. Holly Blackguard was still on her feet however, looking back on where her Water Troopers had been. "They were a bunch of jerks anyway," she shrugged before walking over to where Braker and Johnny piloted the ship.

"Say, handsome," she said, sitting down on Braker's lap, "I don't know if you planned all this or not, but I'm impressed. You know how to show a girl a good time."

"Bad momma," said Johnny Comet.

Chapter Thirteen
Revolting Developments

Dr. Wilde leapt from his bed in the *Flying Electric Laboratory*'s private sleeping quarters. Running down the hall, he burst into the storage room where Bullmack stood motionless.

"Bullmack, wake up!" the doctor shouted, activating the auxiliary sound sensors that would bring Bullmack out of his computerized sleep.

"Good morning, Master," yawned Bullmack.

"Yes, it is good," said Dr. Wilde, wringing his hands. "It's very good because I've made a decision, a very important decision."

"That's nice," said Bullmack.

"Don't interrupt me," snapped Dr. Wilde. "The situation at hand is very grave indeed. We obviously have only two options at this point. One is to run."

Bullmack was happy. "Run, yeah, I like to run. Run is fun."

"That would not be fun; don't you understand? Lord Preposterous will be furious once Prince Tony tells him of what happened earlier today. His entire army will be our enemy. No civilized world will hide us; once we start running, we can never stop."

"I'm scared then," said Bullmack.

"No," the scientist scolded, "don't be scared—be angry. You see, our second option is to fight. And that is exactly what I have decided to do; we will reroute our course as soon as possible and attack Nebulous X with all the force we have left."

Bullmack scratched his nose. "But what if we are too weak to win? They will hurt us."

Dr. Wilde threw back his head in a mad fit of laughter. "Bullmack, you are such a fool. Don't you see? We can't lose. In all the excitement you've forgotten that I brought the Mysteriously Red Reeki Ray with us. We can destroy Lord Preposterous with one blast."

Bullmack clapped with anticipation. "Yeah, the Mysteriously Red Reeki Ray, that'll get 'em! Master, what exactly does the Mysteriously Red Reeki Ray do?"

Dr. Wilde slapped the robot in the head. "What a ridiculous question. It's a mystery, you foot, that's what makes it so dangerous. Even I don't know what it will do." The old man danced around the room. "Think of it, Bullmack, the carnage, the bloodshed, the complete terror in Lord Preposterous's heart as we come tearing through the sky with my untested, unstable, and unexplained Reeki Ray. It's glorious. Bullmack, look at me, look at me! It's glorious. Total war, revenge, and mind-numbing slaughter. What could be better? Ha, ha, ha. Even if we are killed, we'll probably become galactic legends. Tell me—really, I'm asking, what could be better? Forget it; the fact is, I'm hoping that you will die, Bullmack. But only because I want the best for you."

"Thank you, Master," said Bullmack, blushing.

****

Far across the galaxy, Nub Niblet and Roger Godsend, the two masterminds of a secret rebellion growing within the ranks of Prince Tony's fleet, were contemplating their plans within a vacant hallway deep inside the *Maiming Lily*. The discussion was interrupted when Princess Contentious was ushered by on her way to a holding cell; an unfortunate Goon of Doom trudged along beside her, enduring her constant scolding.

"And another thing, who's idea was it for you guys to wear those stupid metal helmets?" she continued, not even noticing the two other men in the hallway. "They look like giant mayonnaise jars. And I bet they're heavy too. Show some self-respect; get a beret. Even a colorful bandana would be better. And try standing up straight, you guys all wobble along like bunch of arthritic apes."

Godsend saluted the Goon and nodded to Contentious as they passed. "Good day, ma'am."

"Sure, sure, nice weather and all that too, right?" Contentious replied. "Stick it in your ear, puke-face, I'm about to be put in solitary."

Godsend stepped in front the princess. "Madame, I mean not to pry, but you seem to be indicating you're having a rough go of it. Do you feel that your rights are being violated?"

"Very perceptive, bub; so what? I can't imagine you being much help."

Godsend took Contentious by the hand. "Please, we're revolutionaries; we care."

"Look, Slim, my planet's blown up, my sister is a love slave to some creepy prince, and I'm about to be put into solitary; I'm really not in the mood to be your sympathy pet for the day."

Godsend released Contentious's hand, walking silently up and down the hall as Nub Niblet and the Goon guardian watched with interest. A look of deep concern etched Godsend's face. Finally, with a burst of emotion, he reached for his holster, pulling out his laser pistol. "That's it!" he exclaimed. "The forces of good cannot take any more! This woman's pain will be the last inflicted upon the innocent. Let the revolution begin!"

"Are you sure?" Nub asked.

Godsend turned his pistol's power level up to "pan-fry", then shot the perplexed Goon next to him. "Let the revolution begin!"

"I think he means it," Nub told Contentious as the roasted Goon fell to the floor. "I'll alert the others."

Nub went scampering down the passage while Godsend and Contentious ran off in the other direction.

"Once the liberation movement begins, I want to be as close to the launch pads as possible," Godsend explained. "I must command all ships."

"You just shot one of your own guys," said Contentious. "Why are you doing this?"

"Because, young lady, I am the cleansing pus needed to purify our sick and ulcerous ruling authority."

"Sorry I asked."

When they arrived at the hanger bay, Godsend and Contentious huddled behind a nearby fighter craft.

"There's nothing to do now but wait," said Godsend, polishing the barrel of his gun with a coat sleeve, "please finish with your history; I'll need to know more if I'm going to be able to help you."

"Well," said Contentious taking a deep breath, "I guess there's this jerk called Lord Preposterous, see, and he's dying to get married, so he snatched my sister and I in hopes of latching one of us. Along the way, we met some real cuties and they tried to rescue us, but Prince Fat-head was too much for 'em. Now princey boy is trying to put the moves on my sis while her real hero is gone."

"And what about the other man? Is he your hero?"

Contentious shrugged. "Well, I guess you could say he's my hero, but he's kind of a clunker. His name's Wayne; he's a space farmer. I am rather fond of him if you really must know—kind of like a soft old bath mat you can never bring yourself to throw out."

"You speak of him in melodies soft and rolling," said Godsend. "You deserve to be together. I shall do my utmost to see that you two are reunited."

"But you have a revolution to fight," said Contentious. "You won't have time to help us."

"Sweet maiden, so innocent and naive. The true revolutionary always has time to right the wrongs he encounters. It is our joyful occupation."

Contentious leaned forward. "Ok, so what is this revolution all about? Why are you doing this?"

Godsend sighed. "Why does a baby fill its diaper, princess? It's just something that must be done."

"Again, sorry I asked," said Contentious. "But at least tell me what a weird little squirt like Nub is doing in your revolution; he looks more like an overworked accountant than a soldier."

"Ah, that's because he is," said Godsend. "In fact, his official title is Chief Accountant to Prince Tony's Profiteering and Revenue Operations. But it's not an enviable position, mostly because of the torturously long hours and Prince Tony's legendary hatred for his accountants."

Contentious scrunched her face. "Tony's some kind of big-shot military officer on a tyrannical planet—he's got alien kingdoms and cosmic monsters to contend against; why would he waste time hating on his own accountants?"

Godsend smiled. "Dear lady, I wouldn't expect one as spotless as yourself to understand the inner neuroses of a hostile aristocrat."

"Try me."

"Well, I suppose it's not that difficult to understand after all; Tony's wealth doesn't really come from any sort of royal pedigree—"

"Son of the Deodorant King, I know," said Contentious.

"Right, not a bad start for a young man, but not exactly upper crust nobility. The prince is nothing if not enterprising, though—fashion design, interior decorating, managing a group of luxury senior centers are but a few of his endeavors. He's also had great success in illegal weapons manufacturing, producing background music for torture chambers, and has a seat on the underground lecture circuit speaking on the stress-relieving benefits of cooking for anxiety-prone tyrants. With such a vast and varied amount of sometimes highly unlawful income, Tony is extremely paranoid about getting ripped-off. Obviously, then, we find the reason for his hostility and distrust toward his accountant staff—they are closest to his valued money."

"Or maybe he just gets a thrill from picking on the nerdy office geeks," said Contentious.

Godsend shrugged. "Could be. Anyway, Tony's harassment of those in the accounting offices proved too much for Nub; despite many seasons of faithful drudgery, the little Niblet eventually found himself contending against that most tantalizing of desires—mutiny!"

"And that's when he met you?" asked Contentious.

"Yes, it was destined to happen, I'm sure, for I myself am well acquainted with personal tragedy."

"I suppose you'll want to tell me your own sob story now," said Contentious.

"I can't, it's unbearable to remember."

"Go ahead, I've got nothing better to do."

Godsend nodded. "Perhaps it is best for someone to know. My misfortune began when I was born into the family of General Gary Godsend, the most famous space officer Nebulous X has ever produced. He was killed in action defending his planet-destroying space fortress known as Gary Godsend's Galactic Garrison Gun, but not before he hounded each of his children to be the best in everything. His legacy of excellence lives on in my brothers and sisters; all six of them went on to become generals, admirals, and fleet commanders while I, despite all my efforts, barely managed to make the rank of sergeant—and that was just honorary because the rest of my company felt sorry for me."

"You can't be that bad of a foul up," said Contentious. "Maybe you just had a few bad breaks."

"Bad breaks?" said Godsend. "You don't know the half of it. I even tried out to be a Goon of Doom but didn't get accepted."

"You couldn't cut it?"

"Not exactly. I wasn't ugly enough. And I'm fully human. They have very strict standards."

"I'm sorry," said Contentious. "But it could be worse; being a space officer isn't everything. And you are very handsome for an older gentleman."

"That's true, but you might be interested to know I also suffer from sore feet, high-velocity gas attacks, and shame-induced bouts of complete insanity."

"Yeah, you're a total wipe-out," said Contentious.

"Quite so," said Godsend, "and therefore the perfect candidate to upturn this corrupt galactic bureaucracy through instigation of a bloody uprising."

"But how did you join with Nub and the accountants?"

"It happened quite by accident," Godsend explained. "I was assigned to escort the accountants to their daily flogging. It was my first encounter with them, and I must say I was quick to recognize their mistreatment. I felt a sudden kinship with those bookkeepers. And that, princess, is when I had my revelation—I was not the failure I appeared to be! Instead, I realized I had been set apart to claim my true identity. I was to become the champion of the meek and lowly wherever they might be found. Yes, I determined to form a fighting legion out of the lowly office staff. And now, with weapons forged from unused paper clips, staple guns, and overlooked tape dispensers we will rise up. Prince Tony and the Nebulous X regime will be the first to fall before the Accountant Army of Revolution. After them, every corrupt galactic system will feel our vengeance. This is only the beginning!"

The hangar's emergency alarms went off, signaling that the revolution had begun somewhere deep within the ship. Moments later, a large group of accountants charged into the hangar, hotly pursued by a platoon of Prince Tony's loyalists. The rebels were shot to pieces before they could even turn around.

Godsend sprang from his hiding place. "Long live the revolution!" he screamed, firing into the enemy troops. "Hail to the violence!"

He single-handedly wiped out half the enemy platoon and sent the other half running back down the hall.

Just as the firing subsided, Nub Niblet came scrambling into the launching bay.

"Sergeant Godsend…" he gasped.

"That's *General* now, little wee bit."

"Yes, sir," said Nub. "But what about *my* promotion, General?"

"Already done, *Corporal*," Godsend announced with a grin. "But tell us—how proceeds the honorable revolution?"

"Sir, I'm starting to wonder if this is going to work," Niblet panted, wiping sweat and dried blood from his forehead.

Godsend laughed. "Nub, what are you talking about? We just captured the hanger bay. How bad could it have gone in the rest of the ship?"

"Well, Prince Tony retreated to his laser proof command center and then ordered all rebel accountants hunted down and executed."

"And the problem?"

"Well, problem is that his troops had laser guns while we mostly had rubber bands and permanent markers. The Accountant Army of Revolution has been annihilated. We're the only ones left."

"But what about the paper shredders I distributed to the men?" said Godsend. "Those should have done some damage."

"They weren't quite as effective as we'd hoped, sir. But we did manage to give them a few nasty paper cuts with some sticky notes, though."

Over in the corner an injured accountant raised himself up on one elbow. "We can still take 'em, General," he said, just before dying of wounds.

Godsend didn't say a word. He calmly laid down his gun and walked to the far end of the hangar. He climbed up on the hood of a star fighter and extended his arms. "At one time, and not long ago—" he began before being interrupted by Nub Niblet tugging on his pant leg. "What is it, little one?"

"Sir," Nub inquired, glancing with obvious discomfort toward the hangar doors, "what exactly are you doing?"

Godsend put his hands on his hips. "I am giving a speech."

"But, sir—"

"I am giving a speech," Godsend repeated.

"Of course, sir," said Nub, stepping back with a bow. "A speech, of course."

Godsend extended his arms again. "At one time, and not long ago, less than five minutes ago, in fact, a great pitched battle was waged within these high, hallowed halls. It was a battle for our dignity, for we are the soiled ones, the foul, rank, and detestable ones, the sour, putrid, and moldering ones. We are the smell of rotten fish on the noses of the 'great' men. We are flung out like so much scum on the seashore, condemned to the most loathsome jobs in the galaxy. And yet this abuse has inspired our noble hearts. As these oppressions have increased, we have begun to march against the sniveling snobs, driving them before us by the shining blisters on our sweating feet.

"Fine gentlemen and ladies, the long-awaited, dream-drenched revolution is now in bloom. The future is ours for the taking. It is a time for the lowest, the shabbiest, the sorriest, most measly, god-awful, and dreadful of us to rise up and claim our dreams. I, your leader, turn now my ear to you, the people, and I ask, 'What do you demand of your future?'"

Godsend's words echoed through the hangar while Nub Niblet and Princess Contentious stared at each other. Finally, Nub smiled his wide, toothy grin. "Well, escape might not be a bad option at this point," he said in his nervous way.

Chapter Fourteen
Prisoners of Nebulous

Johnny Comet's *Asylum* cut through the cosmos with a most unsettling rumble. Johnny and Braker were both doing their best to keep the flight as smooth as possible, but despite their combined efforts the old bus's engine continued to sputter and surge at intervals, at times almost completely dying, and at others sounding like a furnace ready to explode. Knothead Madhouse, apparently unconcerned with the rattling windows around him and the vibrating floor beneath him, lay sprawled out in a front seat. Looking as if he were about to drift off to sleep, at the last moment he drowsily rolled to his side. Turning around, he inspected the three new passengers sitting behind him.

"Well, who are you?" he growled.

"I'm Downer Plasmoe," moaned the short-order chef as he slouched against a window. "I've been thinking about what happened today and I guess I should be thankful you folks saved my life, but I've just got this feeling that none of you really like me."

"We don't even know you," said Knothead.

"I'm just trying to share my feelings," said Downer. "Is it too much to share my feelings with one other fellow being and hope to be understood?"

"Sure, whatever," said Knothead, turning his interest to the pump technician and waitress. "And how about you folks? You got anything to say for yourselves?"

The shifty-eyed mechanic grinned. "Yes, I do. For the record, I just want to say that I'm forever indebted to all of you for saving our lives. Believe me, I would never do anything to stab good people like you in the back."

"Is that so?" rumbled Knothead.

"It sure is," continued the mechanic, "but let me introduce myself, I'm Chuck Weasel, and this is my sugar-heartbeat, my dearest love, Kate Starbrand."

Kate blushed, slapping Chuck on the shoulder.

Wayne leaned across the aisle, smiling. "You make a durn purdy couple, that's right."

"Well, thanks," answered Chuck. "Me and this little lady have been through a lot together. We like to think we've left a trail of love everywhere we've gone in this galaxy."

"Them's real sweet phrases," gushed Wayne.

Knothead couldn't take any more of this kind of talk; propping his feet in the windowsill, he settled in for the nap that had been threatening to overtake him. As soon as the barbarian began snoring, Chuck Weasel crossed the aisle, sliding into the seat with Wayne. "I've got a question," he whispered, "and I wanted to come to you first because you're obviously the most intelligent fellow around here."

"I be?" said Wayne.

"Sure, anybody can see that." Chuck leaned closer. "So, tell me, what is all this running around and fighting about? I mean, what's at stake here?"

Wayne thought hard for a moment. "Love, that's what I'd say—love."

Chuck gave Wayne a disapproving look. "Come on now, hayseed, don't feed me that. What's so important that a whole army would come along blowing up entire fuel stations for you and your gang? And don't you tell me love."

"Well, that's what it is," insisted Wayne. "Braker and I met these beautiful princess sisters but this fella calling himself Lord Preposterous is trying to steal 'em for himself. I tell you that guy would do anything to steal our women."

"Stolen princess sisters, huh? I'll bet somebody from their planet is wanting them back."

"Nope," said Wayne, shaking his head, "their planet got blowed up."

"So why are you trying so hard to get the girls?"

"'Cause of love."

"Come on. What's the real reason?"

"I told you—'cause of love."

"Farmer, don't even try, we're both grown men; what are you guys really after—rewards, ransoms? What is it?"

Wayne looked exultantly at Chuck. "Aww, fella, it's much better than all that—love's got me saddled and cinched, runnin' me harder than a jumpin' pony with a burnin' tail. Don't that tell ya ever'thing you need to know?"

"Oh sure, thanks a lot," Chuck grumbled, abruptly ending the conversation to slip back into the row behind the napping Knothead Madhouse. "Say, buddy," he whispered, nudging the barbarian, "do me a favor, let me in on what all the noise is about? I hear you guy's have some kind of scam cookin' over a couple of princess sisters."

135

Knothead popped open an eye. "You seriously wakin' up a tired barbarian?" he snapped.

"Don't get sore," said Chuck, "I'm just a simple fuel pump technician trying to make sense of this catastrophe so he can keep his sweet and innocent girlfriend safe."

Knothead dropped his feet back to the floor. "Go ahead, go ahead; what is it you're scratching for?"

"That's more like it," said Chuck, rubbing his hands together. "I just want to know what all the commotion's about. What's the big scam, man?"

"Oh yeah, you probably are wonderin'," said Knothead, sluggishly. "Look, it ain't no big thing, really. We're just trying to help a couple of lollipops who got in trouble, you know. Bring a little bit of happiness back to the universe, that's all. Don't worry, it'll all work out." The barbarian snorted and immediately went back to sleep.

Chuck put his head in his hands. He glanced back at Kate Starbrand, widened his eyes, and shook his head. Working his way to the back of the bus he determined to make one last attempt at uncovering the secret. He dropped in beside Holly Blackguard. The solitary water queen was sitting cross-legged, beautiful and poised, the train of her long, black gown draped neatly over her knees. The smiling mechanic pressed close. "And what's a lovely woman like you doing here?" he asked.

Holly stared straight ahead, displaying a wicked grin. "I'm simply biding my time until the moment I can betray Braker's true love into the hands of evil men in order to have the trucker all to myself. Now quit bugging me before I scratch your eyes out."

Chuck slid back into the aisle. "I'm not dealing with normal people here, am I?" he muttered to himself.

As the *Asylum* continued along on its rattling course, Johnny Comet scampered over to Knothead who was back to his convulsive snoring.

"Hey, Knothead," the boy whispered, tugging on the savage's heavy shoulder pad. "Are you one of those space cannibals?"

"What? What's that now?" said Knothead, smacking his lips as he struggled back to consciousness.

"I said, 'are you a space cannibal?'"

Knothead sat straight up, giving up on the nap once and for all. "Cannibal? Nah," he said, stretching. "Them guys are lipless and have massive overbites. I'm a space barbarian."

"Cool!" said Johnny. "What's it like to be a barbarian?"

Knothead rubbed his eyes and put his arm around the boy. "Barbarian life? Oh, it's great, Johnny; I can't imagine anything better."

"Wow—hey, what does a barbarian eat?"

"Raw moon pheasants, Johnny—with plenty of bloody veins."

"And I'll bet you make sure it gets smeared all over your face, too."

"Of course; we never wipe our mouths."

"Do you ever have to take a bath?"

"A bath?! No way, but once I filled a rusty trough with sweat and soaked in it for a while."

"Oh boy," laughed Johnny.

"You're foul," Holly shouted to Knothead from behind.

"You know me too well, baby," replied Knothead, blowing her a kiss.

Johnny was pulling on Knothead's arm. "Knothead, do you fight people a lot?"

"All the time."

"What's the most men you've ever fought?"

"Well, I used to be part of a professional space barbarian fighting circuit. We'd travel around from planet to planet, clan to clan, challenging local chieftains to battles for prize meat. At the time I was in the habit of going out the night before a big match and picking a fight with thirty or forty Bodiki warriors just to get warmed up."

"What's a Bodiki warrior?"

"Oh, them? They think they're all so great, giving themselves fancy names and such; they're just wandering space hobos, really. But they can get right spicy if you get 'em riled up enough."

Johnny's face was aglow with excitement. "And I bet you could beat them all."

"Naturally."

"Did you ever get hurt?"

Knothead laughed. "Get hurt? Of course, that's one of the most important parts of being a barbarian. The more hurt you've been, the tougher it proves you are."

"Really?" Johnny gasped. "Like what? What happened to you?"

"Well, one time a Nihgobian space giant bit my nose off. Then, after I defeated him in a blindfolded duel of whizzle spears I used the giant's own beard hairs to stitch my nose back on. Then there was the time I busted my arm in fifty places. It was so bad I had to cut a hole in the palm of my hand to shake out all the bones. After that I shoved an axe handle in there to hold my arm together.

Johnny Comet was jumping up and down. "Gee, Knothead, can I be a space barbarian too?"

Knothead scratched his hairy armpit. "Sure you can. But I don't imagine you've got any tribal blood in you so you'll have to be initiated."

"Okay," said Johnny, "I'm ready. What's the initiation?"

Knothead squinted an eye while pondering the question. "Well, to make you a true barbarian I suppose I'd have to start by pulling your hair until you go bald in spots."

"Ouch, can't we just skip that part?" Johnny asked.

"Sure, sure," said Knothead. "That part's not so important anyway."

"Great, so what's next?"

"Well, then I'd have to poke you in the eyes for three days straight."

"No way, I'll go blind," said Johnny.

"Want to skip it?" asked Knothead.

"Uh, yeah."

"No problem, you'll find barbarians are pretty casual when it comes to rules and such."

"Sweet. What's left?"

"After that, I suppose I'd have to stomp on your feet while I'm wearing flaming shoes—but only until your toenails fall off."

Johnny lowered his head, staring at Knothead.

"Skip it?" Knothead asked.

"You know it."

Knothead waved his hand. "Consider it gone."

"Hey, this is easy," said Johnny. "Is there anything else?"

"One last thing. And this one you *have* to do."

"Can't get out of it?"

"Not a chance. It's kind of a prestige sort of thing; you understand."

139

"Let's have it, then."

"Okay, for this one, I have to bite your elbow ten times until the wound is large enough for me to stuff a belching bag fly larva into. Then, after the bag fly grows its prickly leather wings and hatches from your arm, you'll have to wrestle it to death and eat it after frying it up in a batter of hot scum and gravel."

Johnny groaned. "Have to?"

"Have to," said Knothead.

"Maybe we shouldn't be rushing into this after all," said Johnny, shrinking back. "I just remembered I've still got some other stuff to do, like grow up, get a job, grow old, and retire first."

"You sure?" said Knothead.

Johnny continued moving away. "Yeah, it's just…you know, responsibilities."

"Always the same," said Knothead as Johnny hurried off. "Responsibilities. Ain't nothing worse."

While the passengers conversed, J.J. was trying to talk business with Braker who was still fighting to maintain control of the bus's giant, bucking, steering wheel. "It's obvious to me that we have to stop and get better prepared to continue this pursuit," said J.J. "We're not in any condition to take on battles like this; consider the ship we're using, and our passengers. Safety measures must be our priority. Perhaps we could even find time to enroll you in a remedial pilot's school."

Braker continued to wrestle the wheel. "We can't stop now, J.J. We've lost too much time. Babe's counting on me. Don't you understand? This is my chance to prove to her and everyone else that I'm someone special. I'm going straight to Nebulous."

"Braker, I'm afraid I must now tell you that you've completely lost your mind," said J.J.

140

"Phase out, knuckle brain," said Johnny Comet, jumping into the co-pilots seat. "Braker's in charge and we're with him. Let's go bust some heads."

"Braker, that's the final straw!" said J.J. "I can't let you do this—even children are being led astray by your madness. I'm older and I'm taking control."

Urged into action by the threat, Wayne and Knothead sprung between J.J. and Braker, their presence forcing the salesman back against the wall.

"Nobody runs this ship but Braker!" Knothead bellowed.

"You want to get killed, is that it?" J.J. shouted back.

"Yeah, maybe we do!" said Johnny Comet, laughing.

"You're an obnoxious child," snapped J.J.

"Hey, I'm just a space orphan," said Johnny, "gimme a break."

"Don't you people see?" cried J.J. "We've barely escaped with my life! You're all mad. Everyone is mad."

Knothead rolled his eyes toward J.J. "We're all gonna be a lot madder if you don't shut up. Now quit pickin' on Braker; he might be a ridiculous bungler but at least he's got spirit. And that's worked fine so far."

"You hear that, J.J?" said Braker. "Everybody trusts me. Now we're going straight to Nebulous to get Babe; you can either make yourself useful or make a disgrace out of yourself, it won't change a thing."

"That scamming salesman is already a disgrace," Holly added from the back. "He's got quitter's blood. Braker's frosty hard. I'll follow him."

"Oh, okay, so now Braker's getting endorsements from a fraudulent black marketeer," said J.J. "You people cannot be serious."

Nebulous X appeared on the space screen. "It's too late to turn back now, J.J.!" Braker cried, his full attention fixed on the dark planet. "We're here. Nebulous X, straight ahead. I'm taking us in!"

Suddenly, Nebulous X guard ships appeared all around them, swinging themselves onto a collision course with the *Asylum*. Hundreds, then thousands, of them closed in, their glowing laser sights twinkling among the stars.

"Hey, this look's serious," said Johnny.

Braker was undaunted by the obstacles. "Take that!" he shouted as the first of a series of blockade ships was rammed out of the way. The *Asylum's* walls creaked and shuddered, large chunks of its outer paneling flying into space.

"Maybe you should slow down just a little," said Johnny Comet, choking back his suddenly rising fear. "I don't really think my ship can handle that kind of stuff."

"Johnny may be right," Wayne added, wobbled by the shuddering floor. "Could be we're bitin' off a bit more cud than we can chew this time, Braker."

"I agree," said Knothead, trying to hold the steel deck plates together.

"Hey, I thought you just got done saying how much confidence you have in me," said Braker.

"Not really," said Knothead. "We just like messing with J.J."

"He's mad I tell you!" said J.J., crouching in the corner. "No one listens to the salesman—but we know things!"

"Leave him alone," said Holly Blackguard. "Braker's flying this ship and he's got it totally under control. Right, Braker?"

"Now where are those brakes?" Braker wondered aloud.

At that moment, a Nebulous X command came over the *Asylum's* voice box. "Foreign vessel, stop your descent immediately or you will be absorbed by the Wall of Darkness, after which you will face the wrathful judgment of Lord Preposterous himself."

"Yeah, right," said Braker.

Suddenly everything went black.

"Hey, who turned out the lights?" shouted Johnny Comet.

****

A short time later, as the captives lingered in the strange, gloomy confines of the Wall of Darkness, Prince Tony finally returned to Nebulous X. He marched confidently into Lord Preposterous's throne room feeling positively feline in his tight black body stocking and crushed red velvet boots. He was quite pleased with the lies he was prepared to tell; with one clever story, filled with half lies and outright fabrications, he would obscure his own abduction of the Princess Babe, the loss of his accountants and several Goons due to the Accountant Rebellion, and the subsequent loss of the Princess Contentious following her last-minute escape with Godsend and Nub Niblet.

"I have important news, my Lord," said the prince, bowing low before his master's big feet.

Lord Preposterous's face was like stone. "Speak to me, my unworthy pawn."

Tony looked up, already sensing the anger in his dictator's voice. "Lord, I understand that you have not heard from me for quite some time and I'm sure it has caused you grave concern. I apologize for that by explaining that my voice boxes were knocked out in my fight to capture your prey."

"Go on," rumbled Preposterous.

"Thank you, Lord. Now, I also realize that in your wisdom you chose the admirable Dr. Wilde to join in the pursuit of the sisters. That matter brings me sadly to the reason my voice boxes were knocked out in the first place. You see, it is with great regret that I inform you of how the good doctor attempted to steal the princess sisters from myself after I had already apprehended them. He did this in a selfish attempt to impress you while blatantly disregarding your best interest of bringing the girls back as swiftly as possible. When I tried to persuade Dr. Wilde to obey your commands a fight ensued. It was in this fight, instigated by Dr. Wilde, that both sisters were killed."

"Both?" Lord Preposterous wailed.

"Regrettably yes, my Lord; killed by the doctor himself."

"And what of Dr. Wilde?"

"Dead also. I myself killed him for such a treasonous act."

Lord Preposterous leaned forward. "Thank you, Prince Tony. Thank you for that kind act of vengeance."

Tony blushed. "You're welcome, sire. Now may I retire to my castle until further assignments?"

"By all means, yes."

Tony turned, and then stopped before leaving. "One last thing, my Lord. My fleet was severely damaged in the battle, a large percentage of my accountant staff is missing or presumed destroyed; may I beg you for reinforcements before another journey?"

Lord Preposterous smiled, his curled, yellow teeth looking like a row of dried corn. "Certainly, it shall be done, my faithful sadist."

"Thank you, my Lord. Thank you."

As soon as Tony was gone, Lord Preposterous roared in fury. "Benchworth, come forth!"

The dutiful manservant shuffled out of the shadows. "Yes, oh furious one."

"I have been betrayed! Dr. Wilde ruined my marriage plans by his greedy treachery! Curse his name forever!"

"Curses, curses," said Benchworth.

Lord Preposterous's voice now decreased to a gentle whisper. "Come now, Benchworth, approach my throne so that I may better vent my anger."

The stiff old gentleman struggled up the impossibly high stairs leading to the throne. "At your service," he said weakly upon reaching the top.

"Away from me!" bellowed Lord Preposterous, sending the man careening down the stairs by a crushing slap to the face. Then, once Benchworth finally hit the floor, Lord Preposterous again reclined on his throne. "Thank you, filthy scum roach, for that stress reliever."

Benchworth cracked his jaw back into place. "No, thank you my most gracious Lord for blessing me with the honor of being so royally abused."

"Think nothing of it," said Preposterous. "Now I shall turn my interests to other matters. Bring in today's prisoners."

Benchworth limped away, again disappearing into the shadows. Soon Braker and his friends stood in the center of the vast throne room.

Lord Preposterous looked down upon the group. "You have all been charged with very serious offenses against this flourishing regime. Do you have anything to say for yourselves?"

Before anyone could speak, Knothead jumped forward. "Yeah, I've got something to say! How would you like four inches of fist crammed up your nose?"

J.J. stomped on Knothead's foot. "Please ignore my woolly friend," he said, smiling apologetically at Preposterous. "He's recovering from a brain removal experiment. It's an honor to be here, sir. Your planet is lovely. I especially like how everything is painted black. Was that your idea?"

"You are a coward," said Preposterous. "Don't ever speak to me again."

"Lay off my friends," said Braker, stepping out from the group. "They didn't do anything to you. I'm the one who crashed through your space barricade; they had nothing to do with it."

Preposterous smiled slightly. "My, aren't you an amusing little ant of a man. Tell me your name."

"My name's Braker Ford and I'm a space trucker by profession, but today I'm here on other business—and that's to bring back the princess sisters you stole."

"Ah, yes, you must be one half of the wandering space trash who interrupted my wedding convoy."

"Wedding convoy?" exclaimed Braker. "Those sisters were doing everything they could to get away from that pack of murderous kidnappers you had chasing them."

Preposterous shrugged. "Everyone has different nuptial customs. What is it to you, anyway?"

"I'm in love with one of those sisters," said Braker.

"An' I'm lovin' me the other gal," said Wayne, stepping up beside Braker.

Preposterous sniffed. "Clearly you are a hillbilly space farmer—"

"Hey, how'd he know?"

"—and I do not address myself to hillbilly space farmers. Step back with the rest of your rabble."

"Who you calling rabble, bub?" interjected Holly Blackguard. "I'm a queen."

Preposterous turned to inspect the crime matron. "Maybe so," he snickered, "but you'll find that besides being passionate about tyrannical power organizations I'm also a very discerning admirer of the ladies. And when it comes to you, you're a tad worn-out to my eyes. That greatly displeases me; I find any deviation from feminine perfection loathsome. I won't even bother to mention that based on the company you keep you must be a very low-ranking queen at that."

"Hey, I'm good-lookin'," Holly protested.

Preposterous nodded. "Granted, you do possess some traces of dusky allure, but you're a tad crusty, my dear, a bit hardened on the edges. At first glance I had considered forcing you into a loveless marriage, but after further consideration I've decided to pass."

"You drooling pouch of stinking space yeast, you've got no room to talk."

"He might be a drooling pouch of space yeast," said Knothead, leaning in towards Holly, "but he's definitely got an eye for real beauty; you gotta give him that."

"Oh, shut up, beast," said Holly.

"All of you are truly a motley bunch," Preposterous continued. "I can find no reason not to torment you for my amusement before finally disposing of you when your suffering has run out of flavor."

Chuck Weasel stepped forward. "Sir," he said with a humble smile, "I'm just a simple fuel pump technician with a heart of gold, but I got one thing that makes my speck of a life worth living and that's this little slice of bliss right here." He took the hand of the blonde waitress beside him. "This is Kate Starbrand. And, sir, if you don't think our lives should count for anything more than a few moments of sadistic entertainment—at least our love should. For Kate's sake—and our love's sake—I ask you to consider maybe just letting us stay on here as your servants. We're real quiet folk, and we just love to serve. That's all I ask."

"I think I'm gonna puke," Knothead whispered to J.J.

"Inspired pleading," said Preposterous. "Keep it up and I might keep you around just so I can hear more of such hilariously heartbreaking beggary.... Just kidding, I would never keep you around."

"Too sappy," J.J. whispered to Knothead. "The kid's got to learn to push the sale, cut right to the deal."

Preposterous inspected Downer Plasmoe, the cook. "I suspect you will now seek to implore me with some poignant rationalization for continued existence."

Downer removed his chef's hat. "It would sure mean a lot if you would hear me out, your Highness. I've had a long string of hard knocks. If it all came to an end like this, well, it would make my life almost meaningless. You see—"

"Shut it!" bellowed Preposterous. "I've decided I'm tired of listening to all this insipid drivel. I will now pronounce judgment upon you and adjourn for my afternoon snack—"

"You'll adjourn to a muffler pipe upside your bloated head, pus muffin!" exclaimed Braker.

As if on cue, everyone in the throne room slowly turned to gaze at Braker in utter open-mouthed amazement.

"What did you say?" stammered Preposterous.

"Basically, he just said he was going to treat you like a public restroom," said Johnny Comet, ecstatic over Braker's boldness.

"Of course, I know what he meant," replied Preposterous. "I'm not some stupid baby dictator who needs every insult explained to him."

"Braker, a little tact might be in order here," J.J. whispered.

"No chance," Braker replied. "We've come a long way for this. Look at that guy; he's a big phony. We're calling his bluff right now."

Johnny tugged on Braker's sleeve. "Dude, you're awesome! You've got some guts!"

"Ignore him, Johnny," said J.J. "He's just trying to act tough. He's a bad example and has no idea what he's doing."

"Hey, kid's love bad examples," replied Johnny.

Braker smiled at Johnny before continuing. "Preposterous, you like to shoot your mouth off like you're some big bully. But I'm not putting up with it today. Like I said earlier, I'm here for one thing and one thing only, and that's to bring back those princess sisters!"

"Yeah, we're gonna bring 'em back!" chimed in Johnny Comet.

Braker continued. "I'm not here to ask for mercy and I'm not here to strike a bargain; I'm here for the takin', and I'll be takin' those women—right now! And just in case you're considering not doing things my way I'll tell you this, and I mean it—I'll pull this place down around your ears."

"Yeah, around your ears!" said Johnny Comet.

Lord Preposterous laughed. "I am the great Lord Preposterous, no one pulls anything down around my ears. Therefore, Braker Ford, in light of your present state of mind, and for your many heinous crimes, including the hindering of my wedding, showing up on my planet uninvited, dragging a feral bunch of delinquents and half-wits into my royal presence, and, especially, for saying a lot of rude things to me, you and all your friends will be executed at my command first thing tomorrow morning. There is nothing you can do about it; you are *my* captives, on *my* planet, surrounded by legions of *my* psychologically messed-up, evil armies. Now think about that tonight, you annoying little blowout."

"Yeah, think about that tonight, you annoying little blowout!" said Johnny Comet, caught up in the sudden power shift.

Everyone looked over to see what Braker's response to Preposterous would be; Braker, stunned silent, looked to Johnny Comet.

Johnny shrugged. "It was fun while it lasted."

As the deflated group marched out of the throne room Wayne whispered into Braker's ear. "Braker, I'm just wonderin' something."

"What is it now, Wayne?"

"Well, I'm just wonderin', when do you suppose we should start pulling this place down around his ears?"

"Be quiet, Wayne."

Chapter Fifteen
Invasion!

At first light, Braker's group was led outside to Lord Preposterous's royal flower garden, the centerpiece of Nebulan beauty and culture—and the envy of every tasteful totalitarian government in the galaxy. Acres of bizarre trees, shrubs, and plants were on display here, each vine and sapling tenderly cared for by dedicated crews of homicidal artists reformed into landscapers and nurserymen. Here, and only here, could one find examples of the fabled Nebulan exploding cacti, man-eating daffodils, and the walking, tentacled tulips constantly speculated upon by interplanetary florists but so rarely ever seen. On the north end of the garden were the sweating lilacs; the south end, the barking rose bushes; the west end, the spitting hemlocks and groping hedge mazes; the east end, the snail ponds and bathing swamp. In the middle of the garden was a courtyard, its center dominated by a huge ivy-covered execution machine. The Nebulous X marching band hammered out the planetary anthem while prancing around the device. Further down the lawn, a party of Nebulan nobility were playing a rousing game of clubs and mallets on the clubbing green. Lord Preposterous and Benchworth were there also, overlooking it all from their private, floating grandstand.

Braker's group was placed in a portable laser cage where they were forced to wait until all the morning's spectators had arrived. The captives milled about forlornly, afraid to get anywhere near the glowing bars after Wayne had lost a bet with Knothead and received a nasty shock due to sticking his tongue on one of the sparking barriers.

Slowly, the courtyard began to fill with dukes and barons, countesses, and earls, all of them eager to socialize while taking in a free public slaying.

As the crowds grew, Benchworth approached the laser cage. "Good morning, all," he said to the prisoners. "Please accept my apologies, I know you must have a lot on your minds right now, but I do have some last-minute instructions for you—and don't think even for a moment this is how we usually do this. Typically, we have at least one rehearsal before the real ceremony, but it seems Lord Preposterous is in quite the hurry to see you all slaughtered today. Now if you can all just smile and wave as the guards lead you to the execution platform, it would be much appreciated. We like to keep the atmosphere festive. No one likes to see these things turn gloomy."

"Anything we can do to help," said Wayne, smiling.

"Thank you," said Benchworth. "That means a lot. You have no idea how hard it is to keep Preposterous *and* the nobility all satisfied at the same time. Believe me, Preposterous is difficult enough on his own. I mean, it's near impossible, as you've probably begun to discover by now."

"You can say that again," nodded Wayne.

Braker slugged Wayne on the shoulder. "Hey, why should we care about their party? We're the ones being executed."

"I don't want to die sour," said Wayne.

"Please cooperate," said Benchworth. "After today you'll never have to see Preposterous again; I've got to face him every morning."

J.J. stepped up. "That's certainly no way to spend a life, let alone start a day. Benchworth, you seem to be a fine old gentleman, you can't really like serving a scrunge like Preposterous, can you?"

"Oh, of course not," replied Benchworth. "I'd rather wear mouse traps on my eyelids."

"So how did you end up as his personal servant?" asked Braker.

"My, but that's an unfortunate story," said Benchworth with a sigh. "I really don't want to depress you kids with the details."

"I honestly don't think you have to worry about that right now," said Braker.

Benchworth shrugged. "Alright. Well, you see, the truth is, Preposterous is not actually from this planet. The universe naturally collects random space contaminants from the solar winds. These clusters of space salts, crud wads, hair balls, and pathogenic fluids then tumble about at extremely high speeds until occasionally colliding with drifting space bacteria; the resulting mutation could end up being nothing more than a sticky intergalactic goober, or, as in Preposterous's case, the living embodiment of an arrogant, festering celestial infection. Anyway, Preposterous continued his high-velocity journey through the outer darkness until he happened to crash-land upon our ill-fated planet of Nebulous X."

"You mean Lord Preposterous is truly just a walking disease?" exclaimed Braker.

Benchworth shook his head. "That's giving him too much credit—he's actually nothing more than a highly-advanced snot rocket."

"Oow-wee," said Wayne. "That's nasty."

"But what does that have to do with you?" J.J. said.

"I was the head of customer service at the finest resort hotel on Nebulous at the time. Lord Preposterous arrived and was, as you can imagine, not terribly well received by the general public. Of course, I never allowed my professional standards to be affected by a guest's contemptibility; I made sure Preposterous's stay was of the highest quality. Indeed, at the conclusion of his stopover he was so impressed that he determined to make Nebulous his new home, and immediately set out to claim total control of the planet."

"But you just said Preposterous was nothing more than a wandering space virus," said Braker. "How easy could it have been for someone like that to take over an entire planet?"

"Easier than you'd expect, sadly," said Benchworth. "Up until then our people had lived for ages in relative ease; not terribly sophisticated, we were tragically unprepared for a hostile takeover. Preposterous found he had great appeal to those malcontents on the fringes of our society. After recruiting them and an army of space thugs, the rest was rather effortless."

"But still, an army of thugs and lunatics against an entire world?" said Braker.

"Let me put it to you this way," said Benchworth. "Back then our planet was led by a committee of retired elementary school teachers. They determined the best way to deal with the threat was a severe scolding."

"Yeah, you guys were kind of asking for it," said Braker.

"Agreed," said Benchworth. "And fittingly I have received the worst of it—Preposterous was always grateful for my courteous treatment of him at the hotel; as reward he ordered me to be his personal manservant. I alone have the honor of trimming his toenails, plucking the hair from his back moles, and preparing his meals, which most nights he just throws back at my face; it is justice, I suppose, as all of the evil our planet must now suffer is a result of the comfort I gave him during that initial lodging."

"Don't blame yourself," said Braker. "You were just trying to do your job. Besides, you could make up for it now and help bust us out."

Knothead shoved his way forward. "Hey, Braker's right, geezer. And if you hate Preposterous so much, why didn't you ever do anything about it?"

Benchworth bowed his head. "Oh, I have been tempted, my son, many times—and I certainly have had ample opportunity. In fact, to this very day I continue to find myself on the verge of assassination but can never bring myself to do it. You must remember, in my youth I was a timid, cowering man; I am even more so now at my advanced age. Bootlicking and submissiveness just seem to come naturally to me."

"Well, you may be a chicken-hearted jellyfish," roared Knothead, "but we're not! Give us a chance to do something!"

"That's right," said J.J. "Try submitting to us!"

"Yeah, how about it, old man," chimed in Chuck Weasel. "Give us a little of that customer service you're so in love with."

"Please," said Kate Starbrand, "we don't want to see an old codger like you waste his life—at least until you've given us a chance to continue ours."

"I would ask you to spare my life," added Downer Plasmoe, "but honestly it's probably not worth saving."

Johnny Comet didn't say a word, he just walked to the edge of the cage and looked up at Benchworth, his child's eyes round and bright, staring away in silent pleading until eventually a single tear ran down his cheek.

Benchworth clasped his head. "Oh, of course I'll help you."

"Sweetness!" exclaimed Johnny Comet with a pump of his arm. "I knew learning to cry on demand would come in handy someday. No one can deny a crying kid."

"And so I cannot, child. Here, let me release you. Then I will provide you safe passage from the garden."

Just then Lord Preposterous set off a blast from his personal air horn canister. Benchworth jumped.

"Oh my," he said. "That's the signal for the execution to begin. I've dawdled too long. He's irked, I'm sure."

"Well, do something!" shouted Braker.

"Too late," said Benchworth, as a company of Goons arrived to escort the prisoners to their fate.

"So that's it?" Braker asked, being led out of the cage. "Can't you do anything else?"

"Oh, yes," replied Benchworth. "I almost forgot, Preposterous wants you to appear in order of height—shortest in front, tallest in back. It just looks better to the crowd; you understand." Benchworth directed Johnny Comet to the front of the line, organizing the rest until Wayne was brought around, forming the rear. "I'm sorry, children. But at least you look good now; that's a smart looking line. I know it's not much but it's all I can do."

"You can say that again," said Johnny Comet.

The courtyard was filled to capacity now with the happy, giggling faces of the Nebulan upper class, each one eager for the commencement of the morning's main event. The prisoners were marched to the execution device, Benchworth veering off to rejoin Preposterous in the grandstand. On the way to their death instrument, Wayne continued to wave and smile at the crowd, Braker repeatedly slapping down his hand. Once the captives were in position, Lord Preposterous raised his arms and everyone fell silent, everyone except for Benchworth who gagged at the smell.

"Today injustice shall prevail," Preposterous began. "For your crimes, Braker Ford, you and your cohorts will be placed in my special Mulch Machine, a unit especially designed by Dr. Wilde to extract the protein from worthless human bodies such as yours and mix it with a top-grade fertilizer that will then be sprayed on my exotic courtyard shrubs. But do not let your excruciating deaths weigh too heavily upon you, for you can rest in the knowledge that your foul lives will, at least in some small way, have brought beauty to a tiny corner of the galaxy."

"Well, thank you," said Wayne.

"Insert them," said Lord Preposterous.

Braker and his friends were led onto a large hydraulic platform beside what appeared to be an enormous blender; a bizarre green liquid bubbled inside. At the top of the container the platform tilted, dumping the prisoners into the green slime.

"Begin the spin cycle," said Preposterous.

A switch was flipped, and the container slowly began to turn. Braker and his friends tried frantically to climb the smooth sides of the immense cylinder but to no avail, they continually slid back into the muck, even as the engines were picking up speed.

In the grandstand, Lord Preposterous gazed at the clouds. "What a beautiful day for a mass liquidation," he sighed just as something above caught his eye. A cluster of black dots appeared in the distance—and they were coming closer. Nebulan security ships, circling protectively in the air, fired on the approaching mass, but were themselves blown into dust by the invading swarm. Soon it was terrifyingly clear who the invaders were—a fleet of lab buses in attack formation, Dr. Wilde's *Flying Electric Laboratory* in the lead.

Alarms went off everywhere as the *Laboratory* released the first blast from its diabolic arsenal of science-type weapons. The doctor used everything at his disposal—Disaster Rain, Shatter Balls, Baby Flingers, and Crowbar Spinners pummeled the compound; a guard tower exploded, then a gazebo; flowers withered, and trees wept. Goons and nobles went racing to find cover from the relentless assault.

Inside the *Flying Laboratory*, Dr. Wilde called out last minute instructions. "Maintain the *Laboratory*!" he shouted to the helmsman. "Bullmack and I will operate the Reeki Craft and destroy Lord Preposterous personally!" Pushing Bullmack before him, the duo entered an elevator that lowered them into the cockpit of a small shuttle docked beneath the *Laboratory*.

Moments later, the compact vessel broke away from its mooring. This was the Reeki Craft, really nothing more than an ordinary sky van, but one that had been retrofitted for the distinct honor of carrying the Mysteriously Red Reeki Ray, a masterwork of destruction so apocalyptic in its potential that even Dr. Wilde had never dared to test it. Within the *Flying Electric Laboratory* there was a bubbling sense of cheerful anticipation; this was the moment the doctor's deranged assistants had been waiting years for—the moment the Mysteriously Red Reeki Ray would finally be unleashed. Crowding the *Flying Laboratory's* observation deck, they pumped their fists in the air, chanting, "Go Red Reeki, Go Red Reeki!"

The shuttle descended until fifty feet above the park. There it remained, hovering silently until its hood split open, a large spotlight rising from within; its red bulb began to glow, accompanied by a crackling hum. A shaft of crimson light streamed out to the center of the plaza, enveloping the entire courtyard, including the deadly Mulch Machine, in its ruby glow. As the ray continued to blaze, the Mulch Machine's glass walls reflected some of the glare back onto the Reeki Craft itself.

"Master, is this how the Mysteriously Red Reeki Ray is supposed to work?" Bullmack asked as he and Dr. Wilde were bathed in the radiance.

"What are you asking me for?" cried Dr. Wilde. "I created the ray to be completely unpredictable."

"It smells like feet," said Bullmack.

"That's probably just you," said Dr. Wilde.

"Nope, this is a lot worse," replied Bullmack, holding his nose.

The Reeki glow deepened, the odor increasing to the point that even Dr. Wilde was covering his face.

"Well, who cares anyway," Dr. Wilde barked. "The ray is working, isn't it?"

"It sure is," said Bullmack. "My nose is starting to bleed."

Down below, the victims of the Mulch Machine found themselves doubly afflicted—not only were they being blended alive, but they were also now forced to endure a stench never before encountered.

"Whoa, something stinks," said Braker as he swirled with the others in the green stew.

"It's like every rotten egg in the universe just got cracked over our heads," said J.J.

"Yeah, that and a million gallons of spoiled milk," added Johnny Comet.

"Kind of gamey, alright," replied Wayne.

"Reminds me of home," said Knothead.

"Shut up, gargoyle," said Holly. "Braker, do something quick, if this juicer doesn't finish us off, the smell will."

"Everyone just plug your nose for now," Braker replied. "We'll have to endure it until we can get out of this Mulch Machine."

"But I can't," cried Downer, "I'm pinching as hard as I can and it's still getting through!"

Things were just as bad outside the Mulch Machine—the Nebulan nobility were coughing and gagging; some crawled; some ran; others just gibbered mindlessly.

In Lord Preposterous's royal skybox the conditions were much the same.

"I think I'm going to be sick," said Preposterous.

"Oh, Lord, I'm frightened," said Benchworth, "I believe the smell is melting my dentures.

In a few more awful moments, the entire flower garden was encased in the unholy aroma. It was horrid, repellent, and raunchy, an unnatural typhoon of nasal flavoring so repugnant that it was fast becoming not just a threat to those in the immediate area, but to all life on Nebulous. Dogs dry heaved; trees dropped their branches; grass turned brown. Inanimate objects felt the strain too—women's hats caught fire, leather shoes cracked and curled;

even the Mulch Machine's walls began to swell, expanding and contracting like a heavy-set man trying to catch his breath.

"What's going on now?" shouted Holly.

Braker glanced around him. "I think it's like when a high-pitched sound causes glass to break, except this time, it's being caused by the vibrations of the stink wave."

"That's ridiculous," scoffed J.J. "A stink can't break glass."

Just then the Mulch Machine's walls burst from the Reeki Ray's pungent strain. The walls shattered, spilling Braker's group onto the ground; at the same time, the ray's reflected funk overpowered the Reeki Craft's engines, sending it plummeting to the courtyard where it crashed onto a Goon guard shack.

A puff of black smoke and a whiff of spicy air told all witnesses that the threat was over—the Mysteriously Red Reeki Ray had destroyed itself.

Far above in the *Flying Electric Laboratory*, the assistant scientists remained pressed to the windows, sadly wailing, "No, Red Reeki! No, Red Reeki!"

From the remains of the smoldering Reeki Craft, Dr. Wilde slowly emerged, stalking forward, his unruly white hair encircling his head like a cloud of noxious smoke; Bullmack trotted happily along behind him, gulping in huge amounts of fresh air.

Lord Preposterous leaned over the railing of his floating grandstand, shaking his fist at the doctor below. "How dare you attack my royal property with the Mysteriously Red Reeki Ray! Not only have you betrayed your rightful lord but now you have compounded the felony by vandalizing my sacred courtyard. Behold, you have pierced the bloated heart of malice and the blood that flows shall be your own!"

"Do you really think you can intimidate me?" Dr. Wilde replied. "Can't you see I came here to kill you?"

Lord Preposterous folded his arms. "I can see every time I am the object of homicide. I can also see that your callous murder of my adored princess sisters failed to satisfy your bloody appetite."

"Murder the princess sisters? Get your facts straight, Preposterous. Prince Tony has those sisters; do you think I'd be here otherwise?"

"My facts are always straight, doctor. Prince Tony informed me that you murdered the sisters, and for that he killed you."

"I'm not even going to respond to that one."

"Master, are you really dead?" asked Bullmack.

"The sisters are alive!" Braker and Wayne whispered, hiding within earshot.

Preposterous stomped his feet. "Prince Tony lied to me!"

"Everyone on the planet lies to you, you dip," said Dr. Wilde. "That's what you do with dictators. The question you should be asking yourself right now is where is Prince Tony?"

"In his impregnable fortress on Mount Rad, of course," responded Preposterous.

"Then that's exactly where I'm going," said Dr. Wilde, with a defiant snap of his head. "I'll get the sisters and force you to stoop before me if you ever hope to be married." The doctor pressed a vacuum button on his belt that instantly whisked him and Bullmack back up to the *Flying Laboratory*.

Even as Dr. Wilde was leaving the scene, Braker and his friends were planning their escape. Still huddled around the smoldering remains of the blasted Mulch Machine, they were momentarily concealed from the Goons in the courtyard.

"Braker, gettin' out of here is gonna be about as likely as a red-haired polecat sneakin' into a speckled henkle-stall," said Wayne.

"Wayne, I have no idea what you just said," Braker replied, "but I do have a plan. It may be a little difficult, but I think it will work. Now listen, everybody, I just noticed the garden has a drainage ditch on the far side of the hedgerow. If we follow it, we can get all the way to the front gate of the palace…"

"Good thinking, Braker," said J.J., "once we get into that palace there will be plenty of room for sneaking and hiding. I guess your judgment isn't all bad."

"Right," said Braker. "Now, getting inside is going to be a problem, but I figure if one of us can just climb the wall up to the tenth-floor balcony, they can sneak back down and open the gate…"

"Braker," Johnny Comet interrupted. "Hey, Braker."

"Hang on, Johnny," said Braker, patting the orphan on the head, "we've got important stuff to figure out and not much time."

"But, Braker, there are Nebulan battle rockets parked all around us with nobody guarding them."

Braker knelt down and took hold of the boy's shoulders. "Johnny," he said tenderly, "don't worry about anything. I'm going to take care of you. I know it's scary, but just give me a minute. I'm going to make everything all right." Then, giving Johnny a reassuring squeeze, he stood up again. "Okay, where was I? Oh yeah, once we're inside we'll have to find an air vent. Then we'll follow it all the way around the palace to get a good notion of the layout. After that we'll have to find a room with paper and pens so we can make a map. Then…"

"Hey, Braker, I've got an idea," said Johnny Comet.

Chuck Weasel whirled to glare at the boy. "Scram, kid, these are adult plans. Way beyond your level. Now keep quiet and knock off the little pest routine." Then, noticing he'd attracted everyone's attention, the mechanic bent over and playfully pinched Johnny on the cheek. "Little boy is so helpful—but don't make grown-ups grouchy-grouchy."

"No more time for plans!" Knothead shouted. "Goons are coming!"

The barbarian pointed toward a pack of Goons bounding forward on the garden footpath.

"Run for the drainage ditch!" Braker cried, directing his gang along the green hedgerow.

Soon the runaways were leading an entire company of Goons down the pathway in a wild race to reach the drainage ditch. The procession charged straight through the killer fruit orchard and had almost made it across the mutagen weed pasture when a Nebulous battle rocket swooped in to block their escape. To their left was the belching pickle meadow; to the right, the clotting mudlands. With no place left to run, it looked like Braker's group was trapped. But instead of a Nebulous pilot at the rocket's controls they saw a grinning Johnny Comet waving them in. Shouting with relief, the escapees piled into the rocket and flew away before the Goons even had a chance to fire their weapons.

"Hooray for Johnny Comet!" exclaimed J.J., leading the rest of the passengers in a cheer. "He ignored Braker's ridiculous plan and saved us all!"

"Sure did," said Johnny. "When you guys all took off, I went in the other direction, toward the battle rockets. No one was guarding them, so it was an easy pinch."

"I was going to help too," said Downer Plasmoe, "but I fell down."

Johnny reached under the control panel as he worked the guidance wheel. "Oh yeah, I almost forgot, here's something else I grabbed on the way. A Goon supply officer was carrying it; but he wasn't paying attention." He tossed Knothead's cherished Molarkian hatchet toward the barbarian.

Everyone cheered Johnny again. Johnny glanced at Braker. "You mad?"

"Mad?" said Braker, happily rumpling the boy's hair. "Johnny Comet, how could I ever be mad? You hijacked an enemy ship, rescued everyone, *and* stole Knothead's hatchet back—you're amazing!"

"Nah," Johnny replied, blushing, "just working on it."

Chapter Sixteen
Assault on Mount Rad

Johnny Comet landed his stolen battle rocket in a small clearing just beyond the torturous path leading into the Blackback Mountains of Nebulous X. The long ridge before them was a nightmarish stack of spiked summits and steep, twisting bluffs. At its highest, most jagged peak stood the heavily guarded castle home of Prince Tony, improbably balanced atop Mount Rad, a pinpoint tip of rock. The mansion itself was an ancient, towering threat with tall spires and winding exterior staircases. But the massive estate was not merely a grim citadel—Prince Tony had taken care to infuse the fortifications with hip exterior design elements; its sprawling terraces were outfitted with hot tubs, outdoor grills, and stone ovens, as well as hanging plants, wicker furniture, wind chimes, and embroidered wall tapestries, all serving to make it the ultimate in sophisticated, party pad strongholds.

As Braker and the others filed out of their rocket, they were quickly aware that Dr. Wilde had beaten them to the scene. The *Flying Electric Laboratory* and its fleet of lab buses were already circling the castle, assaulting it with Heavy Bombs, tiny bean-sized projectiles that would increase any target's molecular structure until it collapsed under its own weight. Thousands of the beads were already raining down on Mount Rad, causing the castle's gyro-stabilized platform to tilt from the increasing density. Prince Tony's defenses were fighting back though, scorching the lab buses with neon laser beams and lightening rays.

"Well, Braker," said Wayne, "looks like Dr. Wilde's already milkin' that heifer. How we gettin' in there now?"

"I'm thinking," said Braker. "I suppose we could just fire up this rocket to full blast and smash our way in."

Holly Blackguard agreed. "Good thinking, as usual, sugar. With all the shielding on this warship we'll be inside with barely a scratch."

"That's a great idea!" said Johnny Comet, pulling on Knothead's gigantic arm. "Let's blow through this place! I'll fly."

"Hold on there, kiddies," said J.J. "Maybe none of you firecrackers have realized it yet but the castle guns are blasting anything in the sky. The odds are not in our favor here."

"J.J., you are one waterlogged loaf," said Knothead. "All you do is complain. I don't think you care about those sisters at all."

"Wrong again, barbarian," replied J.J. "Of course I care about the girls. Why else would I still be here?"

"Maybe because we haven't landed anywhere safe enough for you to make your own getaway yet," suggested Wayne.

"Well, there is that, but don't forget that I'm a used spaceship salesman; I don't often run into people as honest and kindhearted as those princess sisters and I want to give them a break. They need my help. Braker can't do it —I know—I've been watching him. It's time we employ some Whammo strategy."

"I agree with J.J.," said Chuck Weasel. "I love Braker's idea, but I think it's a total flop."

"There's conviction for you," said Holly.

"Well, there's got to be a better way of getting into the castle than smashing through the walls," said Chuck.

"So, what do you professors suggest we do?" said Holly. "It's not exactly like you'll be hiking in."

"Actually, that's not a bad notion," interjected J.J. "There's always more than one way into a fortress; if we just take time to scout the area, I'll bet there's some kind of a trail at the bottom of the mountain that leads to a secret entrance. We did it to get into your place."

"Sure, that's it," said Chuck. "And after we slither in, we can attempt a conference with Prince Tony. Maybe work out a compromise."

J.J. clapped his hands. "Beautiful idea! Now we're talking progress!"

Wayne spit at the ground. "Chuck, you cain't compromise with greed, it'll turn right around and snitch the britches right off ya. Besides, we ain't got that kind of time; them ol' boy's is slapping the fat off each other. We got to get in there before the whole place comes crashing down."

"Wayne's right," said Braker. "We've got to hurry. This is no time for sneaking. Look, the castle's leaning more every minute." He pointed toward the fortress—several walls were buckling, its previous tilt becoming more pronounced. "Let's get the ship ready." He started toward the rocket. "Johnny Comet, take the controls. Holly, man the boom jibs. Chuck, seal the rib knobs!"

"Not gonna do it," said Chuck, blocking the door. "I love your passion, Braker, I really do, but your plan's a dud. I'm going to negotiate with these people. And by the time you come crashing in we'll already be inside and have this little misunderstanding straightened out."

"I think Chuck's on to something," said J.J. "I'm going with him."

Braker pushed Chuck aside and stepped into the rocket. "See you guys in the fortress."

"We're splitting up?" said Downer Plasmoe. "Admit it, this is all my fault, isn't it?"

J.J. and Kate Starbrand followed Chuck down the hill while the other half of the group followed Braker into the ship.

Trudging down the ridge, Chuck looked back in time to see Johnny Comet sticking his tongue out at the defectors. "Lousy brat," Chuck whispered, even while smiling and waving.

Inside the rocket it was all business—Braker and Johnny took their place at the ship's controls; Wayne disconnected the engines' speed restrainers; the others sealed the hatches and strapped in. In a moment they had lift off. The stolen rocket streaked through the sky, dodging diamond beams and glimmer rays coming from the castle defenses.

"Down there!" said Braker, pointing to a crumbling wall. "That's a weak spot if I ever saw one; our best bet—but those walls are still thick. Let's just hope this works."

"On the bright side, if it don't, we'll never even know it," said Wayne.

Johnny Comet grabbed the throttle lever, ramming it into overwork mode. "Let's party!"

The engines emitted an ear-splitting roar, the rocket becoming a sudden gray blur. It sailed past flaming lab buses and twirling death rays, racing directly toward the wall.

"Faster!" shouted Braker.

Johnny pulled the shifter into impractical mode—the engines screamed.

"Faster!" shouted Braker.

Johnny looked at Braker.

"Faster!" Braker repeated.

Johnny used both hands on the lever this time, passing up madgoose mode and going directly to burn out status—the gauges went wild, spinning furiously.

The rocket had become an unstoppable missile now, boring itself into the sagging wall like a drill, and, once through, continued to drive further and further into the castle without showing any signs of slowing down.

"Johnny, hit the brakes!" shouted Braker.

"I'm trying," said Johnny. "But they're not responding. I think we broke 'em."

Rubble exploded out from under the rocket as it plowed on, leaving behind a newly carved tunnel to the outside world. More and more inner walls and barricades were bulldozed until the exhausted engines finally gave up, the rocket coming to a stop somewhere so deep within the castle that the light from the outside was no longer visible.

"Worked," said Johnny.

Smoke was still rising from the surrounding debris when a mob of hazy figures suddenly appeared, all of them rushing wildly in different directions. It was a diverse horde consisting of various human and alien races, the conglomeration displaying only one unifying feature—all were wearing the same gray, numbered uniforms; so many of these runners were crammed into the corridor that Braker's crew could barely squeeze out of their rocket's escape hatch.

"Hey, wait a second!" Braker shouted to one frenzied runner. "Who are you guys?" he exclaimed to another, neither bothering to stop.

Knothead was more direct; he reached out and snatched one runner by the throat, pulling him next to the ship. "Who are you?" he demanded.

The elderly, bald man let out a dry-throated moan. "Stop shaking me," he warbled. "I'm just an old man."

Knothead, seeing the extraordinarily fragile nature of his captive, quickly let go and backed away. "I'm not shaking you, you old clock. I'm not even touching you anymore."

"Well, it feels like it," the man continued to wail, his head rolling from side to side.

"I said, 'I'm not shaking you!'" Knothead exploded, flicking the man on the head.

"You may think you can push me around now, you wooly-faced rowdy," said the man," but I'll have you know I was fight champion for three years running at my old school."

"Yeah, what school was that, tough-gums?"

"How should I know?" the elderly man replied. "That was seventy-five years ago."

"Bah, this old dog is rabid," said Knothead, throwing up his hands.

Braker shoved his way past the barbarian. "I'm Braker Ford, space trucker…"

"Wet Lakeland, dungeon prisoner," came the reply.

"Dungeon prisoner!" gasped Braker. "Why would someone put a harmless old man like you in prison?"

"How should I know?" snapped Wet. "That was over sixty-five years ago."

"Sixty-five years—that's a lifetime!" said the trucker. "Haven't you ever tried to escape?"

"Sure I did, but that was over fifty-five years ago."

"Wait a minute," said Braker, "Prince Tony isn't even that old. How could you have been his prisoner for so long?"

"I wasn't always Prince Tony's prisoner. Space warlords trade their dungeon prisoners all the time; it's a power thing, or a hobby, or…how should I know? I'm just an old dungeon prisoner."

"That's terrible, all those years trapped in these dark, musty corridors."

"It hasn't been all bad," said Wet. "Why I remember back in the old days the dungeon was alive with merriment, people singing and dancing, the torches burning all night until we would finally fall asleep at dawn to the sound of our own laughter…aw, who am I trying to kid?"

"Just my luck," said Downer, "I finally get to visit a castle, and I end up in the prison."

"Great aim, Braker," said Johnny Comet.

Braker ignored Johnny. "Sir, we appreciate your troubles…"

"Call me Wet, son."

"Okay, Wet," said Braker. "We appreciate your troubles, but right now we need to find our way out of here. Do you know the way?"

Wet frowned. "If only you kids had shown up forty-five years ago, I believe I had a map of this place back then, but I think I sold it for a spoonful of soup."

"A spoonful of soup!" said Braker.

"That's right, back in the old days we had it rough—one spoonful of warm pickles and milk for breakfast and one spoonful of cold cream of bologna soup for dinner, and if you wanted any more, you had to find a way to pay for it. Not like today, where all these new young prisoners have it so easy. 'Can I have another spoonful?' they whine in their little baby voices, and of course they get it—and don't think they even have to trade the thinnest blanket for it, neither. We're raising a generation of wind-blown daisies, I say."

Prince Tony's guards were arriving now, firing retrieval beams at the frightened prisoners still dashing about.

"I'm very sorry about the soup," said Braker, "but maybe you know someone who could help us—quickly."

Wet rubbed his sagging neck. "Let's see, my friend Skippy's been out of his cell a lot lately, been working on a new escape tunnel with a few rascals he knows; I'll wager he could help you gather your bearings."

"Where is he now?"

"Well, let's see," said Wet, stretching to look over the crowds. "There he is." He pointed excitedly, seemingly oblivious to the retrieval beams.

Braker's crew was immediately on the move, pushing and shoving their way through the crowds of escaping prisoners, carefully avoiding startled guards and random explosions. At the far end of the corridor, they came up behind an armed prisoner crouched behind a pile of wreckage; he was enthusiastically exchanging shots with an unseen guard.

"Hey, Skippy!" said Wet. "I've brought some friends."

"Glad you found me, Wet," said the man, showing not the slightest interest in the group crowding around him, "I was afraid I'd have to make this break without you."

Braker hunched down next to the man as several incoming laser beams skimmed by. "Hi, I'm Braker Ford, space trucker. I started all this; your friend Wet says you can take us out of here."

The man squeezed off a well-aimed shot, bringing a howl from the unseen guard, and a chuckle from the man. "Ya see that?" he laughed, slapping Braker on the knee, "one more Goon freak becomes a statistic. By the way, I'm Skippy Dodge, military prisoner. And, yeah, I can get you out of here, small reward for you giving me this break. But first we got to make sure this doorway is clear of any more Goons."

"Wait a minute," said Braker. "Skippy Dodge? The Galaxy Saver?"

"Well, yeah," said Skippy, "but I've been a military prisoner longer than a galaxy saver, so, whatever."

"Wow—Skippy Dodge!" exclaimed Johnny Comet. "He's famous. We learned about him in school."

Wayne tapped Braker's shoulder. "Gosh, that sure is Skippy Dodge, all right. The one and only Skippy Dodge, right here in front of us!"

"I know," said Braker.

"He saved the galaxy!"

"I know."

"More than once!"

"I know that too."

"He's a hero."

"Know that too."

"I mean, the ultimate hero!"

"I said I know."

"Kinda just like you're trying to be."

"Got it."

"Cept'n he don't mess up."

"I know! I know! I think we all realize how wonderful Skippy Dodge is, thank you."

Wayne looked at Braker for a long moment. "Jealous?"

"No, I'm not jealous!" Braker shouted. "I'm doing just fine."

A sudden barrage of lasers exploded around the group; more Goons had joined in the fight.

Holly Blackguard looked with contempt at Skippy Dodge. Middle-aged, with gray hair, and a slightly bulging gut, he no longer looked like the dashing space cavalier of old.

"Braker," said Holly, "Skippy Dodge may have been a great hero once, but prison life obviously hasn't been kind; he's way past ripe. Are you going to trust our escape to this rusty old man?"

Skippy's hand shot out to grasp Holly by the face. "Who's the mouth?" he asked, staring menacingly into Holly's eyes.

"The name's Holly," replied the water queen, tossing a punch at Skippy's jaw. Skippy caught her fist with his other hand, twisting her wrist until she screamed.

"You better think twice before you try that again, lady. I'm not a geezer yet."

"Oh great, now we're fighting each other," said Downer Plasmoe as a unit of heavily armed Goons overran their position. "We're a terrible team."

No one dared move, not even Skippy Dodge with his laser rifle. The tiny group was out-manned, out-gunned, and out-Gooned; surrender was their only hope.

****

Far deeper inside the fortress, Chuck Weasel, Kate Starbrand, and J.J. Whammo found themselves marching hurriedly down a restricted corridor after having given themselves up to the secret entrance perimeter guards. They were just now approaching their destination after traveling a seemingly endless maze of passages.

In front of them, a pair of heavy doors were suddenly thrown open, revealing Prince Tony's velvet-lined war office. The prince stood inside, facing a dozen video monitors while directing his defenses through a microphone; in between instructions, he raced back and forth to his wardrobe closet, compulsively changing outfits. Right now, he was squeezed into a scarlet, knee-length topcoat, skin-tight white pants that flared out at the bottom, and a handsome pair of lace-up, pointy-toed boots. A tall metal helmet crowned his head. Princess Babe sat next to him with tears in her eyes.

"Darling," he said, taking Babe's hand, "do not be alarmed, your faithful Prince shall see you through this cowardly attack by righteously destroying each and every one of these cheeky offenders."

"Goons of Doom requesting an audience," spoke one of the soldiers behind him.

Prince Tony whirled. "What is it?" he demanded, rising to inspect the prisoners.

"We have apprehended three interlopers who insist on meeting with you."

Prince Tony chuckled as he looked over the threesome. "So, you 'insist' on an audience with me, eh; at a time like this? Well, this must be quite important; please, speak freely. But mind you, it better be good."

Chuck Weasel smiled. "Trust me, Prince, it is. See, it goes like this—I happen to know that you've got some goods everybody wants. And by the looks of it, things just aren't going your way at this point."

Prince Tony interrupted. "I'm sorry, but what exactly are these 'goods' you are referring to?"

"You know, the Princess. Princess Babe." Chuck clicked his tongue.

Tony laughed. "Oh, yes, I see now; please continue."

"Well, we thought we just might be able to work a deal. If you tell me what she's worth maybe we can come up with something of equal…"

"Say no more," said Tony, holding up his hand. "There is nothing in this galaxy worth so much as my precious Babe, at least nothing you could ever get your hands on. So, this being said, and all transactions forthwith canceled, I will turn you over to the torturers and have your pitiful lives snuffed out with suitable torment."

J.J. Whammo was about to speak in protest when Chuck stepped forward. "I was afraid it would come to this," he sighed, "but you leave me no choice, Prince."

"Yes, yes, whatever, whatever," mumbled Tony, half listening as he turned back to his wardrobe closet. "Goons, please take them far away."

No one moved.

"Goons, remove them!"

Again, there was no response.

Chuck sniffed. "Get 'im, boys."

To everyone's surprise, a pair of Goons drew their weapons at Chuck's command and dropped Tony to the ground with a series of paralysis rays.

Chuck grabbed Babe by the hand, leading her out the door. As he passed the frozen form of Prince Tony he stopped to gloat. Stooping low, he leaned over the prince's contorted face. "I know, I know, you're asking yourself how did he do it? Well, don't you concern yourself with that, Prince Chump, because the deal is done; if I were you, I would be much more concerned with what your attackers are going to do when they find you like this."

"Chuck, come on, let's go," Kate called out as the sounds of battle worked their way closer.

With that, Chuck, Kate, J.J., Babe, and the four Goons slipped quickly away.

Behind them, Dr. Wilde's bombing was having its desired effect—flames whipped through the hallway as a haggard squad of Goons rushed Braker and his gang through the searing vapors and flying debris that led to the war office. With wild-eyed urgency they burst upon Tony's motionless frame.

"Prince Tony, this is no time to be lying down," said the Goon commander.

Skippy Dodge groaned. "He's not resting, you idiot, the man's been zapped with a paralysis ray. Sheesh."

Electric rejuvenation prods were quickly applied to get Tony's nervous system functioning again.

"Oh, my spine," whimpered the prince, rising on wobbly legs. "Where am I?"

The Goon commander shrugged. "In the worst jam of your life I would guess."

"Oh, yes, now I remember. Report, quickly."

"We have captured the crew of the rocket that crashed into the detention center. The pilot calls himself Braker Ford." He motioned toward the trucker.

"Braker Ford!" said Tony. "So, we meet again. Once more though you have fallen short of your goal, for Babe is mine…and gone…and…wait a minute—Babe! Commander, quickly post an alert for Princess Babe, she's been kidnapped!"

"But, Prince Tony, there's not time; Dr. Wilde has almost beaten our defenses. The castle is about to collapse."

"So what; I want Babe. Seal the hanger bay."

"Sir, we must evacuate."

"Absolutely not. Must I kill you to get you to understand—those kidnappers are undoubtedly heading for the hanger bay as we speak; it's their only way out. Now execute these prisoners and retrieve Babe."

"You heard him," said the Goon commander, directing his troops to turn their weapons toward the captives.

Before a shot could be fired, Skippy Dodge yanked the gun from the commander's hand and blasted him with it. Wet Lakeland tried Skippy's trick on the next guard but only managed to jam his finger into the barrel. "Help me!" he screamed, tugging frantically on the gun. Skippy whacked the Goon on the head with his rifle butt before easily mowing down the four remaining guards.

"Shoo-iee!" said Wayne, nudging Braker. "Now that there was a move you couldn't a done on yer best day."

"Big deal," said Braker. "At least we're safe."

"Yeah, and we've got Prince Tony as *our* prisoner now," said Johnny Comet.

"Say, that's right," said Braker. "But, hey, where is he?"

Prince Tony was no longer on the floor, or even in the war office at all—somehow, the ever-wily Prince Tony had managed to slip out during the fight.

"I can't believe it," said Braker. "He's escaped again."

"That Prince Tony is more slippery than greased eyelids," said Wayne.

"I'll bet that means he's gonna get to the princess before us," said Downer, hanging his head.

"Looks like ol' Skippy Dodge isn't so perfect after all," said Holly Blackguard, grinning.

"How's this my fault?" asked Skippy.

Holly snorted. "Well, you shot down all the guards but let their leader escape. I don't call that a flawless performance."

"I didn't see any of you helping," Skippy replied. "I can't do everything."

Holly leaned close to Braker. "Listen to him whine. Stay tough, treasure, he ain't so great."

"I don't care about any of that!" cried Braker, heading into the hall. "And I'm not your treasure. I'm in love with Babe, not you, Holly!"

"Take it easy, boyfriend," Holly replied. "If you're not comfortable with our relationship, you've got no one to blame but yourself. You're the one who came busting into my secret compound, outsmarting my death traps, and killing my best security guard. How was I supposed to resist such a cool operator?"

"I'm not a cool operator!" Braker exclaimed. "I'm not a master criminal, or a great pilot, or a space guardian. I'm just…me, I guess."

"Well, sure, you're not looking so hot right now," said Holly. "But that's just all the tension—it's getting to you. It's all right, though, it happens to the best of them."

"Just stick with it, kid," said Skippy. "I can see you pulling off the madcap mercenary type."

"Thanks, Mr. Dodge," said Braker. "But I'm not interested in that. And I don't want to be a hero—I mean, I did, but not anymore. I don't care about me, or my reputation, or impressing you, or Holly, or anybody. Not even Babe. I just want her back. I just want to be with her."

Skippy nodded. "Say, you're alright."

"No, he's not," said Holly. "That girl's got him all tied in knots. Braker, the sooner you realize she's gone, the sooner you'll snap out of it."

"But Babe's not gone—not yet," Braker replied. "Prince Tony's groggy from that paralysis ray, so there's still a chance we can get to Babe before him."

"Well, if we're going to find this girl," said Skippy, "we better split up 'cause there's a lot of ground to cover in this place. We'll all regroup at the hanger bay on the north tower."

"Is Skippy giving the orders now?" asked Downer.

"Sure sounds like he is," said Wayne. "That's a hotshot major league hero for ya; just takin' charge."

"Who cares!" shouted Braker. "It's a good idea. Now, split up, we'll meet at the hanger! Hurry!"

The desperate rescuers ran off as the fortress walls began crumbling behind them and the deadly explosions grew louder.

Chapter Seventeen
Blood, Bargains, and Betrayal

J.J. Whammo was wheezing and puffing his way down a long castle corridor high in the north tower; Chuck Weasel, Kate Starbrand, and a pair of Goons—one carrying Princess Babe—ran beside him. "Chuck, how did you pull this off?" the salesman panted. "I mean how did you get these guards on our side?"

"Easy," said the mechanic with a self-impressed grin, "when we first got captured, I passed the guards some fake cosmo crystals in exchange for this little favor."

"A bribe. Great thinking. So that's what you were whispering to them about on our way to see Prince Tony."

"Now you got it," said Chuck as they entered the castle's hanger bay. The cavernous docking port was large enough that it not only easily served as the castle's sole launching pad, but also as an exhibition hall for Prince Tony's vast private collection of military and luxury starcraft. Hundreds of priceless vehicles, from armored ozone cruisers to rare space convertibles lined the platform. The grand harbor was one of Tony's favorite hangouts;

in the summertime he would clear out all the starships, open the bay doors and host all night dance parties there.

Chuck approached an aerial troop carrier parked on a display podium. "How's this one?" he called out to the Goons.

The guards inspected the craft, nodding satisfactorily.

"Great, thanks for all the help," said the mechanic, just before shooting the pair down with his amino-pistol. "Top-notch service. I appreciate it." He snickered as the Goon bodies collapsed on the floor.

"Chuck, you just murdered those Goons in cold blood!" shouted J.J.

"Sure I did, slack jaw, but let's get on to more important business: where do we go to cash in on the princess?"

"Cash in? I'm not sure I follow."

"Look, I'm sick of all this nonsense. We're both businessmen here, you can't fool me, I know the drift of things as well as you. Save the cover stories for the other folks and just tell me what this woman is really worth?"

"Great Moons, man, I don't know what you're talking about."

"I'm talking about why half the universe is ready to kill each other over this woman. There must be some reason why and no one will give me a straight answer!"

"Chuck, Braker's in love with her, that's all I can tell you, now come on, we've got to get out of here."

Chuck drew up his gun, grabbing J.J. by the collar. "You fool, I'm gonna get what I want in the end, do you really want me to kill you? Just tell me, is it money, jewels, political favors; what do I get for her?"

The air was hot with tension, ready to explode. The barrel of Chuck's gun was pressed under J.J.'s chin.

"You blithering idiot," said J.J. "You really think this is about money? Believe me, if there was a way to turn a profit out of this I would. But these kids just love each other. That's all."

"Just kill him, Chuck," sighed Kate.

"I can't," grumbled Chuck, knocking J.J. out and tossing him inside the ship, "I need whatever information he's hiding."

Then, just as Kate was pulling Babe into the cargo hold, Holly Blackguard and Downer Plasmoe came dashing into the hanger bay.

"Chuck!" Downer exclaimed. "Boy, are we glad to see you! For once things are going right."

"Let me handle this," snapped Holly, marching up to Chuck.

"Don't try to stop me," Chuck warned, aiming his still-smoking gun at the water queen.

"No problem," said Holly, quickly catching on to the situation. "I just want to know where you're taking the princess."

"Some place I can get a straight answer out of people. This lady's worth something and I'm gonna get it."

"Yeah? Well, just make sure you get it far away, you understand?"

"Oh, don't worry, I'm getting as far as possible from this crazy crowd."

"Good, that's all I wanted to hear. Now scram."

"Holly, what are you doing?" Downer cried.

Holly spun, pointing a finger at the astounded cook. "Shut up, Downer. This is my chance to get rid of this little goody princess once and for all. Nothing's going to stand between Braker and me anymore."

"Well, don't get mad at me," said the cook stumbling across the two lifeless Goon bodies, "I just think…oh, yuck, Holly, look. Chuck must've shot these guys in the back. He's a murderer."

"I had nothing to do with that," said Holly. "That was their business, and this is mine, now stay out of it!"

Downer shook his head. "Well, I'm still gonna tell Braker."

"Don't do something stupid, Downer," said Holly.

"Oh, forget it," Chuck groaned, sending an amino blast toward Downer.

"You're all double-crossers!" Downer yelped as he ran back down the hallway. "And, Chuck, you weren't very nice to work with either."

"Great, he's running back to Braker," said Holly.

"Don't sweat it," said Chuck, "this castle is almost finished. In a minute everyone will be crushed to powder anyway."

As he was speaking, Johnny Comet came sprinting into the far end of the bay.

"Braker, they're in here!" the orphan shouted behind him.

"The brat," snarled Chuck.

"Never mind him," said Holly. "Get lost. I'll take care of this."

Without another word, Chuck ran up the gangplank, into the armored starship, and lifted off. Kate Starbrand blew out the bay doors with the ship's cannon, and with that the deceitful couple flew away with their prize.

"Oh, Braker," Holly cried, running to the trucker. "Chuck's turned traitor. He's taken Babe."

"What? Oh, no," gasped Braker. "How could I be so stupid as to trust a guy with a name like 'Weasel'?"

Holly wept fake tears. "Yes, he tried to kill me, and that coward Downer ran off. I did all I could."

185

The fortress was trembling more powerfully than ever now, the walls about to fail.

Wayne staggered across the convulsing floor, putting an arm around his stunned friend. "Braker, I know you feel lower than a belly-flopped mule right about now, but I just want to remind you the roof's about to cave in and kill all of us."

"Oh, yeah. Thanks, Wayne," blinked Braker. "Is everyone here?"

Huge chunks of ceiling began dropping around them. "Yep, they're with me," said Wayne, "but it don't matter much since we're about to be turned into a stack of griddle cakes."

"Okay, stay calm. What we need is a ship." Braker turned around to discover Johnny Comet had already pulled up in one of Prince Tony's personal cruising sedans. "I should have known," he sighed.

The group was piling in when the hanger bay's outer wall finally came down; Dr. Wilde's lab buses soared inside, blasting everything. In the sudden destruction, Skippy, Wet—and to her unfathomable frustration—Holly Blackguard, all found themselves cut off from Braker's ship; Johnny Comet was forced to fly out into the open or be trapped forever. Skippy, left behind, had only one chance left.

"Follow me or die!" he called to Wet and Holly.

"Oh, decisions," Holly moaned as she raced along the quaking bay.

Skippy had spied a small galactic sportster moored near the back of the bay; he was gambling it would start. He squeezed behind the seat, did some quick hot-wiring, and with his two companions in tow, somehow managed to get out of the bay and into the clear before the total collapse of Prince Tony's fortress.

Never slowing down, they sailed right past Dr. Wilde's *Flying Electric Laboratory* and into deep space.

Wet was ecstatic. "Hurrah, Skippy did it!" he laughed, hugging Holly. "Isn't he great? We made it thanks to good ol' Skippy."

Holly looked sick. "Yeah, good ol' Skippy. Now gimme that voice box so we can talk to Braker."

Skippy shook his head. "Sorry, hot stuff, but this particular ship was in the repair docket, and apparently part of the problem was the voice box." He motioned toward the smashed microphone. "We're on our own."

"Where are we going?" asked Holly.

"Wherever I want—I'm in charge now," came the answer Holly didn't want to hear. "Now quiet down before I turn you over my knee."

Holly slumped back in her seat. It was going to be a long ride.

187

Chapter Eighteen
Heroes on the Run

Braker Ford's pursuit of Chuck Weasel had brought him through two galaxies, and a detour around another under construction, before his stolen starship's power cell finally burnt out, leaving him and his friends' unhappy visitors on a dark, nameless moon.

"This place looks like a dump," complained Johnny Comet, gazing at the endless array of gray rocks that created the dull lunar landscape.

"Don't be a snivel-baby," said Knothead, throwing a space suit to the youngster. "Now get dressed, we're going exploring."

"Oh, boy," giggled Johnny, scrambling into the suit, "maybe I'll find a hideous moon monster to be my pet."

"Never seen a moon monster," said Wayne. "Grampy used to try and scare us kids with stories of 'em when we was bad. But once't I grew'd up and got smarter I stopped believin' in 'em."

"They're real," Knothead warned. "But it's rare to spot one. They don't like to be seen—thankfully."

"Well, we're going to find one today," insisted Johnny.

"I'll help you tame him," said Wayne, "I'm real good with animals—especially imag'nary ones."

Braker clamped down his helmet. "I doubt we'll find any monsters on this rock, but we better find someone with another power cell or we're in big trouble."

"Power cells? Out there?" said Johnny, pointing toward the drab wasteland. "Get real. All we're gonna get is sore feet from wandering around."

"Well, sometimes moons like these have large underground settlements," said Braker. "With any luck maybe we'll find one."

"Okay, you find the hidden city and I'll find the moon monster," said Johnny.

Before long, the group was outside and marching across the soundless moon turf. Hours later, with miles of hiking behind them and still no sign of civilization, they came to a halt on the edge of an enormous canyon.

"Well, fellas," said Braker with an apologetic smile, "I'm beginning to think this moon really is uninhabited."

"Told ya," said Johnny Comet.

"Aww, it ain't that bad," said Knothead. "We'll just backtrack to the ship, set off our distress beacon and wait for somebody to come by."

"Shore," added Wayne. "An' in the meantime we can just huddle up, eat snacks from our nutrition pockets, and tell ghost stories. It'll be just like campin'."

"Neat," said Johnny. "I've never been camping."

"I don't think it'll be that easy," mumbled Braker.

"Sure it will," said Wayne. "What's chaffin' you now?"

189

Braker pointed to the oxygen gauge on his suit. "Check your air supply. I'm less than half—and it was full when we started. If you guys are the same, we'll never make it back."

Knothead and Wayne quickly inspected their own gauges.

"Whoops," said Wayne.

"Say, this ain't right," growled Knothead. "Braker, why weren't you watching our air supply?"

"Me?" said Braker. "Why should I have to?"

"You're the leader," said Knothead.

"So? You've got your own gauge. Why couldn't you check your own air supply?"

"Because you're the leader."

"But I'm not the only one with a gauge," Braker protested.

Knothead folded his arms. "Leader's job."

"All right, sure, it's my fault," said Braker, shaking his head. "So now what do we do?"

"Never argue with a grumpy barbarian," Knothead told Johnny, who was leaning against him.

"We've still got our nutrition pockets," said Wayne. "Let's have something to eat and then we can think about it."

"How we going to eat?" asked Knothead. "Through our helmets?"

"I knew it, we're gonna choke on space dust and die," said Johnny, falling to the ground and pretending to gag.

Knothead looked scoldingly at the boy. "Hey, Mr. Million-laughs, it ain't so funny. That probably is exactly how we're going to die here."

Johnny sat up straight. "Stink. I thought we were having fun."

Braker sat down on a large boulder and gazed into space. "We're not finished yet. Just let me think."

"Well, make it fast," said Knothead. "I'm not real good with tight, airless spaces. And I'm getting short of breath."

"We're not even close to being out of air yet," Braker responded. "Just calm down. Take a minute and look up at the stars. It'll relax you, really."

Knothead frowned, following the trajectory of a shooting star. "It ain't working," he rumbled. "It's getting stuffy in here."

"Well, it's helping me," said Braker. "It's so peaceful I almost feel like I can hear music."

"Oh, brother," said Knothead. "That's probably just the lack of oxygen."

"No, I hear it too," said Johnny Comet. "Sounds funky."

Wayne began snapping his fingers. "That's a right jumpy little tune, alright."

Braker leapt up, running in ever-widening circles until coming to a cleft in the canyon wall. "It's coming from over here!" he shouted.

Just then an angry voice came blaring from deeper in the opening. "And don't come back until you learn how to handle your motor oil!" the voice said.

Braker whirled to see an old, dented robot come stumbling past him.

"I know when I've had too much lubrication," the robot sputtered, wandering off.

Braker was still watching the tottering outcast when the voice came blaring from the crevice again. "Make up your mind, buddy, you going in or you just gonna stand there looking ugly?"

Braker peered into the chasm to see a propeller-headed robot, hands on hips, gazing impatiently at him. Behind him, partially obscured by rock formations, a line of robots, motormen, and artificial persons stood waiting for a place in a tall elevator booth half-buried in the crag.

"Uh…Sure. We're coming," Braker replied, enthusiastically waving his friends over.

"People!" Braker shouted, as the others came closer. "We've found people."

"Not exactly," said Wayne, getting his first look at the line of machines.

"Well, whatever they are maybe they can help us. Let's go in."

"Braker," said Knothead, "don't you realize what kind of place this is? It's a robot bar. You don't want to go in there. They don't like guys like us."

"So what? Just a minute ago you were dying for air. Who cares what kind of place it is?"

"Braker, these kinds of joints are the only places where robots can get away from people and just be themselves. Why do you think it's so hidden? We aren't welcome. Come on, you were right, there is life here; we'll find another settlement nearby."

"Knothead, we don't have that kind of time. Look, I'm staying positive; we'll just go in, take care of our business and be on our way."

The barbarian shook his head. "Alright, but be careful, like I said, robot bars aren't meant for humans; you've got to be pretty rough to even think about going in there."

Brake paused for a moment. "Hey, maybe that could actually work in our favor."

"How's that?"

"Nobody here knows us, Knothead. If we *act* rough, they'll think we *are* rough. And if we throw our weight around, we might be able to get a power cell real quick. Don't go soft on me now; it's time to get mean." He snorted and pushed his way into the line.

"These are the moments I live for," Wayne told Johnny Comet.

The group squeezed into the crowded elevator tube and disappeared underground. Down below, they found themselves in a confusing labyrinth of inter-connecting tunnels filled with wild, cavorting automatons, and a very small percentage of living creatures. A thick, oily haze coated everything while the black walls and red lights cast an eerie glow beneath the low-hung ceiling. A long, make-shift counter ran the length of the main room; it was from there that the mechanical bartender served the motor oil most of his patrons craved.

At the far end of the counter, a tall, shiny robot tipped over, obviously suffering temporary shutdown from flooded oil reserves. Before Braker and his crew knew what was happening, the crowd around the robot threw themselves upon him. In a matter of moments, they had stripped the unfortunate machine of all its gears, chips, and monitor systems, leaving nothing but a collapsed, metallic shell that was quickly brushed into a corner by the crowd as they went back to their revelry.

"Lead on, captain!" said Johnny Comet, giving Braker an irreverent salute.

Braker hiked up his pants, and, followed closely by his friends, marched straight into the masses. Pushing through the casehardened throng, he sidled up to the bar, looking confidently at the bartender.

"Say there, hard top," he began, "I got a little question for ya."

The robot's single scanner eye bounced back and forth in his head. "What is your question?" the toneless voice replied.

Braker sniffed and raised an eyebrow. "I'm looking for a large port power-cell on the cheap, if you know what I mean. Any leads?"

"I do not contain any such information at this time."

"Come on," said Knothead, "this guy's not gonna tell us nothing."

"Hang on," said Braker, "I'm working on him." The trucker turned back to the bartender. "Look, I just want a few leads, that's all. Help us out here, okay, buddy? We're in a hurry."

"I am not programmed to make guesses."

"Oh, you're a stubborn one aren't you."

"I am merely functional as an oil dispenser. I have no capacity to retain further information."

"Oh, yeah?" said Braker, leaning into the bar. "Well, what would you say if I just climbed over this counter right now and tore your little tin body all to pieces?"

"I would say that my heat-seeking laser security beams would vaporize your worthless flesh in less time than it would take your soft, organic heart to pump blood to your smallest finger."

"Okay," said Braker, gingerly backing away from the counter.

"Ready now?" asked Knothead.

"I think so," said Braker.

As they were making their way back through the dancing appliances, Braker spotted a group of humans in the corner. He nudged Knothead. "Fellow humans. What do you say?"

"Don't even think about it," said Knothead.

"Why not?"

"Braker, those guys are moon-scapers—professional men. They don't take to outsiders."

"Wayne, what do you think?" Braker asked.

"Knothead may be right," said Wayne. "They look to be a tad bit unneighborly."

"Well, I don't care what they are as long as they're human. I'm sure they'll help a fellow human being."

Johnny Comet tugged on Knothead's sleeve as they followed Braker across the room. "Knothead, what's a moon-scaper?"

"Those are the folks that travel around and fill up all the craters on a moon before new settlements come in. It's dangerous, rugged work not fit for any decent creature. Only the dregs of the universe apply for the job; I did it myself for a while."

A short, squat, and unbelievably filthy, moon-scaper was leaning against the wall, talking with his buddies when Braker approached him.

"Hey, look what's here, another flesh body," the man laughed, slapping Braker behind the head.

Braker stumbled forward, where he was instantly pulled face first onto the table by a half dozen of the gathered scapers.

The first man came over, leaning into Braker's face. "You must be lost, space boy, you look so sad."

"I'd be more comfortable standing up," Braker grunted as he struggled against the scapers' grip.

"We must be very, very important men," the scaper continued to mock, angrily facing the rest of Braker's friends. "What you want with us, huh? Why you flesh bodies coming 'round here? You look like space wanderers to me. Space wanderers always thieving; you trying to take something from us? We kill thievers right now."

"No, no, we not thievers!" said Knothead, sounding equally angry. "We want nothing, okay? We just want work. Yeah, you got work for us?"

"Work? We're not gonna work for these cree-" Johnny Comet began before Knothead shoved him to the floor.

The filthy lead scaper laughed even harder. "You want to work, huh?" He turned to his friends. "Flesh bodies want scaper work." The scapers all began to laugh hysterically. Knothead was tense, slowly inching his hand toward the trusty Molarkian hatchet slung low across his hip. He tried to stifle his surprise when he discovered it was missing—Johnny Comet had already drawn it and was carefully concealing it behind his own back, ready for action.

Suddenly the lead scaper stopped laughing. "I'm Rued."

"You sure are," said Braker, still spread across the table.

"No, dummy, that my name."

"Your name is 'Rude'?" asked Braker.

"That's what I said, stupid. What, you not understand?"

"No, I get it, it's just, uh, a surprisingly appropriate name."

Rued threw back his shoulders proudly. "I'll take you to big boss, scaper foreman. We'll see who works"—he grabbed Braker by the collar, shoving him into motion ahead of him— "or who dies!"

As they trudged out of the bar, Wayne whispered into Braker's ear. "Braker, I'm just wonderin' something."

"What now, Wayne?"

"Well, I'm just wonderin', are they treatin' us like fellow human beings yet?"

"Be quiet, Wayne."

Chapter Nineteen
Bad Company

Skippy Dodge piloted his escape ship down to the huge orbiting space station. He'd flown through several star systems since the escape from Mount Rad, passing up several well-traveled space routes and civilized planets in hopes of avoiding any chance of a confrontation with roving Nebulous X warships.

"Where are we now, Skippy?" asked Wet Lakeland, just waking up from his position in the co-pilot seat.

"At the farthest outpost in the universe, Wet. This old space station isn't even listed on the constellation traveler's guide these days, but it's got a docking station and a cheap motel inside. We can get some rest and then figure out where to go from here."

"Great idea, Skippy," nodded Wet, "although this has been a rather pleasant escape, I say. Not like the old days where an escape would take a month's worth of nervous, night-time planning by flickering candlelight, hundreds of hours of back-breaking digging, endless days of hunger as we rationed our food and supplies, and countless close-calls with suspicious guards all before that final moment of blithering joy when we would all just give up and go back to bed."

"Wet, I don't remember any escapes like that."

"Well, you were busy," snapped Wet, "but what I'm talking about is how smooth this escape has been, and by gosh, it's been a dandy. What I wouldn't give to be your age again, just to take part in a scheme like this."

"Wet, you are taking part in this."

"Don't tell me my business!" said Wet.

"You always win," said Skippy, shaking his head. "Oh, yeah, that reminds me, you better go unlock Holly now."

"You betcha," said Wet, hustling over to the storage closet where Holly Blackguard was bound and gagged. Once freed, she tossed the old man out of the way, heading straight for Skippy who was guiding the ship into the landing bay.

"How dare you tie me up!" she exploded. "I'm Holly Blackguard, Queen of the Water Works! I won't stand for that!"

"Well, maybe if you'd just shut your yapping mouth once every couple hundred light years you wouldn't have to."

"I've killed men for less."

"Hurray for your side," said Skippy. "Why do you think I tied you up? Now get out, we've landed."

The three fugitives stepped into the landing bay, passing row after row of empty hanger stalls before entering a barren, sterile lobby. At the information center, an automated clerk recited a description of the station's many facilities.

Upon hearing where to find the motel, Skippy started toward the elevator. "Well, this is where we part ways," he said, casting a glance toward the confused water queen.

"What do you mean?" asked Holly.

Skippy sighed. "Look, lady, I've been a military prisoner for fifteen years, just made a narrow escape from one of the craziest battles I've ever seen, and then had to travel the length of the universe with you. Don't you think I'd be just a little bit tired after all that? Now I'm checking into this motel—and you're free to do whatever you want. Goodbye."

Holly grit her teeth. "I don't have a spaceship. I don't even know where I am. How am I supposed to do anything?"

"Well, you're the super colossal space queen for gosh sakes, you must be able to figure out something. Make a few calls; I don't know."

"All right. I'll find my own way out of here," said Holly. "And I'll leave you far behind."

"Okay, goodbye."

"Goodbye."

Later, after a quick meal of reconstituted food pellets in the space station's 'Satellite Lounge', Skippy and Wet went to check into the motel. At the counter they found Holly Blackguard waiting for them.

"Hi, there, Miss Holly," said Wet.

"Hi, scrunge," replied Holly. "Guess what? We're the only ones on this lousy space station. You've probably noticed everything else is automated around here."

"Really?" said Skippy, passing his I.D. to the robot desk clerk.

"Yes, 'really', and you've got the only ship on this place."

"That's too bad. Two rooms, please."

"Make it one room!" Holly shouted to the clerk.

"Hold on a second," exclaimed Skippy.

"Don't you get it?" said Holly. "No one comes out this far. You've brought us so far past the star formations I can't even get a taxi service to come out here. No sir, buddy, I'm with you till we get out of here, and until then it's one room—I'm not letting you and your flunky slip past me and leave me stranded."

"I'm surprised you haven't thought of pulling that trick on us yet."

"Already did, and I doubt you're really all that surprised seeing as how I just discovered you've conveniently removed the engine's compression bolt, making it impossible to start. But that's okay because I've removed the ring magnet, which is just as important, and you won't see that piece again until we're both ready to lift off tomorrow. You're not so smart."

Skippy hung his head. "All right, I guess you got me; one room."

A few minutes later Holly was locked away in the bathroom while Skippy and Wet stared out the window."

"You think she's still mad at us?" Wet asked.

"Probably, but she's quit kicking and screaming so maybe she's got over it by now."

"We gonna leave her in there all night?"

"Heck yeah—I don't know about you but I'm not interested in waking up with my throat slit. She can simmer in there for tonight; we'll drop her off first chance we get tomorrow."

Wet nodded in agreement. "Good plan, Skip, but say, what are you gonna do now that we're free again?"

"Wet," Skippy said, sounding truly tired for the first time, "I'm gonna find my wife."

"Donna?" Wet exclaimed.

Skippy smiled a melancholy smile. "That's right, Wet, Donna Dodge, that big, bold, beautiful gal—my Donna. I left her behind when I decided to save the galaxy—"

"More than once," added Wet.

"More than once," Skippy agreed. "But now I'm back. And my galaxy-saving days are behind me. I mean it this time; the whole celebrity space champion gig, well, it ain't really all that great."

Wet put a trembling hand on his friend's shoulder. "Sure, sure, Skip, we've been through all that, but Donna, well...it's been fifteen years."

"Don't matter, Wet, I'm gonna find her; we belong together. The only thing I'm worried about is if she's sore that I left her behind."

"More than once," said Wet.

"Yeah, more than once," Skippy replied. "And that just adds to the problem."

Wet slapped his companion on the back. "Aww, you know Donna ain't the kind of a gal to hold a grudge. Why, to hear you tell it, she's the most pure-hearted space maiden in the galaxy."

"You bet she is," said Skippy. "But she's also the most helpless; I hate to think what it's been like for her without me all these years."

Wet shook his head. "Poor girl, she's probably still crying herself to sleep every night after kissing your bedside picture and begging you to come home."

"That sure relieves my guilt," said Skippy.

"Well, don't think about that right now. You've got to figure out how to even find her. She could be anywhere."

"I'll track her down somehow—I've got to. Believe me, Wet, she's worth it. What else do you think's been keeping me going all these years?"

"Certainly not that prison food."

"You got that right," laughed Skippy, "but anyway that's what I'm gonna do, but you've got a new shot at life too. No limits for Mr. Wet Lakeland now, right?"

Wet walked to the window, gazing into space. "I guess there's a few things I should say about those limits," he sighed. "I'm an old man, Skippy, as old as the mountains, as old as the weather, as old as the stars, as old as a collapsing star, as old as darkness itself, as old as…"

"I get it, you're old," said Skippy.

"Let an old man speak!" snapped Wet. "It doesn't matter. What I'm trying to say is, in all my years I've never had a friend like you. You've just been the whiskers to me, Skippy. Why I remember the time on Pinko-Kini when you rescued me from the suffocating Death Grip of the Invisible Creep, and that time you traded away your favorite ship to save me from the Boiling Doom Cauldron. And how could I ever forget your last-minute dash across that hot lava bridge to free me from the steaming vapor bonds of the Ring-Men? Who could ask for a better friend than that?"

"Wet, I never did any of that stuff."

"Can't an old man dream?! It doesn't matter, what I'm trying to say is, this universe is a big place—sometimes a little too big for an old man like me. I'd like to stick with a friend. Maybe, if you don't really mind too much, maybe we could find Donna together."

"Sure we can," said Skippy.

At just that moment the outside hallway came alive with the sound of voices and clanking boots. Skippy and Wet crept to the half-open door, quietly peeking out.

Standing in the middle of the hallway was General Roger Godsend, commander of the Accountant Army of Revolution;

Corporal Nub Niblet and Princess Contentious were running up from behind.

"General," said Nub, "we've finished our reconnaissance of the landing bay; no other ships besides our own and that little sportster with the Nebulous X license plates."

"Perfect," said Godsend. "While you were conducting your investigation, I had the clerk give me the room number of the sportster's crew. We've got them trapped behind that door, Corporal; exactly where we want scoundrels of their kind."

"You've done a great job, sir," said Nub. "But what kind of scoundrels are they exactly? That's not a military spacecraft, after all."

"Clearly they're spies, Niblet, sent to track us after we stole our shuttle from the *Maiming Lily*."

"But how would they even know of our departure? I mean, there were a lot of ships besides ours flying about. And besides, how could they track us and get here before us when even *we* didn't know where we were going?"

"Because they're spies," Godsend laughed. "Obviously you know nothing of the subterfuge of war—I'm certain Prince Tony has an assortment of spies spread throughout various space districts, ready to act if there is a spontaneous mutiny. But don't worry yourself with such stratagems; I can handle it. Just bring the rest of the troops forward."

"Yes, sir," said Nub. He looked over to Contentious, then back to the general. "We're all here."

"Excellent," replied Godsend. "Now that we have gathered our full fighting force, we'll clean out this nest of spies and bivouac here for the night."

Contentious stepped forward. "Look, General, I don't mean to delay your beating up on people, but I just want to pose a question before we get started."

"Speak freely, Royal Private."

"Well, listen, you turned me loose from Prince Drippy, so I'm grateful and stuff, but my sister is still back there with him, and so far, all we've done is manage to put more distance between us and her. Now, here we are, still running around, retreating, knocking off spies, and bivouacking, which is all fine for a couple of commando nerds like yourselves, but honestly, I just want to know when we're going back to rescue Babe."

"Fair lady," said Godsend, "of course the rescue of your dear sibling remains a top priority, but when a fledgling subversive movement such as ours has suffered as much catastrophe as we have, constant retreat is the only reasonable way to keep the effort alive."

"But what if no one is even chasing us?" said Contentious.

"Oh, someone is chasing us," said Godsend.

"But we haven't seen anyone this entire time," Contentious protested. "How do you know?"

Godsend smiled. "My lady, for someone to be chasing you, what must you be doing?"

"Well, you'd probably have to be running."

"Precisely. And we are running. Therefore, someone must be chasing us."

Contentious cocked her head. "Now wait just a minute..."

"Truly," said Godsend, "the retreat must continue for the foreseeable future. Soon enough we shall indeed liberate your sister. But for now, there is no more time for talk—we shall lay the rod of vengeance to this gang of spies without any further delay."

Skippy and Wet, who up until now had been listening with bemused interest, suddenly slammed the door.

"They've discovered us!" exclaimed Godsend. "Tricky spies. We cannot afford a prolonged siege; we must root them out immediately."

"What do you suggest, General?" asked Nub.

Godsend rose up to his full height, waving his finger in the air. "Assault the door!"

Godsend and Niblet both charged forward, easily smashing through the thin metal door by the combined force of their weight. Skippy and Wet were slammed to the ground under the wreckage.

"Greetings," announced the general, standing conqueror-like over the inert pair. "I'm General Roger Godsend, commander of the Accountant Army of Revolution. I have just defeated you. Will you surrender?"

Skippy sat up, shoving aside the broken door. "Do I have a choice?"

"None at all. You have been vanquished. You must take your place as the first of our once-pompous, now-disgraced, dirt-eating prisoners."

"Somehow I'm not convinced," said Skippy.

"But you must. I have no more time to waste in defeating you. There is much to be accomplished."

"Like what?" said Skippy.

"Like retreating," said Godsend.

"And finding my sister, the Princess Babe," said Contentious, pushing past Godsend. "She was kidnapped by Prince Tony; maybe you've heard of them."

"Have we ever!" said Skippy and Wet, simultaneously.

Contentious's eyes lit up. "Then maybe you know of Braker Ford and Wayne Musher, our boyfriends. They're trying to rescue us!"

Before Skippy and Wet could respond, there was a terrible scream followed by the crashing of the bathroom door. Like an avenging wraith, Holly Blackguard charged through the doorway, grasping for Contentious.

"Braker Ford's my boyfriend!" she screeched, shaking the princess.

Skippy Dodge grabbed the raving woman by the arm, flinging her onto the bed. "What are you, some kind of a maniac?" he shouted. "You ought to stop treating people like trash, you stupid, ugly, garbage heap!"

"I hope you die!" responded Holly.

"I've heard that before."

"Everyone, please, just calm down!" Godsend pleaded.

"Skippy," Wet demanded, "I don't think what you said to Miss Holly was right."

"Oh, yeah?" Skippy shouted. "How come?"

"Well, because Miss Holly isn't ugly."

"That's it, you're all dead!" said Holly, springing from the mattress. "You're all dead!"

"Prepare to retreat!" Godsend exclaimed, shaking his finger in the air.

"Listen to me!" Contentious howled above all the noise, "I've got to find my sister; won't anyone help me?"

The anguish in the princess's voice caused everyone to pause. Skippy and Wet looked at the floor.

"Please, I'm desperate."

"Well, what do you say, Skip?" Wet asked.

"How can I not help?" said Skippy. "The poor girl's been kidnapped; and who knows what happened to Braker after our escape." He turned to Contentious. "You can count on us; we'll help you find your sister. She's not with Prince Tony anymore but I've got an idea where we can gather some information."

"Thank you," sighed Contentious.

"But, Skip, what about Donna?" Wet asked.

Skippy grinned. "Wet, I know this universe backwards and forwards—I'll find Donna, I know I will; I've always known. But right now, I may be the only chance these kids have left."

General Godsend walked boldly up to Skippy. "I demand a full report on this conversation, soldier. All military decisions must be run by me."

"Well, it's a good thing you asked, Admiral, because we've just made several decisions. Number one—we've decided to not to be your prisoners. And number two, we've decided to help find this girl's sister instead. How's that for a report, Goodsneeze?"

"That's Godsend."

"Whatever."

Nub pulled on Godsend's coat. "General, he called you 'Goodsneeze'!" The little man burst into tears of laughter.

"You are excused, Corporal Niblet!"

"Yes, sir," Nub giggled, wiping his eyes as he walked from the room. "'General Goodsneeze', that's priceless."

"Say, does everyone in this universe have some lame sidekick?" exclaimed Holly.

"Who you calling lame?" said Wet, just as his trick knee gave out.

Skippy gave Contentious a reassuring hug. "Don't worry, kid, if your sister's out there we'll find her."

"I'm very grateful," said Contentious. "But what about her?" She pointed toward Holly Blackguard.

"I'm going with you to get Braker!" said Holly.

"Pipe down," said Skippy. "And by the way, why don't you lay off this Braker kid once and for all? He's clearly not that into you. And why should he be? Sure, you may look like prime steak, but you ain't shown much of value underneath."

"Oh, like you know me," Holly retorted.

"You bet I do," said Skippy. "I know your kind like my own skin—all puffed up, thinking you're something special, believing the entire galaxy should stand up and take notice, and if it doesn't, you're going to squeeze it by the throat until it does. But you know what the joke is, girlie? Maybe you really are something special, but if you don't knock that privileged chip off your shoulder, you aren't going to win over the galaxy—or even a single space trucker. No, you're just going to end up all alone—a bitter, angry, old space hag."

Holly was stunned by the appraisal. "That's not me," she wheezed, sitting down on the edge of the bed.

"That's quite a thoughtful psychological analysis there, my good man," said Godsend.

"Forget it," replied Skippy, "I been around some, that's all."

"Well, I was just thinking, perhaps I myself might gain some benefit if you were to analyze me sometime."

"Yeah, sure, whatever," said Skippy, rubbing his neck, "but right now we've got to get ourselves space-worthy again. You got a ship large enough to carry the five of us? I mean, I'm assuming you do want to help find the princess too."

"Oh, yes, most definitely," said Godsend. "With our increased numbers, I see no need to continue with our previous strategy."

"Then we'll need a larger ship than the little job we came in."

"Have no concern, the one we stole will more than meet our needs. But you must be mistaken, there are six of us, my good man, not five."

"Five," said Skippy, "the queen here can have the sportster for herself."

Godsend moved closer to Skippy. "I have a problem with that suggestion," he said, his tone ominous.

"What do you mean?" asked Skippy.

"A Godsend could never leave a defenseless woman on her own in such a desolate portion of the galaxy."

"Oh, believe me, pops, this one's not defenseless. She'll do fine, just her and the sportster."

Godsend folded his arms. "My good man, I appreciate your concerns regarding the damsel's savage temperament but apparently you don't comprehend the gravity of your own situation—I've already pardoned you for your attempted spying; I can only be so lenient. If you're going to be part of this army, you will have to learn to obey your commanding officer." Godsend tapped the handle of his laser pistol. "Otherwise, you may be looking at a charge of treason, and we don't want that do we, soldier?"

Skippy studied the man before him for a long time. "You're genuinely insane, aren't you?"

"Altogether and completely," said Godsend.

Skippy went back to studying the general before finally throwing back his head, letting out a hearty laugh. "General," he chuckled, "you and I are going to get along just fine."

Soon, Roger Godsend's tiny revolutionary army was off in search of the Princess Babe—while Holly Blackguard sat in the starship's storage closet for one more long ride.

Chapter Twenty
Moon Battle

Braker and his friends shuffled into the cramped underground headquarters of the moon-scapers; of all the makeshift space settlements throughout the universe this had to be the worst. Nothing more than a collection of steel tunnels sealed inside enormous oxygen bladders, the cold, dark surroundings were a great example of the low premium moon-scapers placed on personal comfort. Two types of scapers were on display here—those who lay sprawled and exhausted on filthy mats, and those who sat slumped and exhausted at improvised tables while gambling or drinking homemade ash liquor.

"Home," said Rued with a grand gesture as they arrived at a table surrounded by men that made him look freshly scrubbed.

"Charlie!" one of the men shouted, jumping up and punching Rued in the face.

"Jodo!" Rued exclaimed happily, grabbing a chair and slamming it over the other man's head.

"This is Jodo Durning," Rued announced. "He drives the dirt dispenser with me. He's my friend."

Jodo was a small, hunchbacked humanoid with a smooth, bald head and eyes that looked as if they were set a couple of inches too low into his face.

"I see we have some people here," said Jodo, sizing up the four newcomers. "Don't look like much. You are people though, aren't you? Don't get a lot of people down here. Don't make me mad."

As Jodo was speaking, a man with an astoundingly large belly came bounding forward. "I see we have new friends!" he said. "Now don't leave me out, Charlie. Come on, introduce the new friends you've brought us."

"They say they are men who want work. They carry weapons, too, see?" Rued nodded toward Knothead's hatchet.

The big-bellied man teetered back on his heels, ignoring Rued's implication of a possible threat. "I'm Smack Myers," he declared warmly. "I run this outfit. Hey, you guys really look great; just a great looking bunch. Fantastic. Glad you're here." He gave each one a hug.

"Thanks a heap," said Wayne. "Say, you sure don't seem as scary as we 'spected you to be. We figger'd the boss of these here critters would have to be double fretful himself."

Smack chuckled. "Sure, I get that all the time; moon-scapers have a reputation for being somewhat surly."

"They shore do," said Wayne, "but you're diff'rnt; you seem downright sociable."

"Why, sure I am," said Smack, "and don't think this sunny disposition is just a cover-up for a life spent in grinding drudgery and constant fear of the cut-throat, transient menial workers I'm expected to babysit."

"It ain't?" said Wayne.

"Not at all," said Smack. "Rather, you should consider me to be the pleasantly busy leader to a unique group of highly excitable moon-cavity engineers."

"Say," said Wayne, "that's a durn good way of lookin' at things."

"Sure it is," continued Smack. "And why not? It's not like we're just a haphazard assortment of low-functioning vagabonds destined to roam the butt-end of space while doing the absolute lowest form of common labor imaginable. No, we're hardy pioneers, risking our lives in a black, never-ending frontier, all to develop lunar playgrounds for filthy rich elitists who will exclude us from the very communities we toiled to develop." Smack grabbed his belly and laughed heartily. "But, forgive me, I get carried away sometimes when discussing the adventure that is moon-fissure packing. So, anyway, speaking of work, we've been needing some new guys for the outfit, and here you come along at just the right time. It's just amazing how things always work out, isn't it? Life really isn't just a slow, miserable slog toward annihilation, is it? Life is a charm, just a charm. So, let's do it, huh, what do you say?"

Braker looked at the others. "Well…about that…we're not actually here for work…"

"No work?" interjected Rued. "I knew it. You men too good for scaper work?"

He and the other nearby scapers slowly closed in, their posture menacing.

"Boy, I hope you didn't mean what you just said," said Smack. "Most scapers are pretty sensitive about their jobs; we are crater-filling specialists, you know. When somebody turns their nose up at our chosen profession, well, tempers can flare."

Jodo circled Braker's group. "Scapers teach soft-handed men a big lesson."

"Hold on a minute," said Knothead. "Of course we want work. Why else would we be down here?"

"Sure, sure, that's right," said Braker, his eyes darting back and forth amongst the surrounding scapers. "What I meant was we weren't here *just* to work."

"Well, what else are you here to do?" asked Smack.

"You here to steal from scapers?" demanded Jodo, sniffing around Wayne's shirt collar.

"They're here to see me get trained up in the ways of a scaper too," offered Johnny Comet. "They want to see a kid get raised up right."

"Say, that's fabulous," said Smack, as the other scapers voiced their approval. "What's a kid need with school anyway? School's boring."

"Hey, that's what I always say!" responded Johnny.

"Absolutely," said Smack. "Why, I can't even begin to imagine what my life would be like now if I had finished school." The moon-scaper pinched his eyes shut as if fighting back tears. "Well, let's see then, who's gonna be first?"

Braker shrugged. "First for what?"

"The test, of course."

"Oh, I guess I'll go," said Braker.

"No, don't!" Knothead shouted, but it was too late, Rued and Jodo had already grabbed Braker, shoving him onto a platform in the middle of the room. Then, trembling with depraved excitement, they kicked and prodded what looked like a giant purple pile of clay. But it wasn't clay at all, it was a living creature—a horrible, terrifying creature. A creature the likes of which neither Braker nor any of his friends had ever laid eyes on before!

Slowly it rose, scraping its head on the nine-foot ceiling as it steadied itself on a pair of bowed legs that appeared too short for the rest of its body. Comparatively, its enormous arms were so long that its flipper-like hands dragged on the ground. Its brawny chest was swollen to such proportions that only the creature's eyes were visible above the bulk. A thick, rubbery hide covered this frightful monstrosity.

"Come here," he beckoned Braker, slamming his fingerless fists on the platform.

"It's my moon monster!" Johnny Comet cried with joy.

"Wait a second!" Braker exclaimed, spinning to glare at Smack Myers. "Wait just one second. What's this all about?"

"I'm sorry," said Smack. "It's the test; I thought you knew. It's a treasured tradition among us moon-scapers. If someone wants to be a scaper they've got to prove their strength and resiliency—so we have them fight the strongest member of the outfit. Vigor just happens to be the strongest right now."

"I don't want to fight," said Braker in toneless awe, staring at the monster.

Smack looked good-naturedly at Braker. "Too late now, they already woke him. Besides, you should be honored. These contests provide a fantastic chance for each contestant to search within himself for those great inner qualities of fortitude, perseverance, and courage. Don't think for a minute this is only about the twisted desire of bored moon workers to escape their dismal reality with a sick display of violence and death."

"Oh, good, we're not allowed to kill each other," sighed Braker.

"I didn't say that," Smack corrected. "Actually, Vigor probably will kill you—you just aren't allowed to kill him."

"What? That's not fair!"

"Sure it is. I mean, think about it, we can't take the chance of losing a good worker in tests like these, but you newcomers, well, we don't lose anything if you don't make it. That's just another one of those wonderful old moon-scaper traditions."

"I don't want to be a moon-scaper!" Braker cried just before Vigor slammed him against the wall. The trucker's declaration had no effect on his opponent; the moon monster continued his slow, menacing advance.

Amazingly, Braker somehow managed to wobble back to his feet. "You've been working out lately, right?" he said with an appeasing smile.

Vigor grabbed the trucker, crushing him between his flippers.

"I've got money!" Braker shouted.

"Bah," said Vigor. "I hate money, what good is money when no one likes you."

"I like you!" cried Braker.

"No, you don't. You're just saying that so I don't squirt your insides all over the ground."

"Okay, there is that," Braker replied. "But I don't *hate* you."

"You don't?" said Vigor, dropping Braker. "But I'm trying to liquefy you."

"Yeah, sure, that's a point of concern," said Braker, gingerly feeling his ribs. "But aside from that, it's not like I loathe you."

Vigor gulped. "That's the nicest thing anybody ever said to me."

Braker blinked, hardly believing the conversation he was having. "Well, hey, it's true. I was never even mad at you—and don't even think I would ever want to *fight* you. Although, to be honest, you do look kind of scary."

"I know," said Vigor, "everyone says I'm ugly; that's why they hate me and make fun of me. They think all I'm good for is being strong and mean. I don't want to be mean; I just want a friend."

Braker griped Vigor's arm, at least what he could get a hold of. "Vigor, you don't have to be mean. I'll be your friend."

"You will?" said Vigor with a smile, although you couldn't see it because he had no neck and the lower half of his head was buried behind his heaving chest muscle.

"Sure," said Braker, "I need friends too. In fact, half the universe doesn't even seem to like me right now."

"How come?"

"Well, these rotten guys kidnapped my princess and, well, I've just got to get her back and…"

"You had a girlfriend?" asked Vigor in amazement.

"I guess, for a while."

"I never had a girlfriend," confessed Vigor. "Even the girls on my own planet thought I was ugly—and they look just like me."

"Tough break."

"Yeah, but I feel sorrier for you—you had a girlfriend, and she was stolen. That makes me mad. Can I help you find her?"

"Sure," said Braker. "Vigor, you're a good guy, don't let anybody tell you different."

The entire group of moon-scapers stood riveted in astonishment at the strange scene played out before them.

"Come on, I thought we'd see fighting," complained Rued.

"No fight today," said Vigor. "Braker is my friend, my only friend. No one hurts my only friend."

Smack Myers stepped forward, clapping his hands. "This is great, this is so special, I mean, really, to see this kind of unity between a totally weak human and some kind of freak alien monster is really beautiful. We need more of this kind of thing in our lives." He reached out to shake Vigor's flipper. "Vigor, let me be the first to apologize for treating you like scum."

"Okay," said Vigor.

"I'm sorry too," agreed Jodo. "You're weird. People don't like me either. I'll be your friend. This stinks."

"Well, then," said Braker, a little more at ease with each passing moment, "all we need to do now is find a ship to get us out of here."

"Where's the ship you came in?" asked Smack.

"Braker lost it," said Johnny Comet.

"Maybe we could borrow a ship," Wayne suggested. "Any of you folks got an extra spaceship lyin' around?"

Smack shook his head. "I'm sorry, but moon-scaper crews have no access to long range space travel. The company drops us off at the start of a job and picks us up when we're done. That way nobody can quit early."

"Sounds like a pretty harsh policy," said Braker.

"It only seems that way," said Smack. "It's not just because the company has no concern for the health or well-being of the workers stuck here in the meantime, but it's just that the company doesn't want anyone to miss out on the benefit of seeing a job well done."

"Thoughtful fellers," said Wayne.

"Oh, you should read through our labor contract sometime. You wouldn't believe how much thought they put into it."

"That's all wonderful," said Braker, "but we can't wait around for you guys to finish the job."

"Yeah, you don't want to do that," said Smack. "These jobs can easily take a year or two."

"A year or two!" exclaimed Braker. "That's like a prison sentence!"

"Oh, really it's not so bad when you get used to measuring time in nothing smaller than three-month intervals." Smack paused for a moment. "Now wait just a minute, I think I do know of a ship. Charlie Rued has one he's been building out of spare parts; a souped-up little hot rod that's still in progress, but it runs. I'll bet it could probably make it with just a little bit of faith and a whole lot of love."

Rued looked up from the corner table he was slumped over. "Why should I help? They lost their own ship."

"But, Rued, we're stranded here without you," Braker pleaded.

Rued wrinkled his nose. "What will you give me?"

"Give you? We don't have anything to give you."

"Forget it," was the quick reply.

Braker's face flushed with anger. "Look here, Rued, we need that ship."

"You can charter it."

"I'll charter it," interrupted Vigor, "with my savings from working the moon. Now it's done."

Rued stood up, impressed at the offer. "Vigor wants to give me his money. All right, I'll take the money. But I'm the pilot. And Braker pays for all the damages."

"I'm not running the dispenser all by myself while you have fun," said Jodo. "I'm coming with you."

"Jodo's coming too?" Vigor asked.

Jodo nodded. "Yeah, let's go beat up a bunch of people. We'll save the princess. Why not? I've got nothing better to do. Maybe I'll get something out of it. I hate my job."

"Hold on here," said Smack, "you guys are my best men. I can't just let you go like this."

"What, you going to try and stop them?" said Knothead.

"Try to stop them?" laughed Smack. "Not at all; I'm coming with them. This is a wonderful thing. Besides, I'm their leader; I've got to lead my men."

"This is ridiculous," said Braker. "Don't you guys understand? This isn't a pleasure trip. People are trying to kill us out there."

Smack rubbed his belly. "Braker, moon-scapers aren't afraid of danger; we put our lives on the line every day out here. Hardly a shift goes by without somebody getting plowed under by a moon-dozer, creamed by an asteroid-mover, or sucked into space by a faulty gravity belt—I mean, don't get me wrong, accidents happen, it's not just because caution takes too much effort and we're so exhausted we've abandoned all safety measures. Anyway, my point is, we aren't afraid."

"Yeah, come with us!" shouted Johnny Comet. "It's fun! Just wait till you meet all these crazy folks we've been chasing. Boy, are they nuts. You guys will fit in great!"

"But, Smack," Braker continued, "you have responsibilities. You can't just abandon your life's work."

Smack's face grew solemn. He folded his hands silently. "Braker, moon-scaping is my calling, my life's work. Obviously, nothing means more to me than filling up moon craters with dirt all day, every day without end. But I'm coming with you, and it's not because my life has no meaning, or because if I remain on this moon for one more day I'm going to have a complete nervous breakdown. I'm coming because it's the right thing to do."

Braker looked to Vigor.

The moon monster shrugged. "You can resist, but just remember, most guys who argue with the boss accidentally fall into the meteorite chipper."

And so, after Smack left some hasty instructions for his remaining moon-scapers, he led Braker and the others to the underground maintenance shop where Charlie Rued was already waiting.

As they entered the garage, Knothead dropped back to walk beside Vigor, who was bringing up the rear of the group.

"So, you're a pretty big guy," said Knothead. "I bet you think you're as tough as me."

"Yes, I believe I probably am," Vigor answered.

"Well, I'm a space barbarian, and that means I'm dangerous. You think you're as dangerous as me?"

"Yes, I believe I probably am," said Vigor.

"All right. Well, have you ever swum the terrible Kytuuk River on the mud planet of Myuuk using just your teeth to haul a barge full of wounded mud soldiers while having enemy bog warriors pelt you with poison-tip arrows from the shore?"

"Yes," responded Vigor.

"All right, but have you ever been the sacrifice at the center of an evil death cult ritual on the demon planet Wango-Maroon, yet somehow managed to escape only to realize you were being followed, so you doubled back, trekking on foot over the haunted Dezztom Mountains, leaping from the edge of a crumbling cliff to destroy the cultic village with the yellow-tongued sociopathic spiders you collected and carried in a two-hundred-pound sack on your back?"

"Yes."

"Well, has a lunatic space baron from the planet Ikil ever dipped you in hot tar and pinned you to the ground with a burning stake through the heart, but you managed to escape and heal yourself through sheer will-power, after which you returned to your home to find everyone you've ever known murdered by the baron's army, so that very night you dug a hundred-foot volcano trench to their memory before you scaled the impossibly high walls to the baron's fortress where you called down lightning from the sky to destroy his entire court while you flew to safety by grabbing hold of a passing Folly-Bird's tail feathers?"

"Yes."

Without a word, Knothead turned around and lifted his long, red ponytail. Branded on the base of his neck was a small circle with two crossed battle-clubs. "But do you bear the Mark of Fangbaum, the sacred symbol given to all true space barbarians at birth?"

Vigor solemnly peeled back some of his enormous chest muscle to reveal the exact same symbol on a hidden portion of his neck.

"I guess there's just no reasoning with you," said Knothead.

By now, the group was well into the hangar, far enough that they could see Charlie Rued rolling happily in the dust as he waited for them. "Now you meet my ship, the *Rued Star-One*," he announced proudly, jumping to his feet. "Sure is pretty, huh?"

"Pretty?" Braker fumed, staring at the rocket. "Rued, it's a two-seater mini-craft, it can't even carry all of us."

"Don't worry," said Rued, tossing garbage out of the cockpit, "it just looks small, come on in."

For the next half hour Braker, Wayne, Knothead, Jodo Durning, Charlie Rued, Johnny Comet, Smack Myers, and Vigor all took turns squeezing in and out of the cockpit in a hopeless attempt to find a configuration that would include them all. Finally, Vigor ripped out the seats and glovebox to make the extra space they needed. After that, they all managed to pile in, although Johnny Comet was wedged under the steering wheel and Braker and Wayne had their faces pressed so tightly against the windshield they were both finding it hard to breathe.

"Aah, here we go!" exclaimed Rued as the ship lifted off. "But I better warn you of one thing."

"What's that?" gasped Knothead, trying to move Vigor's feet from off his face.

"Well, I'm not so good with stopping and starting yet, so don't be surprised if the landing's a little rough."

"This is no way to rescue a princess!" Braker cried as they burst into space.

"Say," Wayne muttered to himself, "I wonder if anybody even knows where we're going?"

223

Chapter Twenty-One
Chitchat with a Criminal

The treacherous Chuck Weasel was quite pleased with himself as his stolen spacecraft raced through the cosmos with its illicit cargo.

"How about that getaway; pretty smooth move for the old Weasel-guy, huh?" he snickered to his adoring female cohort, Kate Starbrand.

"As if it could ever be otherwise," said Kate, plastering an overly dramatic kiss on the cold lips of her swaggering boyfriend.

Behind them sat J.J. Whammo and the Princess Babe, both tied to a row of exhaust tubes.

Kate turned to Babe. "You got a problem with staring?" she shouted, as if the captured princess could help but notice the theatrical passion between the two.

"I'm sorry if I spoiled your moment," Babe apologized.

Kate leapt over to where the bound princess sat helplessly, slapping her across the face. "You snotty rich girls make me sick! You're probably used to getting everything your way. Well, around here you'll find you big hair-do types don't rank so high."

"I'm sorry," said Babe.

"Oh, I'm sure you are. And you'll be even sorrier once we bust in on your secret. Right, Chuck?"

"Yeah, right," said Chuck, pacing the room. "All I gotta do now is figure out what that secret is."

"You and Kate are just pathetically confused," said J.J. "There is absolutely nothing to be gained by this woman."

"Don't tell me what I can gain!" Chuck snorted. "If I have to, I'll drop you both off at an alien food factory as vitamin supplements, so don't push me!"

"Chuck, think about what you're doing," Babe pleaded, "you and Kate are just making yourselves sick over all this. You have each other, why not just settle down and enjoy what you have?"

"Enjoy what I have?" laughed Chuck. "Maybe you don't realize who I *really* am. Most people know me as—Mike Tomorrow!"

Babe gasped. "The Cosmic Super Thief?"

"That's right. Obviously, you've heard of me."

"I can't believe it," said Babe. "If you're Mike Tomorrow then that means Kate Starbrand is really—"

"Candi Thornapple, the High-heeled Bandit," Kate announced with a toss of her hair.

"You guys are in the news reports every day," said J.J., "but I'd heard you two were killed in your last hold-up."

"That's what we wanted people to believe," Chuck responded. "I'm pretty crafty. After that last job, I decided we should lay low for a while. A guy like me has connections, so I made a few calls and the next thing you know Mike Tomorrow and Candi Thornapple are goners."

"So why get tangled up with me?" Babe asked.

225

Chuck strutted across the room. "I'm a big wheel, princess. I require certain luxuries in my life that can't be fulfilled on a fuel attendant's salary. You're nothing more than a few extra bucks to tide me over till better days."

"That's exactly where you're wrong," said J.J. "You just picked up a galaxy-load of trouble. We're probably being followed right now."

"By who; Braker Ford? I left him eating my dust."

"Braker! You've actually seen Braker?" cried Babe.

"Sure did," Kate scoffed. "What a goof."

Babe wasn't even listening to them anymore. "I knew it, I knew it," she muttered aloud. "He didn't give up on me. Braker never gave up. He's still trying to find me."

"Good luck to him," snickered Chuck, "you're mine for now, at least until I figure out what makes you so valuable."

"It's not what you think," Babe insisted.

"Sure it is. You're worth something big."

"There are some things worth more than money," said Babe.

"You talk to us like we're crud!" Kate exploded. "You think we're lower than you because we have to work for a living!"

"Calm down," said Chuck. "You got too much fire in you, girl. Why don't you go up front and check on that automatic navigator, it's been a while, you might have to crank it up again. I'll finish with these two."

"Alright, Chuck," sighed Kate, draping her arms across Chuck's shoulders, "but don't be too long, I need my big, handsome man around." She shifted her eyes toward Babe. "You know it's not nice to be all alone."

"Get out of here," Chuck giggled, slapping Kate's thigh as she sauntered out of the hold.

Once she was gone, Chuck sat down in a chair directly across from J.J. and Babe. He sat there for a moment, not saying anything, just slouched over as he rubbed his temples.

"I got it! I've got a way to cash in on you two!" he finally shouted.

"Please tell me it has nothing to do with alien food factories," cried J.J.

Chuck sat straight up in his chair, one leg bouncing excitedly. "Much better than that, pin cushion. I'm sure even you have heard of the Crossroads of the Universe, where all the galactic express lanes converge at a gigantic toll station; well, there's also a huge entertainment complex there—casinos, malls, amusement parks, everything a bored space traveler needs, and I happen to know I can haul in a pretty good sum for two humans like you."

"Oh, no," gushed J.J. "we're going to be auctioned off to some strange, traveling caravan of space oddities!"

"Not quite," said Chuck. "Plan on spending the rest of your lives toiling as witless slave labor at the Crossroads. It's a big place; they pay a high premium for able bodies."

"I will do my best to prove worthy of whatever price I may bring," said Babe.

"Only problem is," said Chuck, "the Crossroads is a long way from here; but this ship is pretty sturdy, I think we'll make it just fine."

J.J. hung his head. "Why couldn't this have been one of my ships?"

Chapter Twenty-Two
Room of Terror

The dust from Mount Rad's smoldering ruins had not yet settled before Dr. Wilde's minions began scavenging for survivors, most notably the princess sisters and Prince Tony.

Meanwhile, inside the *Flying Electric Laboratory,* Dr. Wilde finished interrogating the last of Mount Rad's captured defenders. "Do we have no more captives?" he screamed to his subordinates after failing to gain any useful information from the beaten Goons.

"I'm sorry, Dr. Wilde," apologized one brave attendant, "but those are the last ones we found. I guess there is one other, but he wasn't a soldier. He appears to be a cook; probably just another of Prince Tony's prisoners."

"I don't care what he is!" shouted Dr. Wilde. "Let me speak to him, I must find someone who knows if those sisters are alive or not."

"Yes, sir," answered the underling, quickly exiting the room and returning with the dazed but still living Downer Plasmoe.

Dr. Wilde's face twitched with intensity while staring at the despondent cook. "You—I recognize you. Yes, you were one of the men in Lord Preposterous's compound when I attacked. What's your name?"

"Downer Plasmoe," said the cook, miserably.

"Have you heard of the princess sisters?"

"Yes, you guessed it. That means I'm in more trouble now, right? That's the way it goes for me. I'm just the unluckiest—"

"So, you do know of the sisters!" said Dr. Wilde. "You *will* tell me of their location."

"I doubt I can."

"That shall swiftly change, you flimsy minded fool; I will extract the information from you." Dr. Wilde clapped his hands. "Take him to the brain workshop!"

Gasps filled the room, followed by silence and then hushed murmurings among the surrounding guards.

"Take him!" Dr. Wilde repeated. Downer was promptly dragged down the hallway as the grinning doctor followed.

A speedy elevator ride to the deepest depths of the ship brought the group to a tiny, dark corridor, a single steel door at its end. The door opened slightly. Hot steam exploded from within. Downer looked on in horror as a sagging prisoner was brought out by two pasty-faced guards.

"Don't let them take you in!" the man cried. "They're monsters I tell you!"

"Be quiet" demanded Dr. Wilde, "or you'll get the Treatment again."

The prisoner's lips curled in terror. "Oh no, not the Treatment! Oh, please, anything but the Treatment!"

The screaming man was put into the elevator even as Downer took his place in the terrible room. Inside the red, glowing workshop, Downer was introduced to an incredible world of bubbling test tubes, sparking energy magnets, steaming hot jet burners, and a small kitchenette for preparing snacks.

"Awaiting your orders, sir," an eager assistant announced as Dr. Wilde tied on his lab apron.

With incredible speed Dr. Wilde spun around to glare at Downer Plasmoe. "Strap him to the Hydro-Electric Gizmo Unit!"

"Go ahead, I don't care," Downer groaned as he was led to the hideous machine's examination table.

"You will care," said Dr. Wilde. "You will care very much. Soon you will beg for mercy you don't deserve as you tell me all you know."

Downer grimaced as he was bound to the table. "Bad things happen to guys like me all the time," he said, the table rising to a sharp angle. "I guess I shouldn't be so surprised." A gleaming metal brain box was placed over his head.

Dr. Wilde's eyes were wide with delight. "You are probably wondering what evil things I'm about to do to you."

"Not really."

"You must be!" Dr. Wilde exploded. "There is no other mind like mine in the entire galaxy; you must be petrified at what I can do."

"Whatever you say, I guess."

"Aren't you in torment as you consider the rueful fate that awaits you?"

"Sure, but why should this be different from any other day?"

"You are a very depressed person," said Dr. Wilde.

"I am not," Downer whined.

"Whatever, it doesn't matter," said Dr. Wilde. "Your emotional status won't affect the Hydro-Electric Gizmo Unit. You see, in just a moment the unit will send fiendish electrical impulses to specific target areas of your worthless brain, temporarily liquefying any areas that are resistant to my commands. You will then answer all my questions without hesitation. Regrettably, the process will not be very painful, although you will become extremely thirsty."

"A brain's a brain," said the cook.

Dr. Wilde flicked on the unit with a dramatic twirling of his wrist. "Let's begin."

The nefarious machine rattled as it built up power. Shortly, its liquo-meters read a full hundred percent. Downer's brain was ready.

"I'll start with a few simple questions," said Dr. Wilde. "First, who is Braker Ford?"

"He's a nice guy, much better than me," answered Downer in a dull, monotone voice.

"Who are the princess sisters?"

"Real nice girls who would probably never even dream of dating a guy like me."

"Hmmm. Answer this—where is Prince Tony?"

"I don't know, probably some place better than where I am."

"Where are the princess sisters right now?"

"One is with a mean guy named Chuck Weasel who wanted to shoot me."

"And the other?"

"I don't know, but I'm sure she's some place I'd rather be."

"I see, well, obviously that one is irretrievable, so tell me more about this Chuck Weasel. Who is he?"

"He's the mean guy who stole the princess. He's probably smarter than me."

"Where did he go to?"

"I don't know, but it's probably a better place than I could ever think of."

Dr. Wilde began to pace the room, scratching his head. "Where, where, where would I go if I had just kidnapped a princess?"

Unable to arrive at a suitable conclusion, the mad doctor slammed his fist onto the experiment table. "Assistants, reconstitute the cook's brain and take him to a cell until further notice. Oh, and do an all-over, thorough exam, and get a tissue sample; maybe we could make some kind of depression serum out of his blood or something."

Dr. Wilde's helpers quickly set about reversing the Gizmo Unit's effects as their leader stormed out of the room.

"Where, where, where?" the doctor repeated to himself as he rode the elevator back up to the command bridge.

"Good afternoon, Master," said Bullmack, standing by the door.

"Silence!" screamed Dr. Wilde. "Can't you see I'm deep in thought?"

"I'll be very quiet then," replied Bullmack.

Dr. Wilde grunted as he paced the floor.

"What are you thinking of?" asked Bullmack.

"Nothing!" screeched the doctor.

"Oh," said Bullmack.

Dr. Wilde continued to pace back and forth; he was beginning to make Bullmack dizzy.

"You must be thinking about nothing very hard," said Bullmack, trying to keep his balance.

Dr. Wilde raced up to the robot, his fists clenched.

"As a matter of fact, I am using my fantastically unlimited amounts of intelligence to figure out where a pathetically foolish man would take one of the princess sisters after kidnapping her, but I cannot properly concentrate with your continual interruptions of stupidity!"

"I'm being very quiet again," said Bullmack.

Dr. Wilde went back to his pacing, more frantic with every step. Bullmack went back to being dizzy.

"Master," Bullmack finally spoke.

"What now?"

"If I stole a girl, I would take her to a mall to get something to eat because she might be hungry."

"Yes, yes," said Dr. Wilde, "that's because you're an idiot and—that's it Bullmack, your pointless comment helped my massive brain figure out where the princess is!"

"Eating at a mall?"

"No, you machine, she's at the Crossroads of the Universe, I'm sure of it."

"Is she going to eat there?"

"I don't know, but I do know there are many other things there that could be useful to a kidnapper with a princess."

"So, am I very smart for discovering the plan?"

"No," exclaimed Dr. Wilde, "you are very simple indeed. Why, for example, would you take the princess to a mall when any old restaurant would do?"

"That's because after we eat I could take her to all the little shops and buy her lots of pretty dresses and flowers."

Dr. Wilde pulled at his swirling white hair. "Why would you ever want to do that? That's disgusting!"

"Isn't that what you do for beautiful ladies?"

"No!" bellowed Dr. Wilde. "That's not what you do! You rip them to bloody shreds in savage fury, scattering their severed limbs across the land, you ignorant mess."

"Oh, yeah," said Bullmack, "I forgot about ripping them to shreds; severed, bloody limbs, much better, yeah."

Dr. Wilde turned to the pilot of the ship. "Captain, direct us to the Crossroads of the Universe, and I mean fast. Break all the traffic regulations."

"Yes, sir," said the pilot in a strangely familiar voice.

Dr. Wilde was so ecstatic as he rushed from the room that he never noticed the pilot's smug vocal quality, or the hateful face partially obscured behind a pair of huge space goggles. If he had, he would have discovered that it was Prince Tony himself who was now secretly guiding them to their fateful destination!

Chapter Twenty-Three
Crossroads of the Universe

"All right, folks, take a good look at The Spaceman's Paradise because it's our next stop," said Skippy Dodge, piloting his shipload of rescuers toward an enormous space city surrounded by a dozen smaller, orbiting space stations.

Roger Godsend was the first to arrive at the windshield. "So, this is the Crossroads of the Universe, is it?"

"Well, not exactly, General," Skippy explained. "The true crossroads—the exact center of the universe—are those toll stations we just went through. What we're looking at now is an intergalactic resort called The Spaceman's Paradise, but it's what most people are thinking of when they refer to the Crossroads of the Universe. Being near the middle of all creation, it makes for a busy intersection, so, years ago, some wise guy got the bright idea to build a mega tourist center here. It's got everything—spas, eateries, nightclubs, you name it. I'm surprised you haven't heard of it."

"I've heard of it, of course," said the general, "but certainly you can understand how the life of a paranoid militant is unlikely to include jaunts to floating circuses."

"Oh, sure," said Skippy. "But we're not here for a holiday, either. The Crossroads is a popular spot, which means that underneath its bright lights, there's lots of money, and wherever there's a lot of money, there's also shady business and underhanded deals. If you want to pick up word on something dirty that's happening in the universe you can usually find it right here. And I'm willing to bet this is where we get our first lead on Princess Babe."

Contentious and Nub squeezed into the cockpit now. "I've never seen what's so special about this place," said Contentious. "The entire joint is nothing but tacky shopping outlets and gaudy stage shows."

"Gee, I came here with some of the other accountants one time, and we didn't think it was gaudy," said Nub. "We bought red dwarf space shoes with telescopes in the heels and got to watch Albert Frenzy conduct his exploding lithium worm orchestra."

"I stand corrected," Contentious replied flatly.

In front of them, the space city was tall and sprawling, its many stores, hotels, and theaters all lit from the flashing billboards and glowing marquees that were contained beneath a protective, transparent dome. Great throngs of spacecraft swarmed around the outside of the station, each awaiting admittance to the interior through various access ports located in the city's bubble covering.

Due to the congestion, Skippy was forced to orbit the station several times before finding an accessible portal. Once inside the dome, he then had to await an open parking spot on the landing docks that surrounded the city like scaffolding; hundreds upon hundreds of these crowded platforms were stacked from the lowest of the city streets to the top, all of them connected by large elevator transports and miles of gorgeous, if impractical, spiral staircases.

At its lowest level, the city appeared to be flooded under a thick, rippling layer of multihued liquid.

"It looks like your resort has a plumbing issue," said Godsend.

"Not at all," Skippy responded. "That's no leakage; it's supposed to be there. What you're looking at is Aqua-thite. It provides the artificial gravity inside the station. It's a particularly outdated technology; whoever owns the Paradise probably still uses it just to keep costs down."

The Aqua-thite's constantly changing color showered the dome with exquisite reflections. "It's beautiful," Contentious admitted, gazing at the strange fluid.

"Yeah, beautiful from a distance," said Skippy, "but you don't want get near it, that junk is packed full of toxic chemicals that act like acid on contact with skin. That's why you hardly see anyone use the stuff anymore."

Wet Lakeland leaned in. "I remember one time back in the old days when I was part of a construction crew building a star bridge over a black hole cluster, these two Thaglians got to horsing around and spilled a container of that Aqua-stuff all over their feet. Next time I saw them they were just a couple of talking heads hooked up to a computer terminal."

"That's awful," gasped Contentious.

"Not really," said Wet. "After that, they got a big promotion as safety advisors, going around giving lectures to different crews on the hazards of interplanetary construction work."

"Skippy, it doesn't make any sense to keep using something that dangerous," said Contentious. "The entire lower level of the city is unusable. That's impractical."

"Impractical but cost effective," replied Skippy. "Anything to save a buck. That's what this place is all about—saving money and making money."

Skippy guided his ship to a recently vacated spot on a crowded platform and shut the engines down.

"There is no place for greed in a just universe," said Godsend, marching toward the gangplank. "I shall cleanse this place of its piggishness even as I release the captive princess from its ravenous clutches." He was halfway down the ramp when Skippy came running up behind him. "General, I was just thinking, umm, maybe Wet and I should do the snooping around while you and the others guard the ship. You know how important the ship is to us."

"A fine idea, Private," said Godsend, saluting, "consider it an order."

"Yes, sir," said Skippy, grabbing Wet and hurrying toward an elevator.

Godsend was just starting back into the ship when a cheerful female attendant approached. "Hello, up there," she called out.

"Why, hello, young lady," said Godsend in a chivalrous tone, "how are you today?"

"I am happy," replied the girl, "we're all happy at the Crossroads."

"What's going on, General?" inquired Nub, walking onto the plank.

"Merely exchanging pleasantries with a young employee of the station," said Godsend. "The poor girl failed to address me as 'General'—somehow she didn't recognize my rank." He motioned toward the stripes he had drawn on his uniform collar with an orange marker. "I'll let it slide this time, seeing as how we are new here."

"Good thinking," said Nub.

Godsend turned back to the still-waiting attendant. "What is it I can do for you, miss?"

"I am the docking bay attendant and I'm here to collect on your fees."

"Young lady," said Godsend with displeasure, "this is a military transport, and we are on a mission of grave importance. I would suspect there are exemptions for persons in such cases." He turned to the listening Nub Niblet. "How was that?"

"Very official," said Nub.

The attendant paused for a moment before giving her reply. "We are very happy here," she said, "we are all very happy here. Unpaid docking fees make us unhappy; we cannot accommodate you under such conditions."

"I believe this whole affair could be quickly settled if I could just speak with your superiors," Godsend replied.

"You do not agree to pay—we must correct the problem."

"Aah, she's going to get her superiors," said Godsend as the woman turned to leave.

Moments later, Contentious sat staring out the front windshield when she noticed a flurry of sudden movement beside the ship. "General," she exclaimed, "I think something's wrong out there!"

Godsend and Nub hurried to the cockpit in time to see the female parking attendant leading a team of six guards, each carrying high-powered laser whippers, fully energized.

"General," Nub said nervously, "I'm afraid their superiors outrank our superiors."

Godsend raced for the hatchway. "You may be right, Nub. I suggest evasive maneuvers—everyone run for your lives!"

Godsend burst onto the open gangplank to find the parking attendant already awaiting him, a whipper at the ready. "Surrender; resistance equals destruction."

Godsend whirled around, intent on sealing himself inside the ship; instead, he slammed directly into Nub and Contentious who were running up from behind. The general hung his head. "Young lady," he told the attendant, "if it were not for the presence of these unarmed comrades behind me, I would make my last defiant act one in which I bare-handedly thrashed you and your entire platoon of miscreants into a state of swooning insensibility."

"Then you agree to submit?" asked the attendant.

"I would prefer to label it a tactical yielding."

"I can't believe it," said Nub, "we've been taken prisoner by a parking attendant."

Godsend squared his shoulders, holding his head high. "Surrender with dignity is never shameful," he explained as they were led away.

"Yeah, but a parking attendant," complained Nub.

"Now, now, little Niblet," said Godsend, "do not withhold credit to your adversary where it's due; obviously this one's quite crafty. And do not despise her for a lack of rank—remember from what lowly state you once arose."

"Yes, of course you're right," replied Nub. "How pretentious of me; she did a fine job and got the jump on us fair and square."

"Now you're talking like a true gentleman warrior," said Godsend. "I'm proud of you, Corporal."

Nub blushed, standing a little straighter himself as they marched.

"How about we save the award ceremony for later, okay?" said Contentious. "The truth is the parking attendant just fed you your own underwear. How about we just figure out what to do now."

"A fine suggestion, Royal Private," Godsend said with a resolute air. "Free or captive, a soldier's duty is never done. And escape is a prisoner's first priority. We'll begin planning as soon as we arrive at our new location."

"General," said Nub thoughtfully, "you're a great man."

"Yes, I am, Nub," Godsend replied as he stepped into the elevator that would take them to the detention level. "Yes, I am."

Chapter Twenty-Four
Two Queens and a Broken Heart

On the other side of the Crossroads, Skippy Dodge and Wet Lakeland were having little success in their search for clues; right now, they were conversing with a card dealer in one of the city's more posh casinos.

"We are all happy here," the dealer said cheerfully, "I do not understand why you think we would not be happy."

"I know you're all happy here," said Skippy, "you're all crazy, jolly, happy here; I'm not arguing that. I'm trying to find a girl who might just possibly be unhappy because she was kidnapped, okay? Can any of you grinning gargoyles understand that?"

The dealer's beaming smile disappeared. "We don't know anything about kidnappings here. I suggest you seek your diversions elsewhere." His smile quickly reappeared. "Thank you and have a happy day."

"Yeah," rumbled Skippy, walking away, "have a stinking, rotten, happy, day yourself."

Outside on the street, Wet looked disappointedly at Skippy. "I don't get it, Skippy. Seems like these young folks are trying so hard to be friendly these days, it's making them just plain dumb. No common sense anymore, I say."

"Friendly as a bunion on a sore foot," said Skippy. "Something's wrong here. This place was always pretty sleazy but this is weird. It's like everybody's personalities have been erased. I'm not ready to give up yet, though. There's one more place we can try; it's an old pilot's hangout not far from here. We may be able to get a straight answer there."

"Let's try it," said Wet as they started down the bustling street.

They didn't notice the shadowy figure that trailed along behind them, or the ground skimmer that weaved through traffic staying just out of their sight.

Near the end of the block their shadowy pursuer gave a signal and instantly the crowds parted, leaving Skippy and Wet isolated on the walkway. The ground skimmer came crashing onto the path, zapping them with an Enfeeblement Ray that allowed its two victims to be easily pulled inside. Moments later a blast from the skimmer's roto-boosters sent the vehicle shooting down the street to an unknown destination.

"What's the big deal?" raged Skippy, fighting against the Enfeeblement Ray's effects that kept most of his body useless.

"Good afternoon," spoke one of the Crossroads' security officers next to him. "Please relax, our ride, and the debilitating numbness you feel, will last only momentarily. Then you will have the pleasure of meeting our queen."

"Great, how's my hair?" snarled Skippy.

"Free taxi service and visits to royalty," said Wet. "Boy, these kids are nice. Too bad they're so dumb."

A short time later the skimmer screeched to a halt inside a dark, cavernous parking garage. Skippy and Wet were put on carts and hauled into an elevator; after a quick trip to the top of the Crossroads highest tower, they entered a huge, ornately furnished penthouse. In the center of the apartment, a long banquet table was laden with an array of the finest foods available anywhere in the universe; a man and woman dined at each end.

Before anyone could speak, something rose from under the feet of the woman. It flew straight toward Skippy and Wet.

"Stop, Meat!" the woman commanded. Immediately the creature stopped where it was, floating lazily in the air.

"You will have to forgive my pet, Meat," the woman apologized as Skippy stared at the slimy, pulsating ball of shapeless flesh and wiggling tentacles. "He is easily excitable and becomes overly curious when visitors arrive."

"He looks like he could become a little overly vicious too," said Skippy.

"Not really," replied the woman. "His brain quit functioning years ago and he's blind in his only eye."

"Gee, does he bite?" Wet asked, reaching out to pat the creature.

"No, don't!" shouted the woman. "He has no mouth, but his tentacles carry an electrical current that can burn a man down to ashes in seconds. As I said, though, he is more curious than anything."

"Well, that's all really heartwarming," said Skippy, "but I doubt you brought us here just to expound on the qualities of your adorable pet. Who's black nightmare are you?"

The woman threw back her head. "I'm Donna Dodge, Queen of the Crossroads."

Skippy's jaw dropped. "Donna!" he gasped.

Dressed in a black mini-skirt, high-heels, and a long red cape, this wasn't the Donna that Skippy remembered. The hardened, make-up layered features of her face betrayed shock at the sight of her long-lost husband—but only momentarily. She quickly regained the callous confidence of her cold demeanor.

"Skippy Dodge, still alive; I should have known you'd still be scraping around out there."

Skippy's face went slack with disbelief. "Donna...you've changed. I...I sure missed you."

"I'll bet you did."

The man at the table stood up now. "Aren't you going to introduce us, Dee?" he asked in a soft voice that slurred his words into a whispery hiss.

"Of course, dear," said Donna. "Skippy, this is my faithful husband and business partner Donny Beautiful."

"Hi," rumbled Skippy, glaring at the man in the white jumpsuit.

"Greetings to you, old bird," grinned Donny, his perfectly smooth and sculptured face revealing more teeth than Skippy had ever seen in a human mouth. "I've heard so much about you. It's truly a pleasure to meet—at least the antiquated version—of the great Skippy Dodge."

Skippy ignored Donny completely. "Why did you bring us here?" he asked Donna.

Donna sat down in an overstuffed lounger. "I got word someone was sneaking around the Crossroads asking a lot of questions about a missing woman. That doesn't win many friends around here."

"Really? I'm surprised not since everyone seems so happy these days."

"Real good kids you got here," said Wet.

"And why shouldn't they be happy? I run a tight operation. Everyone here is treated fairly."

"Try again," Skippy demanded. "What's your scam? You're different, this place is different, the whole lousy joint is like a creep house."

Donna leapt up. "Don't come back to me fifteen years late, complaining about what I've become. I've built a business for myself, got a husband who does everything I tell him—"

"Thank you, darling," sniffed Donny, sipping from his drink.

"—and I've got workers, loyal workers, who are glad to be here. This is my life now."

"I'm not buying it. Those people aren't happy to be here, they're practically comatose. What are you hiding?"

Donny Beautiful quickly swallowed the last of his drink. "Brain chips, old man, brain chips. Very simple; cost effective."

"Now you've spilled it!" shouted Donna, slapping Donny. "Go sit down."

"Sorry, dear," moaned Donny, going for another drink.

"What's wrong with you?" exclaimed Skippy. "You've put brain chips in these people's heads so you can control their minds?"

"I have to survive somehow. I can't afford to staff this place any other way; employee benefits and insurance are killing me. And don't even get me started on that new chain of anti-gravity bowling alleys popping up in every other galaxy; you wouldn't believe what they're willing to pay their people."

"So you steal your employees' ability to think?"

Donna shook her head, looking at the floor. "This is really funny, you acting like you care what I'm doing all these years later."

"What are you talking about? I do care."

"You didn't care too much what happened to me all those years ago when you took off to save the galaxy."

"More than once," added Wet.

"More than once," Donna repeated, spitting out the words.

Skippy shook his head. "Are you seriously telling me you're mad because I saved the galaxy?"

"I'm mad because you didn't save the galaxy for me—or for anybody else. It was all for you, for Skippy Dodge, the great Galaxy Saver. Everyone's idol."

"I was fighting for freedom."

"Don't make me laugh."

"What did you want me to do? Not fight?"

Donna snatched Donny's drink away from him, gulping it down herself. "Sure, you had to fight, of course you did, you were the cool hero-guy. But did you ever think about me? I had to fight too—I had to fight to make it on my own. And that's exactly what I ended up doing. I crawled and scratched for years. You have no idea what I went through to get to this level of corporate leadership. Now I'm on top and you don't like it."

"It wasn't easy leaving you," said Skippy, the fire in his voice gone now, "but I believed in what I was doing."

"Yeah, you always had something to believe in, didn't you? As long as it got your name broadcast as a great man. I suppose that's part of the reason why you came here today; the great Skippy Dodge returns on a benevolent mission to save a missing princess. That would look good added to the legacy. Well, none of that matters now—you know too much. My guards will be escorting you and your friend to the edge of the city where you'll accidentally fall into the Aqua-thite basin; it happens from time to time."

"But I can't swim," said Wet.

"Shut-up," said Skippy.

"Really it won't be that bad, old shoe," clucked Donny Beautiful, "you'll probably disintegrate before you drown."

"Shut-up," said Donna.

Skippy glared at the Crossroads queen. "You know me, Donna, I'll fight my way out of here if I have to and I'll warn you not to stand in my way."

Donna chuckled. "Skippy, from the looks of you these days you couldn't fight your way through an open screen door. Besides, I doubt you're completely over the effects of the Enfeeblement Ray, so, please, just shuffle on out of here before you embarrass yourself."

Attempting to move, Skippy realized Donna was right, he and Wet could barely keep their balance as the security guards prodded them into the hall.

"Pleasure to make your salty acquaintance," Donny Beautiful called out perkily as the door slammed shut.

Skippy shuffled down the hallway, grief and frustration finally overcoming him. He spun around, clenching his fists. "Donna, maybe what I did was all for myself, but I never meant for all this to happen! I never meant for you to become a corrupt space resort manager!"

"Continue moving forward," ordered the security captain, "and please don't disturb us with another outburst. Instead, we suggest you consider happiness as a primary emotion."

"I kinda like him the way he is," said Holly Blackguard as she emerged from around the corner. She was packing a deadly five-barreled heat blaster in her hand. "I'll be taking over from here. You dopes get lost."

"But these are our prisoners," said the guard captain.

"Well, they're my prisoners now, so drop your shooters and take off."

"This is rather unpleasant," said one of the guards as the detachment laid down their weapons and walked away.

"They'll alert others," said Skippy.

"We'll be gone by then," Holly replied. "Anyway, I couldn't stand to shoot them."

"Couldn't stand to shoot them; when did you develop a conscious?" said Skippy. "What's come over you? And how'd you get here, anyway?"

"Godsend and the others were captured soon after we landed. I escaped from the storage closet and wandered the streets until I happened to see you get kidnapped. After I hijacked a taxi to follow you, I clobbered a guard to get this gun. I heard your whole conversation with Donna from out here."

"I'm sure you got some big laughs from that," said Skippy, turning to face the wall.

"No, I didn't get any laughs. But I think I finally understand what you've been trying to tell me."

"You're still not making any sense," said Skippy.

"Sure I am; just listen to me for once, will you?" Holly closed her eyes, embarrassed at what she had to say. "I've been an evil woman, Skippy, as rotten as they come; I see it now. But what has it gained me? What will it ever gain me? I could run the entire universe and end up only kissing myself in the dark. I suppose you—and Donna—are the only ones that could teach me that."

"What in the world are you getting at?" asked Skippy.

Holly sighed. "Skippy, you're rough and tough, a real hard-boil, I know that. But you've got a heart under all that guff, a real heart, a heart I can understand, and, well, Skippy, I just want you to know—I love you. There, I said it, and it's true. I think I've loved you since I met you. And I know I could never begin to replace Donna, I couldn't even try, but if you'll have me, I'll be your queen."

"But you said you loved Braker Ford."

Holly shook her head. "For all the wrong reasons, I mean, Braker's a great guy, sure, but let's face it, I was attracted to Braker because I thought he was a killer deep down inside. But that's all so wrong. I'm sick of all that now. I want to change. I don't want to end up like Donna. I want to start over—with you." Holly's big, dark eyes swelled with tears. "Skippy, you're a grumpy middle-aged space hero, and I'm a young, evil space queen, but together, maybe we can make each other better. So, you gotta tell me, Skip—will you have me?"

Skippy kissed the water queen on the forehead. "Little lady, I'll let you in on a secret. You really are as rotten as they come. But it never bothered me half as bad as I let on." His hand enclosed around hers. "I love you too, kid. I got a feeling we're both opposite sides of the same coin. You're right—we belong together. Now let's go find the others and start our lives over."

The couple hurried down the hall while Wet followed along behind, shaking his head. "I guess it don't matter how old you get," he said to himself, "there are just some things you aren't ever going to see coming."

Chapter Twenty-Five
Big Trouble, No Relief

Chuck Weasel guided his spaceship into the traffic lanes leading to the Crossroads of the Universe.

"Take a look at the rest of your life," he taunted Princess Babe, who slumped behind him.

"I'll try to make the best of what's given me," Babe responded.

Kate Starbrand shouted at Babe from across the cockpit. "You will not, you rich brat! You'll be miserable just like you deserve. You always try to act like you have it so together."

"Kate, you're only hurting yourself by being so unpleasant, let's be friends instead."

"You're not so beautiful," sneered Kate.

"Alright, knock it off," said Chuck as the craft landed. "I'm trying to plan a crime here."

"Chuck," J.J. pleaded, "you've got to believe me, you're heading for a disaster. There are some very dangerous folks after this princess."

Chuck snorted. "You want to talk about dangerous folks? No one is more dangerous than Mike Tomorrow. I'm big; I'm a star;

I'm an exploding ball of gas. Let me tell you something Mr. I-can't-do-anything-better-than-sell-used-spaceships, I've got this whole thing figured out. I'm gonna be rich while you and little Miss Princess are gonna be zombies!" He slapped J.J. in the face and whirled toward Kate. "Let's go, sweets, time's wasting."

Soon the entire, miserable party was piling out of the ship.

****

Far above in the darkness of deep space, another group of mismatched travelers were about to join the scene. Braker Ford and his would-be rescuers were approaching the Crossroads in the rollicking starship *Rued Star One*.

"What's going on out there?" groaned Braker from his position against the windshield. "Where'd all the traffic come from?" The trucker was watching the endless stream of spacecraft that rushed past them.

"I think we've just entered the toll lanes," confessed Charlie Rued, turning down the ear-splitting rock music coursing through the *Rued Star*'s speaker system.

"Great, just what we need," said Braker, "backed-up traffic and expensive tolls. I hope you've got a toll card."

"I got one in the ash tray, but I can't reach it," explained Rued, trying to stretch his hand over the pile of bodies crammed into his tiny craft.

"I'll get it," said Johnny Comet, reaching into the tray. A second later his hand was covered with a greenish-brown goo. "Oh, gross, what is this stuff?" he cried.

"Don't worry," said Rued, "that's just something I spilled last year."

"You're sick."

"Did you get the card?" sighed Braker.

"No, and I'm not reaching in there again," coughed Johnny, trying not to throw up.

"So, what do we do now?" asked Rued.

"Turn around, just get out of the lane!" Braker shouted. But it was too late—they were already next in line at the floating tollbooth.

Rued smiled unhappily at the robotic toll-taker as its communicator electro-arm attached itself to the ship.

"Toll card, please," spoke the robot.

"Aah, got the card, can't reach it," said Rued.

"Toll card, please."

"I can't reach it. Spilled my lunch."

"Toll card, please."

"I can't reach it..."

"Toll card, please."

"Really, I spilled my lunch."

"Toll card, please."

"I can't reach it."

"Toll card, please."

"It's in the ash tray, stupid machine! I spilled my stupid lunch on it, now I can't reach it!"

"No card. Prepare to be escorted to the security platform."

"I got a card."

"Toll card, please."

"I can't reach it."

"Toll card, please."

"I told you, I can't reach it."

"Prepare to be escorted to the security platform."

253

"Here's my card, stupid machine!" shouted Rued, slamming on his turbo-boosters and shooting past the booth, the severed electro-arm still dangling from his ship.

Instantly the flashing lights of four nearby security ships surrounded the *Rued Star*.

"What'd you do that for?" exclaimed Braker as demands for their surrender blared through the voice box.

"That's my style," said Rued.

"I'm gonna pound you!" roared Knothead.

"Here we go," said Jodo, "trapped by police. I'll fight. Don't like uniforms. My feet hurt."

The screaming security vessels demanded all other spacecraft out of the way, forcing the *Rued Star* through a suddenly vacant portal in the bubble dome surrounding The Spaceman's Paradise; inside the dome, they escorted the *Rued Star* toward a small detention base on the nearest landing platform.

"See, my style works," said Rued. "We got a parking spot and didn't even have to pay the toll."

"You're an idiot," said Braker.

They had almost touched down when Wayne noticed a group of sightseers on a nearby terrace. "Hey, Braker," said the farmer, his face mashed tightly against the windshield. "Look down there. Them folk look familiar!"

Braker rolled his eyes toward four tiny figures waiting for an elevator to the markets below.

"That looks like Chuck Weasel and Babe!" the trucker exclaimed. "It is! It's Babe! It really is! Rued take us down!"

"But, Braker, the security ships," said Wayne. "Them law ponies don't want no more misbehavin', that's fer shore."

"Forget the ships! Ditch 'em, Rued! Hurry!"

Rued was more than happy to comply. With an eager snort, he rolled his ship to the side, slipping between the two closest vessels and diving beneath the leaders.

"Good going!" said Braker. "Now all we've got to do is swoop down and pick up Babe; we can explain everything to the security guys once she's safe with us. You can slow down now, Rued."

Rued looked vacantly toward Braker, his cheeks trembling from the violent pulse of the overcharged engines.

"Rued, I said slow down! Chuck's right below us; just bring us in for the landing!"

"Hang on, this is always the hard part!" Rued cried, finally getting his voice back.

"Hey, Braker, ain't that funny," said Wayne, "Rued sounds just like you when you're tryin' to land a ship."

"Shut up, Wayne!" said Braker.

The *Rued Star* was rocketing toward the terrace at a speed that made landing impossible; Rued pulled up at the last second, the scalding breeze of his engines knocking Chuck Weasel and every other patron on the platform off their feet. Then, as the unwavering security ships continued closing in, and everyone in the *Rued Star's* cockpit shouted frenzied instructions, the panicking Rued circled around for another attempt. This time though he was not only coming in faster, but also unintentionally far below the intended platform. Three levels too low, he careened through row after row of unoccupied starships until ramming to a stop against the elevator shaft at the far end of the platform.

"Not so bad," said Rued.

"Hey, I'm used to it," said Wayne as he and Braker both threw off the ship's fragmented canopy.

On the uppermost platform, Chuck Weasel and his startled companions had no idea as to the reason for the sudden cataclysm, but not waiting for answers, Chuck slung Babe across his shoulder and made a run for the stairs. Kate did likewise, heaving J.J. onto her back as she followed close behind. Above them, more security ships arrived on the scene, circling in utter astonishment.

"This is going to cost you," Rued told Braker as he surveyed the damage to his mangled ship.

"Bill me later!" said Braker. He pointed toward the stairway. "That's the only way down now that you blew out the elevator. We've got to get to it before Chuck and Kate!" The trucker jumped out of the *Rued Star* followed by the others. He started toward the upper stairway, then dropped to the pavement. "Leg, leg!" he screamed in agony.

"What is it, Braker? What's wrong?" shouted Wayne.

"Leg's asleep," groaned Braker. "It's killing me. I'll never make it up the stairs!"

"Boy, oh boy," said Wayne, "it couldn't get any hotter if'n we were slurpin' on chili pepper lollipops."

****

Back in the prison sector, Nub Niblet and Princess Contentious watched as General Godsend paced their cell.

"Have you thought of a plan yet, General?" Nub asked with an expectant grin.

"Nub, I always have a plan, in fact I have several; my task at the moment is to mentally file through them and select the one most perfect for this situation."

"I knew it!" shouted Nub, clapping his hands.

The cell door opened. Two guards walked in flanking a man with slicked-back hair and a greasy face. He wore a long, white operating gown, its pockets crammed with sharp instruments.

"All smile," commanded the guards. "The doctor has arrived."

"Smile this," said Contentious, kicking the closest guard in the shin.

"Calmness, everyone, calmness," said the doctor in a soft, warbling voice. "Allow me to introduce myself, I'm Doctor David Birth, Chief Surgeon of the Crossroads. I'll be the physician attending to you today. And how is everyone this afternoon?"

General Godsend stepped forward. "Sometimes I get these incredible headaches that feel like someone is pushing a drill into my brain—but then the tormenting voices come back and I realize everything is okay."

David Birth studied the man before him. "What's your name, sir?"

"I'm General Roger Godsend. Some call me the Intergalactic Madman, but in reality, I'm the leader of the Accountant Army of Revolution."

"That's me," grinned Nub, coming to attention.

David Birth nodded slowly. "Yes, very compelling, and the beautiful young girl—what's her name?"

"'A poke in the eyes', if you come any closer," piped up Contentious.

David Birth laughed quietly. "Gentleness before violence, my dear, silence before fury." He quickly exited the cell, calling over his shoulder to the guards— "We shall do the woman first, gentlemen. The Armies of Revolution can wait."

Before anyone could react, the guards yanked Contentious from the cell, locking the door behind them.

As the door clanged shut, Nub raced around the room. "General, that mad scientist is going to do something terrible to poor Contentious. We've got to rescue her right away."

"Precisely right," replied Godsend, reaching into his mouth to pull out a small silver object.

"What is that, General?"

"It's my micro-voice box I keep hidden under a false tooth just for emergencies. I think I'll call my good friend, Stedman T. Boyle, time-traveler. He should be able to get us out of here." Godsend fidgeted with the tiny instrument. "Blast myself!" he finally exclaimed. "I always forget to replace the batteries."

Nub threw up his hands, circling impatiently. "What now, General?"

Godsend pulled the glove from his left hand, revealing his index finger to be false. He popped off the top. "This is Chlorium Monotron 638," he explained, shaking out a yellow powder into his other hand. "Its explosive energies come unleashed when it makes contact with metal. It should create a huge explosion that will blow this door completely away."

"General, I love the idea, but I'm sure you've considered that the explosion will probably blow us away along with the door."

Godsend poured the powder back into his finger, closed the top and put his glove back on.

"There's still got to be a way out of here," said Nub.

Godsend sat down on a bench, yanked off his boot and unscrewed his right foot. Reaching up into his hollow leg he retrieved what looked like a small pistol.

"Melt Ray," he announced.

"Perfect!" shouted Nub, dancing around the room. "But, sir, you must be half hollow from the looks of things."

258

"Yes, it's true, Nub," confessed the General, "but never forget—half a Godsend is better than none."

****

On the other side of the city an unhappy guard rushed into Donna Dodge's throne room. "My Queen," he cried, "Skippy Dodge and his companion have escaped—"

"Oh, my heart, protect me, Donna," blurted Donny Beautiful.

"Pipe down," scolded Donna. "Guard, continue."

"The report is that Skippy escaped with the help of a mystery woman. We don't know where they are, but we have word of a ghastly disturbance taking place on landing platform nine with a crashed spaceship and all kinds of commotion. It could be the escapees. Attending security ships are circling the area awaiting your command."

Donna stood up from her throne, snatching her cape from a nearby sofa. "Listen carefully, tell the security ships to continue their holding pattern. Post all other guard units on alert. They are to make no definite action until I arrive."

"Yes, Queen."

Donna flung the cloak around her shoulders. "Donny!"

"Yes, dear," responded Mr. Beautiful, pouring himself yet another drink of blue liquid.

"Go downstairs and prepare my personal craft. I want you to drive me to platform nine. Skippy Dodge will regret this awful day." The Queen of the Crossroads stormed out of the throne room followed by her faithful pet, Meat.

"Oh, my heart," gasped Donny Beautiful, gulping down his drink. "Oh, my heart."

Chapter Twenty-Six
Doomed to Death

Finally arriving to what was quickly becoming a major conflict, Dr. Wilde's fleet of lab buses closed in on The Spaceman's Paradise. The *Flying Electric Laboratory* led the procession, smashing through the galactic tollbooths before bullying its way through a portal in the bubble canopy. Searching for a parking space, one of the *Laboratory's* navigators noticed something on the space telescope.

"Dr. Wilde, you had better come see this," announced the technician. "It looks like they're having some kind of a spaceship festival down there; maybe a demolition derby—there's a crowd of people, smashed up spaceships, and lots of smoke and fireworks."

Dr. Wilde stomped over; grabbing the scope, he was astonished to see a highly magnified image of the havoc now engulfing the Crossroads' landing platform.

"This is no demolition derby, you beefhead!" screamed the doctor. "It's the princess! That disgusting, moronic interloper

Braker Ford is fighting to get her back. We must—" Dr. Wilde stopped in mid-sentence. He put his fingers to his lips, breathing deeply. "—we must be very, very careful. We cannot afford another mistake this time.

"Pilots, have our fleet of buses spread out across the city to avoid early detection. Only the *Laboratory* shall approach the platform. But we must wait for the perfect moment."

Meanwhile, Braker and his band of rescuers—Wayne, Johnny Comet, Knothead, Vigor (who was now carrying Braker and his tingling leg), and the rest of the moon-scapers had succeeded in cutting off Chuck's stairway escape route. The bandit had no choice but to turn around and take his contraband back to where they had just come from; back on the top platform, Chuck raced past startled bystanders until finally cornered against the railing. Undaunted, the Cosmic Bandit turned, already fashioning a hasty bargain that he hoped might prevent a costly last stand.

"Well, well, if it isn't the true-hearted space trucker and his devoted companions, all come back to retrieve the beloved princess," he said, leaning casually against the rail. "Come on, I'll make a deal with you. If you guys won't come clean with what this little jewel's really worth, how about we just cash her in here and all walk away with a cool pay-off we can all just divide up."

Braker winced. "We're not making any deals with you."

"Hey, it's a lot better than fighting it out," said Chuck, twirling his gun.

"Look, Weasel, I love that princess and I'm getting her back, whatever it takes!"

"It's gonna take you and a lot of your friends getting hurt," said Chuck. "My pistol is at full power."

"Make a deal, any kind of deal!" said J.J., still hanging from Kate Starbrand's shoulder.

"Yes, make the deal, Braker," said Babe, still hanging from Chuck's shoulder. "I don't want you or any of your friends hurt over me."

"No deals!" Braker insisted.

"That's real tough talk coming from a guy snuggled in the arms of a moon monster," snickered Chuck.

Braker, suddenly realizing he was still being cradled by Vigor, hurriedly ordered to be placed back on his feet.

"Haw, haw," Chuck scoffed. "Hey, at least you'll die standing. Any last words?"

"Please, sir," Vigor interjected, polite as ever, "I don't know why you are so angry at my friend, but he is my only friend. If you shoot him, then I'll be alone again. And then I would be very sad. And then I would have to give you a squeeze you'd never forget."

Chuck burst out in cruel, mocking laughter. "Oh, is ugly blob monster going to give me a big scary hug? Well, watch this, tubby. I'll air out your friend and then trim some size off you."

As Chuck raised his pistol, Vigor bounded forward with a tremendous roar. Tearing Babe from Chuck's shoulder, he seized the bandit in his gigantic arms and pressed him into a tiny ball. Then, with a great heave, Vigor pitched the frothy blister far away. The grotesquely compact body sailed across the expanse before bouncing off the bubble dome and falling into the Aqua-thite below.

Everyone was frozen in shock except for Kate Starbrand—before the nugget-sized version of Chuck Weasel had even disappeared from sight, she had grabbed his gun from the ground and sent a laser blast through Babe's delicate, twisting body. The princess was slammed onto the concrete, flames whipping from the hole in her side.

Braker Ford dropped to his knees. "You've killed her! You've killed Princess Babe!"

"And your cuddly moon monster just turned my boyfriend into an oily peanut, so good riddance," said Kate. "Now back off or you'll get the same as your precious debutante. You lousy cowards, ganging up on a defenseless couple like Chuck and myself; you don't deserve a princess. I always had more finesse than that prissy sugar cube ever had, anyway." She waved her gun at the group, using it to gain access to the stairway. "Now spread out, you bunch of slobs; I'm getting out of here. Chuck's problem was thinking he could be as good a negotiator as he was a thief. Well, I'm not making that mistake. I know when to quit a scene. I've got street smarts; that's enough to take care of myself." From there she ran down a dozen flights of stairs before finding another elevator that brought her to the city streets below.

Hurrying across a busy intersection, she located a security ship parked by the corner; tossing her gun aside she flung herself onto the guard standing nearby.

"Help me, help me!" she exclaimed. "Please, there are men up above at the top of the platforms; they threw a man over the side and shot a woman! Now they're trying to kill me. Take me away. They're awful."

"Climb in," offered the guard. "I'll take you to our laboratories. Our scientists will see to it that you're made quite happy here."

"Thank you, oh, thank you," blubbered Kate with self-satisfaction as the last half of the galaxy's most notorious crime team was lifted into the sky and toward an unexpected fate.

263

Back on the platform, Wayne was the first rescuer to inspect the princess. "Braker, Babe's shot up pretty bad, that's for sure, but she ain't dead by any means. You're more confused than a blind badger runnin' backward up a downhill road. You're all messed up."

Braker's joy at the news was quickly overshadowed by the thundering arrival of the *Flying Electric Laboratory*. Dr. Wilde, having witnessed Babe's apparent murder through his space telescope, lost no time in dropping onto the scene; the ship hadn't even fully landed when Dr. Wilde came racing down the gangplank followed by Bullmack and a team of conceited lab assistants.

"You squirming bag of idiots!" the scientist shouted, pointing toward Braker and the others. "Your incompetent bungling has managed to get the princess shot! Apparently, you don't care that her death would seal my fate with Lord Preposterous!"

"Wow, that might be the most out of touch statement I've ever heard," groaned Johnny Comet.

"At least he's a doctor," said Wayne. "Maybe he can help Babe."

"A maniac doctor is more like it," growled Knothead. "If this old sawbones gets ahold of her, she's likely to end up barking like a dog."

Dr. Wilde raced up to Knothead, his raging face tucked directly beneath the barbarian's bristly chin. "You brainless space amoeba, you floating astro-germ, your stupid barbarian insults are meaningless—don't you realize that you and all your bobble-witted friends are now my prisoners? I will restore the princess to health while you losers sit helpless in the *Flying Laboratory's* confinement cells. And if you don't behave Bullmack will beat you senseless!"

"That's right," nodded Bullmack, "I can be pretty mean sometimes."

"Enough, Bullmack! I will have no fraternizing with the prisoners."

"But I was just threatening them, I was just—"

"Silence! Take them away!"

"Please, just help Babe!" Braker pleaded as he and the others were marched into the *Flying Laboratory*.

Dr. Wilde and Bullmack both looked down at the unconscious princess. Kneeling beside her, Dr. Wilde checked for signs of life. "Still live—but just barely. This looks like a job for the Parametric Rejuvenation Disc. Bullmack, take this woman to the ship's Rejuvenation Room and place her on the Disc."

Bullmack clapped his hands with glee. "The Disc, the Disc. Whee, I love the Disc!"

Trembling with excitement, the robot scooped Babe up and raced into the *Flying Laboratory*. Dr. Wilde was close behind as Bullmack burst into the Rejuvenation Room, tossing Babe onto what looked like a giant circular steel table wrapped with blinking lights.

"Stand back!" Dr. Wilde ordered as he strapped Babe to the table. "The Disc is about to spin."

"Can I ride it next, Master?" Bullmack asked.

"No, now quit interrupting."

The Rejuvenation Disc began humming as its speed increased, revolving faster and faster until Babe was nothing more than an intense blur.

Bullmack was enthralled. "Is the lady having fun spinning, Master?"

"No, she is not having fun, you big mistake. The Disc is not a toy, it is a highly sophisticated medical instrument that you could never even begin to understand."

"Yes, Master, but the Disc is still my friend. Did you know that, Master? The Disc is my friend. My good, old friend. My very, very good, old friend, the Disc is."

"No, it's not!" screamed Dr. Wilde. "The Disc is not your friend. The disc can't even think, and neither can you! Go do something useful; go guard the prisoners and make sure they don't escape."

"Yes, Master," replied Bullmack, sauntering jauntily off.

With Bullmack gone, Dr. Wilde went back to studying the Disc's control panel. Behind him a new figure entered the room; it was a lab technician wearing full operating gear and a large germ mask.

"How is the patient doing?" the man asked flatly.

"Very well, very well," Dr. Wilde murmured, not bothering to turn around. "She's almost completely healed. Go inform the pilots we're ready to lift off."

"I don't believe we shall be departing so soon," the technician replied. "Step away from the machine."

"What is this?" exclaimed Dr. Wilde, spinning around to find a laser gun pointed at his chest.

"I'll be taking over from here," said the technician.

"There's only one man who would speak to me with such arrogance!" said Dr. Wilde, ripping the germ mask from his adversary's face.

With his mask now gone, the gunman slipped out of his operating gown, revealing himself to be garbed in a much more vibrant ensemble than his simple outer robes would suggest. The double-faced cashmere jacket, fitted suede pants, and ruffle-topped leather knee boots left no doubt—the doctor was staring into the eyes of his arch-enemy—Prince Tony, the Glamour Boy of Gunberry!

Chapter Twenty-Seven
Falling into Chaos

Deep in the heart of the Crossroads detention center, General Roger Godsend and Nub Niblet had succeeded in melting through their prison door thanks to the general's secret melt ray and were now dodging guard patrols as they searched for Princess Contentious.

Making their way to the medical aid station at the far end of the detention center, they found a narrow, black door marked as the entrance to Dr. David Birth's examination ward. What lay beyond they could only wonder.

"Now what, General?" Nub asked as he and his commanding officer crouched beside the door. "Princess Contentious must be in there."

"Of course she is, Nub, and that is why we must make our attack at once."

"But, General, we don't have any weapons."

Roger Godsend leaned back against the wall, closed his eyes, and smiled. "Little Niblet, how much you still must learn about the art of warfare. This is a rescue type of attack; weapons are not necessary. All we have to do is get in, get the girl, and get out. Surprise is our key, speed our weapon."

"Yes, sir, General," grinned Nub, "surprise is our key. I wish I could have thought of that."

"Someday maybe you will, Nub. But for now, it's on to glory; we haven't a second to waste. The order is attack!"

A single, combined kick easily smashed the door open, and the two soldiers stormed inside to the sound of their own exhilarated double war-whoop. A moment later, the ecstatic rescuers screeched to a dumbfounded halt—a squad of gun-wielding security guards was already awaiting them just within the threshold.

"Welcome!" said David Birth, stepping out from behind the guards. "We've been expecting you. Come in, please."

Nub shook his head in disbelief. "General," he said thoughtfully, after regaining his ability to speak, "you were right, surprise really is a great tactic."

"Yes," Godsend replied, slouching with disappointment, "unfortunately it's also a very popular one."

"Have a seat, gentlemen," continued David Birth. "When I heard you had released yourselves earlier, I suspected you would be coming here. I certainly don't blame you; this is much more interesting than being in that drab cell." As he was speaking, he brought the gagged and handcuffed Princess Contentious out from behind a curtain, shoving her into a metal chair in the center of the room. "I postponed the operation until you could arrive; I thought you might enjoy watching since you are next on the list. Knowledge through education, you know. But enough chitchat, let's begin, shall we?"

David Birth ignited a red laser scalpel and signaled for Contentious to be strapped into her seat.

"General, do something!" Nub whispered as guards approached the princess.

General Godsend glanced around the room, his eyes darting wildly.

"Doctor Birth?" he finally exclaimed.

"Yes, Mr. Godsend," answered the surgeon.

"That's General."

"My apologies; General."

"I was just wondering…um…what exactly is the procedure you're about to perform?"

"Oh, pardon me, sometimes I can be so absent-minded. Enlightenment brings pleasure, of course. Forgive me." The doctor pulled a small micro-chip from his pocket. "This is the Z-2 Contemplation Dispensator. Once attached to the base of the patient's skull it will impair her mind until she is incapable of developing any independent judgments. She will then be trained to do our biding, whatever it may be; quite a remarkable little tool."

"And we're going to get these too?" Godsend gulped.

"Yes, or at least one similar to it. You see, no two minds are alike; each chip must be custom made after a thorough computer scan of each patient's individual brain waves. That way we ensure proper behavior."

"Incredible. May I see it?" Godsend asked.

"So inquisitive; that's very healthy," commented the surgeon. "Of course, study it all you want. I'm an admirer of these little gems myself."

David Birth handed the chip to Godsend who looked it over carefully before popping it into his mouth and swallowing it down.

"Ha, ha!" the general laughed. "I've eaten your chip, you malevolent dissector; now free the girl, I've spoiled your plan!"

"That's the General for ya!" said Nub.

David Birth's eyes narrowed. "I see you have only feigned interest in the Z-2 Contemplation Dispensator." The doctor's voice grew more chilling. "Your attempt at resistance has only delayed the inevitable. You shall see that the chip will be quite simple to retrieve. Guards, hold him."

David Birth brought the glowing laser scalpel closer to Godsend's mid-section.

"Nub, help!" Godsend cried. "These cranks are going to split me open!"

"No problem, General!" shouted Nub, leaping up to send a brutal punch into his commanding officer's belly. "See, doctor," he grinned, continuing to pound on Godsend's quivering stomach, "a few good wallops in the old bread-basket and that chip will come right back out."

"That's not exactly what I had in mind!" wheezed Godsend.

David Birth and his guards stepped back, watching in amazement as Nub continued slugging away at the stumbling and groaning general.

"Cease this madness!" David Birth finally shouted. "Guards, eliminate them. I must get the chip; I have many more patients to see today."

Godsend and Nub both jerked upright as the guards raised their weapons. At that moment Princess Contentious shot out of her seat and head-butted David Birth, sending him careening into the nearest guards.

"Now we've got them, Nub, grab a gun!" Godsend ordered as weapons scattered across the floor.

Nub snagged a rifle while Godsend grabbed a pair of pistols; in an instant both sides were blazing away as the newly armed Army of Revolution traded sudden violence with their startled enemies. A berserk storm of unceasing laser fire exploded in every direction.

"Come to me, come to me!" Godsend cried, firing from both hands as he raced around the room, picking off guards at random. "Come receive justice, perverted deviants of science!"

The general made several laps around the ward before stumbling across Nub who was taking cover behind a demolished antitoxin cabinet.

"How goes it, Nub?" Godsend asked breezily.

"Not so good. Don't think I'm going to make it."

"Nub, how dare you say such a thing?"

"General, I've been shot five times."

"No whining in my army, soldier! Now go out and conquer. We're of sturdier stock than that."

"Yes, sir," moaned Nub as the general dashed back into the laser blasts.

Amidst the firing, David Birth made his way to the rear exit. "You can't get out alive!" he shouted to Godsend as he smashed the controls to the steadily closing power door. "I've just released my Purple Poison Gas. All the other doors are jammed, and you'll never make it to this one in time. That'll teach you to mess with public health services!" With a pleased pucker of his lips, the homicidal surgeon ran unhindered into the open hallway.

"It's closing too fast!" Nub cried, watching the remaining security guards making their own hopeless attempt to reach the door.

Godsend looked around quickly, noticing a nearby motorized examination table on wheels. Throwing himself on top, he went rolling forward, working the controls with his feet. "Jump on!" he yelled to Nub while speeding by.

The little soldier leapt aboard; Godsend grabbed Contentious around the waist at the same time, bringing her along for their last-minute salvation ride.

"On freedom's road we fly!" Godsend exclaimed as the trio shot through the doorway.

They continued down the hall, moving with such speed that they overtook the still-running David Birth, pinning him to the front of the bed. With the doctor screaming all the way, they drove onward, never slowing down until they slammed into a wall far down the corridor. The hysterical David Birth was knocked unconscious upon impact, while the others were tossed to the floor.

"Now that's what I call an escape," said Nub, with a satisfied nod.

****

Skippy Dodge, Wet Lakeland, and Holly Blackguard were high above the city, making their way down from Donna's penthouse by way of an old, exterior catwalk that connected the tower to a series of landing platforms; they thought they had gone undetected until a long, luxury sky-sled floated up beside them.

With soundless precision, the gleaming vehicle's convertible top rolled back. Donna Dodge rose from within, leaning over the windshield. Hatred ran rampant across her face. "Did you actually think I wouldn't be able to find you in my own city, Skippy Dodge? We've got unfinished business; you've been my own personal curse for too long. Now I'm going to end it. Do you hear me?"

Skippy continued walking toward the convertible. "Donna, I'm sorry for the past. I never meant to hurt you."

"Stick it in your ear."

"Donna, your bitterness is going to destroy you," Skippy continued. "Please, listen to reason."

"Destroy me?" Donna laughed. "My bitterness is going to destroy you! You're going to pay."

"But we don't have any money!" Wet exclaimed.

Skippy glanced over to see Holly Blackguard drawing her stolen weapon from the folds of her cape.

"Don't worry, I've still got my gun," she whispered.

"I heard that," said Donna, flipping a switch on the dashboard that sent the gun flying from Holly's hand and left it sticking to the magnetized bumper of her sky-sled.

"Donna, just let us go, that's all I ask," pleaded Skippy. "You'll never see us again."

"I know that's a lie as much as you do, Skippy. Now that you know the secret of the Crossroads you won't be able to keep from trying to rescue my poor, defenseless mind-slaves. And that just won't do. No, I think you've had this coming for a long time."

"Ram them!" she ordered, sliding back into her seat as Donny Beautiful slammed on the accelerator and Meat blissfully bounced around on the back cushion.

"Hit the deck!" shouted Skippy, shoving his friends to the steel grating as the roaring sky-sled surged over them.

Barely missing its target, the vehicle crashed through the catwalk's outer railing before swinging around and coming to a jolting stop that left it hovering far above the shimmering Aquathite basin.

"Ouch, Donna, I'm bruised," Donny Beautiful whimpered after whacking his head on the steering wheel.

"Quit whining, toad," snarled Donna, "we're making another run at them. Get going."

"Here they come again!" cried Holly, watching the sled come hurtling back.

"We're doomed," bawled Wet.

The sky-sled rushed closer. It was almost on top of them when its main guidance fin suddenly blew apart. The craft whirled crazily in the air before plunging straight into the poisonous Aquathite with Donna and Donny still inside.

Skippy collapsed exhausted on the catwalk. Holly looked over to see him holding a smoking pistol.

"My gun, that's my gun!" she exclaimed, taking her weapon from Skippy's hand. "How did you get it back?"

"When the sled made its first pass at us, I just waited until the last second and yanked it from the bumper. It was our only chance."

"Sure was, Skippy," sighed Wet, gazing over the railing, "but we're okay now."

As Wet was speaking, Meat came soaring up from below the catwalk. Its giant eye was bulging, its electric tentacles flailing wildly. It was confused and angry, lashing out at anything in its way.

Wet stumbled backward. "Good Meat, good Meat," he purred.

"It can't understand you!" Skippy exclaimed. "It doesn't have a brain!"

"Bad Meat, bad Meat," scolded Wet.

"It does have a brain," said Holly, "it just doesn't work!"

"Whatever!" cried Skippy, narrowly sidestepping a flying tentacle.

Holly was just about to blast the repulsive creature with a heat ray when Meat knocked the pistol out of her grip. Holly fell to her knees, her hand shaking from the brief electrical charge.

"Holly, get back!" Skippy shouted as the monster closed in on the dazed woman.

There was no time for Holly to react; Meat was directly over her. With astonishing speed, it rolled forward, whipping its tentacles downward.

Holly dropped onto her back, her hand brushing against a piece of severed metal railing. Without thinking, she heaved it at the beast. The bar sailed up, cutting all the way through Meat's saggy, pulsating body. The alien deflated with a blast of escaping air and floated lazily back down into the Aqua-thite.

Holly stood up slowly, leaning on Skippy's arm for support as the tired threesome continued down the catwalk. No one spoke for a long time. The day's events carried a heavy impact for all involved. It was a time for quiet, deep reflection.

Finally, Wet spoke. "Gee, Miss Holly," he said with a sigh, "you sure do have a way with animals."

Chapter Twenty-Eight
Braker's Last Chance

In The *Flying Electric Laboratory's* Rejuvenation Room, scientist and prince were preparing for their final showdown.

"My good doctor," said Prince Tony, holding his foe at gunpoint, "it would seem our intriguing game has reached its conclusion. I will now seal the contest by terminating you and reuniting with my beloved Babe."

"I'm not that easy to take down," said Dr. Wilde. "And you forget I can still use my knuckles."

The feisty scientist leapt forward, battering Prince Tony's jaw with a well-executed speed jab. Tony flew backward, his gun skidding into a corner.

Dr. Wilde pressed closer, giving Tony no chance to recover. The prince collapsed onto a counter filled with flaming Q blocks. He grabbed one, tossing it at Dr. Wilde.

"Careful with that," grumbled Dr. Wilde, catching the block. "My laboratory is full of fascinating and dangerous items."

"A detail wholly inconsequential to you now," said Prince Tony, slamming Dr. Wilde into a large metal cabinet.

"Keep away from this machine!" shouted the doctor.

Tony laughed, grabbing Dr. Wilde's face and dribbling it off the cabinet's control panel. The console caved in from the impact, setting off a flashing red light and the wailing of a siren.

"I…I can't move," gasped Prince Tony as he and Dr. Wilde both stood frozen before the machine's red light.

"Of course, you fool; you've just activated my new, experimental Pain Transverser."

"So what?"

"So what?! Our molecules are about to be absorbed into its assimilator vortex from which there is no escape. I told you to be careful."

"Sorry," moaned Prince Tony.

"Oh, how I hate you," Dr. Wilde replied as the two mortal enemies were suddenly sucked together into the machine's intake vent.

With both men now permanently absorbed inside, the siren automatically switched off, plunging the room into an abrupt, eerie silence, broken only by the hollow moan of the Parametric Rejuvenation Disc's constant mechanical whirling.

Meanwhile, down in the prison section, Braker and his friends were getting reacquainted with Downer Plasmoe as Bullmack stood guard.

"Howdy, Downer," said Wayne, "boy are we glad to see you alive, we thought something awful bad like gettin' killed happened to you."

"No, nothing like that," said Downer, "just more like getting my brains melted down and shoved back in. I should be thankful, I guess."

"Well, at least we're all together," said Braker. "Now we've just got to figure a way out of here."

Bullmack had been listening through the voice box in the prison walls. "You prisoners can't escape," he said through the speaker. "Master says to hold you here until he finishes with the pretty girl."

"What's Dr. Wilde going to do to her?" demanded Braker.

Bullmack scratched his ear. "I believe he's going to rip her to shreds."

"Rip her to shreds?" shouted Braker.

"That's right," said Bullmack. "That's what Master says we do with pretty girls."

Braker dashed over to Vigor. "Vigor, you heard what Bullmack said; these guys are crazy. We've got to get out of here. Babe's life depends on it. Do you think you can smash your way out?"

"I'll try," said Vigor, throwing his full weight against one side of the room. The resulting dust cloud, although impressive, failed to hide the fact that Vigor had only managed to ram his head through the wall.

Bullmack, startled by the partial emergence of the prisoner, instantly began hammering on Vigor's face. "Don't try to be escaped!" he said between blows.

Vigor, trapped where he stood, reared back, slamming the wall with clenched flippers until it crumbled to the ground.

With no barrier left between them, Vigor and Bullmack now stood face to face. The two muscular giants studied each other carefully.

"Wanna wrestle?" asked Bullmack.

"Okay," said Vigor.

The brutes charged forward, toppling to the floor where they continued their contest as a thrashing, bucking heap.

Braker ran past the violence, shouting all the way. "Come on, to the Rejuvenation Room before more guards arrive!"

The escapees disappeared down the hall, leaving Vigor and Bullmack to battle alone.

After a short dash through the *Electric Laboratory's* antiseptic hallways, Braker and his friends burst into the Rejuvenation Room to find Babe still spinning on the Disc. Wayne flipped the power switch, bringing the Disc to a stop; Braker unbuckled the straps on Babe's wrists.

"She's waking up!" cried Braker.

"Braker, you're really here!" said Babe, opening her eyes for the first time.

"You bet, Babe," said Braker. "And don't worry about a thing. I've got it all under control now."

Before Babe could be lifted from the Disc, the back wall of the Rejuvenation Room exploded inward. As the dust settled, Benchworth came lurching through the newly gaping hole. The old gentleman was reeling under the weight of the oversized blast helmet on his head and the enormous rocket launcher on his shoulder.

"Salutations, good people of the cosmos," announced the butler, coughing on the smoke. "Prepare yourselves for the most meaningful moment of your lives! The joy of the universe is here, making a rare, one time only unscheduled appearance. All hail the dazzling, the delightful, the stunning, the sumptuous, the pleasing, the plump—"

"Watch it," said a voice from outside.

Benchworth coughed. "Your oppressor and mine, His Majesty, Lord Preposterous!"

As Benchworth spoke, two small space trolls dressed in matching red uniforms marched in and took their places on each side of the opening. Blowing a shrill tune on a pair of brass horns, they snapped to attention. Lord Preposterous had entered.

"You've got to be kidding," said Braker. "This cannot be happening."

"All under control, Braker?" said J.J.

"Braker's sense of timing has never been real good," Wayne told J.J., who nodded in agreement.

Lord Prespostorous stood before them resplendent in flowing black robes, his ample alien bulk eclipsing the light from behind him. "Good afternoon, losers. I'm here to collect my princess."

"Well, you can't have her," said Braker.

"Oh yeah, that's going to just turn him right around," groaned J.J. "Don't be a pansy; give him a reason to fear you. He's got to feel threatened, boy. Intimidate."

"But last time Braker tried that we got thrown into a giant blender," said Wayne.

"Point well taken," replied J.J. "Braker, don't do a thing. Leave it to me, as usual." Shaking his head, he turned to Lord Preposterous. "Your Majesty, if I may borrow just a quick moment of your time, I'm well aware of your determination to entertain a relationship with this young girl, as any right-minded lecherous sheik of your caliber would, but I feel I must inform you that we as a group regrettably find ourselves in disagreement with such a pursuit, and even more regrettably, we have a filthy, hairy-backed space barbarian embedded in our tiny band. He is especially loyal to your feeble opponent Braker Ford. And where your rival has neither the resolve nor the might to take you on directly, this barbarian possesses no such liabilities. Believe me, he is a violent, filthy, zoological specimen fit only for the harshest of confinement. Considering his barbaric, unrestrained nature and his opposition to your romantic undertaking, you may find it in your best interest to divert immediately from this endeavor."

Preposterous studied Knothead, who for his part, was just staring at J.J. with an annoyed frown. The dictator folded his arms.

"I can't control him," said J.J.

Preposterous looked at the ceiling. "I am not impressed."

"He's liable to go off without any provocation."

Preposterous tapped his foot.

"He cares nothing for his own health or safety."

Preposterous examined his fingernails.

"I mean it," said J.J. "Look at that man. He is marinating in his own filth. His own bodily fluids coat him in some sort of gritty, blighted, perspiration-generated body wash. He smells like sardines, and I think that's black mold under his lower lip. Such a creature would think nothing of sacrificing himself to the sweet release of unmanageable rage!"

"Disgusting, but of no consequence to me," sniffed Preposterous.

"That does it!" J.J. exclaimed. "You have insulted him for the last time. The beast can take no more. Knothead, wreck your havoc. I will no longer attempt to restrain your boiling thirst for honor and juicy gore!"

Knothead continued looking at J.J. while shaking his head. "You are such a weird creep. What do you want me to do?"

"You're a barbarian—do something barbaric and unrestrained!"

"Like what?" asked Knothead. "I'm just a crummy mud-coated varmint, right? You can't expect cruds like me to be very creative."

"Don't do this to me," said J.J. "I'm just selling the product. Now do something crazy."

"Be careful, cave man," said Preposterous. "I'm in love; that can make me very unforgiving."

Knothead surveyed the room, then walked over and snatched Benchworth's rocket launcher from the butler's shaking hands.

"Good move," said J.J. before turning to glare at Preposterous. "See what I mean? Completely unpredictable. I had no idea."

"He intends to kill me, of course," Lord Preposterous sighed. "I suppose it's inevitable. But it will not stop me."

"Pfftt. Yeah, just keep telling yourself that, bigshot," said J.J.

"Oh, no, please don't," Babe pleaded, trying to dissuade Knothead from his violent intent. "Preposterous truly is a horrible goblin, but I cannot bear to see anyone hurt, especially on account of me."

"It ain't nothing personal," Knothead told the princess. "But this really is the sort of stuff we barbarians do. I mean, just imagine if we went around behaving decently. What would people say? Besides, you got to admit he does have it comin'."

"Please, listen to me," Babe continued. "No one can truly win by resorting to hostility. Consider kindness as a way of life instead."

"Nope, I'm committed to hostility," said the barbarian. "It ain't never failed me yet."

Knothead pulled the trigger, sending a rocket screaming into Preposterous's unmissable gut. The dictator was lifted high above the floor by a red shockwave before landing on his feet again.

283

Smiling, he leisurely dusted himself off as the smoke cleared. "You underestimate me," he snickered.

J.J. was dumbfounded. "Laser rockets don't hurt you?"

"What do you think?"

"That's preposterous."

"Exactly."

"That does it, I'm committed to kindness," said Knothead, tossing down the rocket launcher.

Preposterous walked toward Babe at the Rejuvenation Disc. "You don't become absolute ruler of a planet for nothing," he told the others. "I can crush every one of you. Now, I suggest you delay me no further in my nuptial preparations. I have a wedding party complete with impatient royal priests aboard my ship. They shall perform the ceremony immediately, forever bonding Babe and I in that honored union of master and slave."

Preposterous draped Babe over his arm and turned to go, Benchworth hobbling unsteadily along behind them.

"You really got to stop him now, Braker!" said Wayne. "That lugger is 'bout to abscond with your gal. An' fer the final time, too, I think!"

"Yeah, I can see that!" Braker cried. "But what am I supposed to do? How do I fight somebody with that kind of power?"

Wayne thought for a moment. "Let me try," he said, hurrying after Preposterous who was making his exit through the *Laboratory's* ruptured wall.

"Hey, don't go yet, P'ostrous!" Wayne shouted.

Preposterous paused, giving Wayne a glance from over his shoulder. "And what do you want, fiddlestick?"

Wayne stood still; his hands clasped in front of him. "Well, sir, I'm just a simple space farmer but I would like to share a story with you."

"A story?" said Preposterous. "It's my wedding day. For what possible reason would I listen to a story?"

Wayne looked at the floor. 'Well, it's real important, sir. And it's about yer wedding. You see when I was a boy, I managed to find a Gooblie when it was just a baby, an' I raised him as my own—"

Preposterous stepped back inside. "What in the world is a 'Gooblie'?" he asked with distain.

"Well, sir, they're these cute little creatures that grow in the moss pockets of low traveling asteroids. They got a soft little frog face on a piglet body with a monkey tail. They're real hard to find. But I got me this one and I done just loved him. I taught him how to fetch, and roll over, and he'd even snuggle with me at night under the big 'ol country quilt Grammy Delba made me. But there was this mean, nasty boy named Stink Lumpkiss who lived down the road in a big plantation his daddy owned. Well, Stink, he wanted a Gooblie fer himself, an' like I said, they're real hard to find, you got to be in just the right place at just the right time, standing under just the right asteroid. An' you know that ol' Stink, he weren't of a mind to settle down fer that kind of waitin', so you know what he did?"

Preposterous shook his head.

"He done snatched up my Gooblie when I weren't lookin'. I tell you I searched high and low, but I never could find my little Gooblie again; I had no idea he were just down the road the whole time in Stink's holdin' pen. Now, I was just a boy, but my heart felt like it'd been poured out like a speckled duck egg over a patch

285

of sour potatoes. Ever' night, tucked alone in my bunk, I soaked Grammy's quilt with my sad cryin'. It weren't 'til years later Stink admitted to what he done, but by then it were too late. He said my Gooblie never took to him like he did to me an' eventually my lonely Gooblie run away. But Gooblies ain't got such good eyesight—that's 'cause they sprout out there in space where it's dark all the time—an' he never found his way home. I had lost forever my precious Gooblie an' all those won'erful times we could have had together." Wayne paused, interrupted by the sobbing coming from the other listeners in the Rejuvenation Room.

"Hush up, vagrants!" Preposterous shouted, his own face streaked with tears, before ordering Wayne to finish the story.

Wayne choked down a lump in his throat. "Well, sir, I hope you can see that this princess is Braker's Gooblie. Them two love each other. She ain't never gonna be happy with you, an' because of that you ain't never gonna be happy with her. In the end ever'body's just gonna be heartbroked. I'll never get my Gooblie back, but, maybe if'n you're just willing to let this one go, this pair wouldn't have to be run through the briars like I were all them years ago."

Preposterous wiped his eyes, nodding as he softly whimpered to himself. "Yes, yes, I see now," he said, finally. "And I want you to know, as unlikely as it is, cowpie, you, out of all these who have opposed me, are the very one who has come closest to actually stopping me; that is the most heart-wrenching story I've ever heard. But there's just one problem—I don't care about anyone except myself. Bye."

Preposterous grabbed Babe's arm, forcing her to wave a final farewell before carrying her back through the hole in the *Laboratory's* side.

"I won't let you go," Braker shouted, as he and the others followed Preposterous outside.

"I have proven myself to be the supreme galactic evil," Preposterous replied without turning around. "What can you do against me?"

"Come back! This is not over!" Braker cried.

Preposterous kept walking. "Fool, please."

"I'll fight you!"

"You are a speck," said Preposterous, continuing on. "You have already admitted you cannot win."

"I'll never give up!"

Preposterous slammed Babe to the pavement. "You are a tenacious man. Somehow you have survived every disaster that has befallen you and yet you insist on ensuring your extinction. Very well, if you intend to continue this harassment, I will fight you. To the death."

"Yep, definitely better than moon-scaping," said Smack Myers.

Wayne grabbed Braker by the shoulder. "Braker, can I tell you something?"

"Sure," said Braker, still looking at Preposterous. "What is it?"

Wayne leaned close. "You're weak," he whispered.

Braker glared at Wayne. "That doesn't help."

"Well, gee, Braker, Preposterous is a big fella, and don't forget, even that rocket launcher couldn't hurt him."

"You don't have to point that out! But what else can I do? I've got to try. I have to. I just hope that if I don't make it…well…I just hope Babe never forgets me."

"After the thrashing you're about to get?" said Wayne. "I doubt she ever could."

J.J. pushed Wayne out of the way. "Braker, are you mad? I know it appears you have no other options but it's clear now Preposterous can't be beaten, especially by the likes of you. I have an idea, let Preposterous take the girl; we'll steal a ship and follow them. We can rescue the princess at a more appropriate time."

"J.J., you heard what Preposterous said; he's got impatient priests waiting to marry them right now. I can't let them go. I believe I can do this; there's always a glimmer of hope."

Smack Myers came rushing up, shaking Braker's hand. "I just want you to know this act of pointless sacrifice is a radiant ode to love; you're an admirable man, Braker. It's been nice knowing you."

Jodo Durning nodded in agreement. "Stinking dictators; always taking stuff."

Braker looked over at Johnny Comet standing alone at the edge of the platform. The young boy's face was puckered with sadness.

Braker held out his hand. "Johnny, what do you think? Can I make it?"

Before Braker could say another word, Johnny Comet ran to him, embracing the trucker like he would never let go. "Preposterous is going to kill you, Braker," he cried. "I want to stay with you. I was hoping you could adopt me or something. You could teach me how to be a space trucker; maybe we could tool around the galaxy together."

Braker choked back tears. "Johnny, I'd love to do that, but you're still a kid, you've got to be in school."

"Well, just forget it then," said Johnny.

Babe lay on the ground where Preposterous had thrown her. "Braker, you really don't have to do this."

"But I do, Babe," said Braker. "Because it's the only thing I can do. Sometimes you have to fight—even if it means taking on the whole universe and coming up short. And if it does end up being the last thing I do, it'll be the best thing a guy like me's ever done."

"Oh, Braker, you grand, ridiculous, brave boy," said Babe, her voice filled with an inextinguishable joy. "You are so much more than a space trucker. Whatever happens, you will never be lost to me."

"Hey," shouted Charlie Rued, "if this guy dies, who's gonna pay for the repairs on my ship?"

"Alright, that's enough of all the tenderness," said Preposterous. "Now brace yourself, trucker, and come get your paddling; I'm growing antsy."

Braker took one last look at his friends, then, moving unsteadily at first, danced up to his opponent, weaving and swinging his fists through the air. "Here I come, Preposterous," he shouted, "get ready to taste trucker justice!"

Lord Preposterous stood ramrod straight, hands at his side as he watched the trucker impassively. "How fitting it is for a man of your caliber to reduce a conflict of this magnitude to the level of a common street brawl."

Braker was still jumping about excitedly when he suddenly reached out, striking Preposterous on the nose with all the force he could muster.

A faint smile flickered across Lord Preposterous's face. His chest heaved from a sudden outburst of dark, insidious giggles.

"Why are you laughing?" asked Braker.

Preposterous shook his head in amusement. "Because now I know exactly what you can do."

Startled, Braker began backing away just as Preposterous's fist came plunging forward, mashing into the trucker's jaw.

Braker squatted down, carefully placing both hands on the pavement. His unfocused eyes rolled back and forth. "Is it over? Did I win yet?" he asked.

"Not even close," said Johnny Comet.

"Someone help him," Babe cried.

"No one interferes," stated Lord Preposterous. "The trucker claims the princess and he must rightfully face me alone. It is his last chance."

"I'm okay," said Braker, rising to one knee. "I won't give up."

Clenching his fists, Braker had just started forward when Vigor came bounding unexpectedly from Dr. Wilde's ship. The creature's appearance injected the onlookers with newfound hope.

"Try and stop this interference!" shouted Johnny Comet.

"Vigor!" Braker gasped with relief.

Lord Preposterous looked nervously at Benchworth.

"I'll be with you in just a minute, Braker," Vigor panted, his body covered with bruises.

Moments later Bullmack came charging out of the ship. Sheets of torn flesh dangled from his battered face while gears and wires fell from his twisted and exposed metallic skeleton.

"I've finally found someone who knows how to play right!" said the robot, gleefully driving his shoulder into Vigor's belly. Stumbling backward, they both went careening over the platform and into the poisonous Aqua-thite depths.

"No!" shouted Johnny Comet, jumping onto the railing in time to see the last rippling effects created by the monsters' tremendous splash.

As quickly as he had appeared, Vigor was now gone. And so was the momentary hope he had provided.

"Well, trucker," huffed Preposterous, tapping his foot, "I am still waiting for your participation in this fight."

After a long moment, Braker painfully made his way back within striking range. Preposterous took a wide, wild swing, smashing Braker's chest with inhuman power. The trucker crumpled, instantly bombarded with a rain of punches.

"You're no competition," Preposterous roared. "I haven't even broken into my typical exercise-induced lather of rancid body sweat!"

Braker could offer no resistance as Preposterous slugged him again and again to the deck.

"Well, one thing we know," said Smack, "the boy can't fight but he sure can take a beating."

Skippy, Wet, and Holly arrived now but there was nothing they could do. They stood with the others and watched in silence.

Braker rose once more to his feet. Lord Preposterous pumped his fist into Braker's side with machine-like quickness. "You arrogant little human," he boomed, "you really couldn't see how very small you actually are!"

Braker hit the ground again. He rolled onto his back, his eyes swelling shut. "Please...don't hit me anymore," he whispered.

Lord Preposterous threw back his arms with delight. "I've broken you already! Ha, ha, ha. What an inferior specimen!" He pressed his foot into Braker's throat. "Now to do the universe a favor and finish you off for good!"

Chapter Twenty-Nine
A Day to Last Forever

Lord Preposterous's heavy boot pushed further into Braker's neck.

"Stop!" cried Babe. "You've already hurt him enough; just take me, he's no threat to you now. Please, let him live."

Lord Preposterous looked down at Braker's purple, bulging face, and drew back his foot. "Yes, bride, I will let Braker Ford live. I will let this battered bit of refuse suffer a life of humiliation as my personal servant—every day watching helplessly as we revel in a state of blasphemous matrimony. Yes, he will know that I was made owner of Princess Babe because of his own abysmal smallness. He will know that I, Lord Preposterous, exist as manifestly superior to him in every conceivable way—I'm stronger, smarter, and much better looking!"

"I might give him the first two, but definitely not that last one," J.J. whispered to Wayne.

"You're not better than Braker," said Babe. "All you really are is a selfish space braggart, swollen with your own pride. You may be stronger than Braker, but you're not better than him—you can have all the power in the galaxy, and win every fight; you can cause everyone to bow down to you and have the adoration of millions, but have *you* ever really cared for someone else? Have you ever cried for someone, given of yourself until there was nothing left to give for someone? Have you ever been swallowed up in the sweet agony of desire, bound by joy, lost in the richness of serving another whose own happiness now means more than your own life ever could? No, you haven't, but Braker has; just look at him, he's absolutely emptied himself for love, and it's a richness someone like you could never understand. You're not superior to Braker, Lord Preposterous, not even close. You care only for yourself, and you don't even realize it—but you're all alone."

Lord Preposterous flared his nostrils. "Apparently, princess, you misunderstand why one chooses to become an evil tyrant in the first place. But, no matter, I've gotten what I wanted and now it's time for you to begin your life of servitude to me." Preposterous swept Babe up in his arms. "Benchworth, let us be going."

Until then Benchworth had been unneeded and virtually unnoticed. But now all attention turned to the elderly butler as he remained motionless following his master's call.

"Benchworth, I said, 'Come'."

Benchworth looked up into the face of his master, his lips moving silently.

"Benchworth, account for yourself, what is wrong with you?"

"Lord Preposterous," spoke Benchworth, trembling, "I'm an old man, but I don't want to be alone."

"You're not alone," said Preposterous, "you have me." He flashed a quick, embarrassed smile toward Braker's watching group.

"I don't believe that is totally correct, sir," sniffed Benchworth. "I don't mean to complain but it's just that sometimes I really can't stand you."

"Benchworth, how dare you. I believe you are suggesting I might have some slight imperfections."

"No, it's not like that. It's not because your eyes are too close together, or because your head is too long and pointy, or because your skin is clammy and mossy green, or even because your nose is always runny. But it's because you're cruel; you beat me, call me names, and treat me like I'm less than nothing."

"That's your job. Stop grumbling."

"Yes, Lord, but these young people, they care for each other. I think it's very nice."

"You're obviously senile. Say no more. Later I will see that you are well-disciplined for attempting a coherent thought."

"Thank you, my Lord," said Benchworth, bowing his head, "but I still don't believe I shall be going with you."

"What?" exclaimed Preposterous. "Have you gone insane?"

Benchworth wrung his hands. "I fear I must explain more; you see for many years now I've been putting poison in your dinner…"

"My only weakness! Benchworth, you cankerous horse pustule, I told you about that in confidence—as friends. How could you?"

"Yes, very shameful indeed. I could never bring myself to go through with it though and I always put the antidote in your dessert."

"Excellent, a true friend, indeed…Benchworth, did I not cancel dessert tonight in order to more hastily retrieve the princess?"

"Yes, sire, tonight we skipped dessert."

Lord Preposterous pursed his lips, swallowing hard. "Benchworth, is it possible that you might still have this antidote?"

Benchworth turned away, looking to the sky. "Forgive me, but I'm afraid that requires one last bit of explaining."

"Speak—quickly."

"Well, do you remember how you beat me one last time tonight for walking too closely behind you?"

"Yes, yes, vaguely something of that nature."

"Well, sir, the antidote was in my shirt pocket and—"

"And when I gave you my patented chest punch…?"

"You smashed it."

Preposterous laid his hand on Benchworth's shoulder. "What exactly does this poison do?"

"Well, sir, very simply it penetrates your molecular structure, reducing you to your basic elements. You'll know it's kicking in when you begin perspiring heavily."

"Nonsense," said Preposterous, sweat pouring down his face.

Benchworth sighed. "I'm afraid it's true, sir, very soon you will be nothing more than a puddle of smelly sludge."

"Hey, Babe wasn't kidding when she called Preposterous a space sludge!" said Wayne.

"We're saved!" Babe exclaimed, struggling to break out of Preposterous's clutches.

But the poisoned ruler wasn't overcome yet. Tightening his grip on the princess, he raised her above his head. "You are my property!" he screamed. "I control your fate—and I choose your death!"

Before everyone's horrified eyes the sweat-soaked dictator tossed Babe over the railing. Without a moment's hesitation, Holly Blackguard jumped between Babe and the barrier, deflecting Babe's fall with her own body. The collision sent both women tumbling in opposite directions, Babe rebounding to the safety of the platform, Holly into the open air. Once again it was only the water queen's spring-like reflexes that saved her from certain doom—she caught hold of the railing's bottom rung with a single hand; it was a tenuous grip. She began slipping away almost immediately. Babe leaned over, reaching out to her.

"Don't!" shouted Downer Plasmoe. "She betrayed you and Braker. She's not on our side."

Babe hesitated; Holly stared up at her, saying nothing. Then, as quickly as she could, Babe stretched out, grasping Holly's wrist. With Skippy's help, she pulled the dangling woman back to the platform.

Regaining her footing, Holly stood before Babe, regret bearing down on her.

"Whatever you've done, you have a second chance," said Babe. "Run with it."

"Thank you," Holly said quietly, holding tightly to Skippy's arm. "I will."

"Just great," said Downer, "I suppose it's just like me to say the wrong thing at a time like this."

"Hey, everybody, look at Lord Preposterous!" Wayne exclaimed. "He's a puddle of smelly sludge!"

A communal gasp escaped the lips of all who turned to see the thick yellow ooze that stained the very spot where Lord Preposterous had just stood. No one spoke; all were struck silent, studying with disbelief the bizarre remains of their arch foe.

Then, as Braker himself struggled to his feet, Johnny Comet dashed across the platform, jumping into the trucker's arms so that they both went crashing back to the ground. As if on signal, a mad celebration broke out with wild cheering and dancing, everyone jumping up and down, laughing joyously together.

"It's over!" Johnny Comet cried, still holding on to the trucker. "You made it, Braker! You made it!"

The landing bay was alive with merriment; Babe was hugging Benchworth while Wet danced around the smelly puddle and J.J. tried to convince Knothead that he knew rockets wouldn't work on Lord Preposterous all along.

Amid the jubilation, General Godsend, Nub Niblet, and Princess Contentious came running up. Babe and Contentious embraced while Skippy Dodge saluted the general.

"Conty, oh, Conty, I thought I'd never see you again!" wept Babe. She was still speaking when Wayne came bounding up, all aglow.

"Contentious!" he blubbered. "I missed you a whole mess, gal! Seeing you again is better than stepping into a warm pile of smiles."

"You're a real poet," groaned Contentious.

Wayne continued to stare at her adoringly. "Did you miss me, too, apple eyes?"

"Oh, I definitely missed you too," replied Contentious, "the whole time I was fighting for my life out there in the dead of space and you were nowhere around. Care to explain where you've been?"

"Oh, puppy dog, I been all up and down this galaxy lookin' fer you."

"Well, it sure took you long enough to find me. I could have been killed while you were out parading around. What kind of a boyfriend does absolutely nothing to rescue his girl; it took two doofy army men to actually save me."

Wayne blushed. "Girl, I know I'm late but I'll be darned if your scoldin' didn't never sound sweeter. There just be somethin' 'bout the way you slap me down that plucks them sugar-coated banjo strings o' my heart."

"Well, get used to it, because we've got a lot of work to do to get you housetrained."

"So, you ain't mad? You still gonna take me as your own lovey-dovey?"

Contentious sighed. 'Yeah, why not, after all I've seen I'm pretty sure I could do a whole lot worse."

"Yay-Hoo!" shouted Wayne. "If that ain't the biscuits and gravy! Hang on, girl, 'cause you 'bout to get schooled in chickens, dirt, an' feed stompin'."

"I suppose," said Contentious, "but don't get too excited because you've got some education coming too. You're about to learn how to speak in an intelligible language, how to bathe, and how to wear clothes without built-in bibs.

While royalty and country were coming together, Smack Myers gave the sulking Downer Plasmoe an exuberant bear hug.

"Congratulations on surviving your ordeal," said Smack. "You made it, man. You must have one wonderful story to tell."

"Some story," said Downer, "I ruined everything, and I'm left with nothing."

"How can you always be so depressed?" asked Smack.

"How can you always be so happy?" responded Downer.

"I deal with my soul-shattering misery by wearing a shallow veneer of happiness," said Smack.

"That's funny, I deal with my soul-shattering misery by wallowing in it," replied Downer.

Both men stood silently for a moment in a sudden, profound appreciation for the other's own unique emotional artistry.

Across the platform, General Godsend was busily describing his impressive rescue of the Princess Contentious to an enthralled Skippy Dodge.

"So, as you can see, we were determined to perform our duties even to the point of sacrificing our own bodies," he said, motioning to Nub Niblet whose jacket bore the marks of a dozen laser scorching. "And we're not ones to complain either, isn't that right, Corporal?"

"Yes, sir, General," answered the cheerful little soldier, "although fainting isn't out of the question."

"Might I say," interjected Benchworth, overhearing Godsend's conversation, "that after your stalwart deputy has received a suitable patching of wounds, your apparently abundant command skills could be greatly used in the stewardship of Nebulous X now that Lord Preposterous has so hastily vacated his throne."

"An excellent idea," said Godsend. "It would be a privilege to serve Nebulous X once again, this time in the interest of prosperity and justice. What do you say, Nub?"

"I like the part about getting patched up first."

"Nonsense," exclaimed Godsend, already looking for a starship. "Honor awaits!"

"What a leader," sighed Nub, finally collapsing.

Nearby, Knothead gave J.J. a pat on the back that almost tipped the little salesman over. "Well, it's finally over, you old rascal; you made it through safe and sound. What are you going to do now?"

"Funny you should ask," said J.J. steadying himself. "I've got a feeling this Crossroads may be in the market for new leadership. A man with my experience might just be able to turn this place into a somewhat respectable operation after all."

"Need a bodyguard?" Knothead asked.

"Friend," J.J. grinned, leading the barbarian toward the Crossroads offices, "have I ever got a deal for you."

As everyone continued to rejoice, there came a great trembling that shook the entire platform. The quaking grew stronger until Vigor came into sight climbing up the outside support beam.

"Why if it isn't good ol' Vigor," said Smack Myers. "We gave you up for dead, Vigor. But welcome back, anyway."

"Glad to be back," responded the alien even as his previously unrelenting enemy, Bullmack, clamored serenely over the railing beside him.

"Good evening, fair people," Bullmack intoned, sounding uncharacteristically articulate.

The group drew back, shocked at the brutal robot's reappearing.

"Oh, don't worry about him," said Vigor, holding up a fistful of electrical cables, "I've been doing a little rewiring. I kind of dabble in computer programming."

"That is correct," said Bullmack, removing the top of his metal cranium and holding it next to his chest. "Vigor's timely intervention has redeemed me of my more violent anti-social tendencies."

"Well, that's just dandy," said Wayne, "but, Vigor, how did you survive falling into the Aqua-thite? Them toxins will kill a feller the minute they're absorbed into yer skin."

"That's simple," said Vigor, "my species doesn't have any skin!"

A huge round of cheers burst out; even shoppers and tourists who had no idea what was going on joined in the party. As the celebration rose to even greater heights, Wayne showed Vigor the puddle of smelly sludge that used to be Lord Preposterous, and Bullmack went around shaking hands with everyone.

"Does this mean what I think it does?" Jodo asked Smack over the shouts of victory.

"Yes, Jodo," Smack beamed, "it's time to head back to the moon and resume our hard, yet honest labor, all the while cherishing the wonderful memories we've gained from this fantastic adventure."

"I thought so," said Jodo. "Life stinks."

"It sure does," agreed Smack.

While the others talked and laughed, Princess Babe moved quietly through the crowd of friends. She was looking for Braker.

She found him alone, leaning on the railing far at the other end of the landing bay. He was reading the hastily written repair bill Charlie Rued had just handed him for the *Rued Star One*.

Babe gently touched the trucker's cheek. "How's your face?"

"It hurts," said Braker. "But I think that's a good sign. At least I can feel it again. How's your laser wound?"

"Like it never even happened," replied Babe.

Babe took the paper out of Braker's hand, gently putting her arms around him. She looked into his face, tears shining in her eyes. "Braker, I can hardly believe that a short time ago I thought

301

this was the worst day of my life, but right now it feels like a day to last forever."

"Babe," Braker smiled, pulling her close, "every day with you is a day to last forever."

Then, as the reflection of a thousand stars shone across the glittering Aqua-thite waves, one ordinary, insignificant space trucker finally kissed the princess he'd fought a universe to find again.

About the Author

James A. Fyerman grew up loving comic books, sci-fi, and just plain silliness. While the other kids were outside playing with balls, he was roaming the aisles of his local library in search of rocket ships to other worlds. Today, when not working as a firefighter/paramedic in central Ohio, he writes breezy, lighthearted space operas in the tradition of classic Flash Gordon and Buck Rogers comic strips. Except, of course, his come with a farcical twist. He also enjoys being home with his wife and two children watching old black and white movies, most likely something with spaceships or the Marx Brothers. Braker Ford's Adventures in Space is his first published novel.

Made in the USA
Columbia, SC
06 December 2022